MATTIE MASTERS SMITH

(Mattie Masters Smith Series)

K.S. Riggin

Table of Contents

Prelude

Mattie Masters Smith pops her eyes super large and glares at her best friend, Jimmy. "How dare you say I can't be a space captain? I will be. I will be. I will. You hear me?"

Poor Jimmy can't answer because Mattie is sitting on his chest, her fist in his mouth.

That's the last time Jimmy ever makes such a statement, even though, as a seven-year-old, he still believes it. After all, everyone knows the Lunar Academy only accepts males, but Jimmy wisely, never mentions that fact again.

When Mattie turns ten, someone else repeats it, but this time it's a teacher at school. Mattie can't hit a teacher, but she stops bringing him apples and the wild flowers she finds on the way to school. She no longer sighs over him, either, or writes a thousand times in her notebook: Mattie loves Mr. Depore. She decides that her teacher is just like everybody else — except her best friend, Jimmy, who now says he believes in her.

The next day, Mattie tears out all the pages in her binder that say: Mattie Smith Depore. Then she vows that she'll find someone better to marry, someone who has faith that she really will become a spaceship captain.

Mattie, at that age, has absolutely no doubts she'll one day go into space. It's all she thinks about and all she dreams of.

Her Uncle Theodore is already a real space captain. He's her father's brother, and although she's never seen him, he sends interspace messages to them every now and then. Mattie has a postcard from Mars. It's hanging on her bulletin board, right over her desk.

She has a picture of Uncle Theodore, too, in his space uniform from when he was at the Lunar Academy twenty-two years ago. Mattie stares at that picture each night before she goes to bed, promising that someday she'll wear that same uniform.

"I'm going to be a space captain just like you," she promises her uncle each and every night.

Mattie's younger brother, Simon, teases Mattie constantly about having Uncle Theodore's picture in her bedroom. He makes fun of her for being in love with her teacher, too.

But the day when Mattie finally tells her brother that she hates Mr. Depore because of what he said in front of the whole class, Simon doesn't laugh at her.

Instead, he nods sagely and lisps angrily. "What does he know? That teacher's an idiot. You'll go up there. I know you will."

Mattie stares at her little brother. Her mouth drops open, and she has to struggle to close it. Simon never defends her. Not ever. Suspiciously, she backs away and retreats to her room.

But Simon has joined her side. He also believes that Mattie can do it.

****

Chapter One

A Few years later, Mattie and Simon's father announces at dinner that Uncle Theodore is planning to visit them. In fact, he's actually already on his way.

Simon smiles, glances at Mattie, then grabs a carrot stick. He figures that his uncle's visit will be something different, a great adventure that he can talk about at school. While he's pondering that, Simon's baby teeth crunch at the carrot, rabbit-like.

To Mattie, the announcement is more like witnessing the arrival of an angel. She gasps. Her hands drop into her lap, and she's suddenly paralyzed with breathlessness. Her uncle's coming. The sound reverberates in her head, a cascading waterfall of delight.

Mattie often views the future as being a long tunnel with lots and lots of corridors. She thinks she can see sunlight streaming through each of the openings as she peers down into them. She believes she can walk through any one of those passages and get to whichever ending she wishes if only she chooses correctly.

Finding out that Uncle Theodore is about to visit them represents the light that Mattie knows will guide her down the correct corridor. Mattie, overcoming her incredulity, backs out of her chair and runs to her father to hug him. Then she kisses her mother for good measure.

"Thank you. Thank you!" Mattie cries out. "When will he be here?"

Her parents are smiling, sharing her joy. The family is sitting around the plasticized wooden table in the kitchen. They've just eaten vegetable lasagna and salad made from the lettuces that they grow in the garden. Their plates are full of the remnants of the meal, but the dessert is still sitting, ready to be dished out and passed. Peach cobbler. Mattie's favorite. It's a good day for all of them. The return of the uncle has been long awaited.

Mattie's eyes scan the scene, recording it: The curtains in the window, dancing in the evening's slight breeze, the clock on the opposite wall — a wooden cuckoo that no longer pops out on the hour, beating its rhythm into minutes with a steady click, click, click. She studies her Mom in the lemon-yellow pants and top. She's trim and young-looking. Mattie sometimes notices that she's even pretty. This is one of those times.

Her dad is wearing the one-piece orange polo he prefers at home, the one with the silly painted-on tie. He's starting to lose his hair at the front, but his large olive-colored eyes are full of smiles. Mattie adores him. He's her favorite person in the world — next to her best friend, Jimmy.

Simon is sitting across from her parents, his freckles are plastered across his face like a real-life dot-to-dot, his grin almost connecting them. Mattie scoops all this up into her memory, wanting to keep this moment always, this spot of light that highlights the opening to her chosen passage.

She draws in a deep breath. "Does Uncle Theodore know about me, Dad? Have you told him?"

Her dad looks puzzled a moment. He glances at her Mom. Then his smile widens, and he chuckles. He understands what Mattie's asking. He nods then and says. "You mean how you want to go to the Academy?"

Mattie's mother pokes him with her elbow. Then she shakes her head. "Matison, don't encourage her. You know we've talked about this."

Strangely, Simon is silent. His eyes are as wide as Mattie's, though slightly worried as he studies his mother's face.

But Mattie's dad isn't troubled. He turns and looks down at his daughter. He smiles.

As if that's a sign, her mother begins lecturing, like she always does whenever the subject of space comes up. "Mattie," she says, "you know that's never going to happen. We've told you that going to the Academy is impossible. We've said it over and over."

Mattie's chin hits the sky. Her lovely blue eyes grow gray with seriousness, but she doesn't respond to her mother. She's watching her father, her lips firm with determination yet trembling almost imperceptibly because she's not 100% certain he'll back her up.

Her father sees all that and winks. "That's for you to decide, sweetheart," he tells Mattie gently. "Nothing's impossible if you really want it enough."

Mattie's mom groans, "Mattison!" she howls with displeasure.

Her husband turns and looks at her. His eyes soften with love. Then he folds his arms around his wife and gives her a kiss right in front of the kids.

Simon lets out a thoroughly disgusted, "Yuck! Don't do that where we have to see it!"

But Mattie, still caught up in the words of her father, isn't even aware of the kiss. The words are hanging in front of her, coloring the air, a neon sign for her to hug against her soul. She's hardly aware of anything else. She's staring into her future, seeing herself in an astronaut's uniform, standing in front of Lunar Academy.

"We were talking about Theodore's arrival, everyone," Mattison instructs his family. He clicks his fingers in front of Mattie's dazed eyes, claps Simon on the back, and places a kiss on the back of his wife's hand. "I'm sure Theodore will have lots of stories to entertain us with. We'll get the chance to hear about his space adventures, and Mattie, you can do some telling of your own dreams, right? After all, dreams are what make each of us special."

Mattie's mom is shaking her head again, mumbling, "Stop encouraging her, Matison. You know she…"

"Having dreams never hurt a single person, Clare. Let Mattie have her aspirations. Who knows? It's possible. Our Mattie *may* change the world, even the universe. We've gotta let her try."

Mattie's mother sighs and stands so she can dish up the cobbler. Her dad, realizing that he's forgotten the dessert bowls, jumps up to go get them.

"Will you bring the ice cream?" Mom calls out.

****

Mattie blinks. That scene is gone. Life rushes by.

Mattie hands in her research paper on inventions and gets it back with a perfect score. She takes a math test and an English test. She does reams of homework assignments and as always, gets the highest scores, but the truth is that she's only sleepwalking. She mentally records none of it because it's not important to her. Those moments don't walk her down the passage of her dreams. Only at night, when she looks at the picture of her uncle and she talks to him, only then does she see more clearly.

Of course, Mattie continues to spend time with her best friend, Jimmy. She tells him all about her uncle — everything she knows, at least. Sometimes, she goes on and on about him until Jimmy gets bored and storms away. But mostly, she and Jimmy are in one accord. They spend their time making up stories of alien planets, adding in an alien monster or two because Jimmy likes the excitement of them. Sometimes, they make up problems with the spaceship. Those are Mattie's favorite times.

Mattie has a book full of ship diagrams. She's memorized the layouts. She knows the function of every complex instrument on each and every panel in the control room. She knows the power sources, the number of rooms, the passageways, and the shortest routes in all directions. She even knows the kind of cargo and tonnage the ship can carry and the amount of fuel it requires.

And when she closes her eyes, she can almost see herself walking along the wide corridors heading for the Power Room or her own quarters. At night she dreams she's there on the ship, and then the stories she and Jimmy have talked about come alive. In every dream, she is the captain.

In that way, the year passes, and Uncle Theodore's ship will soon be landing.

Chapter Two

The day Uncle Theodore's ship lands, I don't go to school. Instead, the whole family travels to Los Angeles International Space Port. Strangely, we have to park in a completely different city called Inglewood. There, we're inspected by our fingerprints, eye prints, and brain scans. That is all an interesting experience, and I'm quite happy to be officially imprinted into the system. I view it as a step forward in my plans, but Simon fusses the whole time, especially about the brain scans, although there is absolutely nothing painful or distasteful in the process.

The checkpoint process takes the better part of an hour, and then we're whisked away to the actual port. The ground trembles as we near. A supersonic has just come down, and the air feels electric, almost as if it's rippling with static electricity. My throat grows dry, my eyes burn, and I feel slightly faint. Getting so close to a dream can do that, I guess.

Dad puts his arm around me and hugs me. "Pretty exciting, isn't it?" he asks, and I am very glad he understands, even though I can't speak of it. I hug him back and then stand, staring out the windows, transfixed by the sight of so many landed ships.

Mom has brought some yellow daffodils for my uncle. She figures that they're something he probably hasn't seen in a long time, so she holds the bouquet in her arms, even during all our tests and the transit ride to the port. The flowers are wrapped in pseudo paper with a layer of water so they won't wilt, and, of course, the pseudo paper's lining keeps them from dripping.

Mom and Dad grow the flowers in our front yard. We have lots of them there, but enclosed in the transit, the smell of them permeates the air.

"I've never smelled daffodils before," one of the other passengers tells my mother. "They smell just like roses."

Mom immediately dives into a conversation with the lady, telling her all about the new grafts that my father genetically altered to produce daffodils with both scent and increased longevity. Mom is still talking about it when the transit slows and stops.

Mom slides one of the daffodils from its pocket in the paper and gives it to the lady. She's always doing sweet things like that.

The transit and the Port corridor form a tight seal between them, so we step down into the building where we're supposed to wait for Uncle Theodore. Dad puts his handprint on the door, and it slides closed. The transit rushes off. Mom waves goodbye to the lady she was talking to. She makes friends everywhere.

Simon has run ahead. He's trying to act "cool" about our visit to Space Port, but I think he's as excited as the rest of us. Simon calls back that he's heading for the bathroom. Mom decides that's a good idea, so we all trail behind. I don't want to leave the wide picture windows, but I know better than to argue. Once Mom sets a path, we all have to follow it.

After that, my parents offer to treat us to drinks in the *Outer Space Bar*. Simon and I giggle and exchange looks. We know my parents are desperate for another cup of coffee. That's why we get to order something.

The *Outer Space Bar* is decorated with black walls and ceilings. It's dark inside, but the artificial shine of fake stars scattered across the walls lights our way. We find an empty table and sit down. Almost immediately a standard server robot slides over to us. My parents order their coffee, Simon asks for a soy milkshake with blackberries and peaches, and I order my usual Space Juice, which is pretty much carbonated water with flavoring and sweetener — at least that's what Dad keeps telling me.

We've arrived at the Space Port early so we can relax a bit before Uncle Theodore's ship lands, but it comes in early. We're still sipping our drinks when the loud speaker announces its approach.

"Oh, no!" yells my mother. "I left the flowers in the bathroom."

I volunteer to retrieve them, but Mom won't let me go alone, so we both go running back to the restroom. Unfortunately, someone has taken them.

Mom rages. "After I carried them all the way here," she complains. "And I kept a hold of them all through the probing at the Entry Port. I can't believe I set them down and walked off. I just can't believe it!"

When we rejoin Simon and Dad, my brother suggests that we try the *lost and found*. No flowers there. Simon and I hurry back to the gate.

Then we see the daffodils. A young and very pretty woman is carrying them.

"Hey, those are our flowers," Simon yells out.

The lady ignores him. She's looking at the gate door, watching for it to open.

Simon, whose hand I'd grabbed to keep him from making a big deal out of the situation, breaks free and sprints over to the woman, "Those are *our* flowers, ma'am," he says, with the very demanding and extremely loud voice of a five-year-old boy.

Just at that moment, the gate door opens, and the woman pushes Simon aside.

Dad rushes over and orders us to retreat. He doesn't want the sudden crowd of adults to run us down. I try to pull Simon back, but he isn't budging.

"Those are Mom's flowers," Simon yells over the noise. "She can't just steal them."

Dad mouths, "NOW." I can't argue with what Simon is saying. He's right. It isn't fair that a strange lady with a red beret on her head has our flowers, but Dad is glaring at me. I grab again at Simon, but he dodges away. I shrug and return to my father.

"That woman has our flowers," I tell Dad, pointing in the direction where Simon is. "My brother told her the flowers were ours, but she's ignoring him."

"That's not important," Dad tells me. "We have lots more at home. You go cheer up your mother. I'll grab Simon."

It's a good thing he does so because Simon is trying once again to get the woman's attention. This time, he pulls at her jacket, and she screams. Dad pushes forward.

All this is happening while the ship is unloading its passengers. Streams of people are pushing through the waiting crowd. Cries of "Oh, Harry! I've missed you so much," "Look how much you've grown," and "Welcome home," surround us. Some couples are kissing. Others are hugging each other in wild and exuberant dances of enthusiasm.

Uncle Theodore apparently walks down the entrance path, and no one cries out to welcome him. That's because Dad and Simon are arguing with the lady about whether she should call the police because Simon attacked her. Mom and I are standing back away from the crowd, and we can't see a thing. So Uncle Theodore just keeps on walking, figuring that because his ship has arrived early, no one is there to meet him.

Thus, by the time the incident with the flower woman is cleared up (quite unsatisfactorily since the woman still claims the daffodils are hers) and the ship is all unloaded of people, we are empty-handed. No flowers. No, Uncle Theodore.

Dad checks the passenger and crew list. His brother was definitely on the ship. Yet, it appears to us that he hasn't gotten off. Mom tells the officials at the desk that they've lost somebody and need to go search the ship. The officials shake their head, shut off their computer terminals, and stand up to go.

"I'm sorry, ma'am," they tell her. "There's nothing we can do."

It's a terrible moment. Mom sighs heavily and slumps into one of the ugly plastic chairs, Dad lectures Simon, and I go over to stare out the window. I imagine anyone watching thinks I'm just staring up at the ship, but the reality is that my eyes are dripping, and I can't see a thing. The long-awaited event has not happened after all — it's Uncle Theodore's ship, but he hasn't come in with it, and I'm utterly crushed.

I don't know what would have happened if Uncle Theodore hadn't decided to check back at the gate. He tells us later that he'd been hit with a very strong urge to return to the site of his arrival, but Dad, who doesn't believe in ESP and all the other pseudo sciences, interrupts him and says, "You mean, you decided to come back and wait for us here so you could take a nap?"

When he says that, Uncle Theodore laughs and the two of them come together, embracing in the way males do — with lots of backslapping.

While Uncle Theodore is engaged in his reunion with his brother, I get a good look at the man. My uncle's taller than my father and skinnier, too. Dad isn't fat or anything because he's really active in the garden, but my uncle is wiry and agile — more panther-like. He acts like he's got springs on his feet — although I don't know how that could be with the heavier gravity of Earth. Yet there's something in his tread, the way he places his feet down so cautiously, it's as if he's ready at any moment to jump to the side and dart off or attack.

Apparently, feeling my eyes on him, he scans me a moment, and then he smiles. That brings me the shivers. Uncle Theodore's eyes are very much like my father's eyes, but they're different, too — more alert and cautious and most peculiarly vibrant. I look away. I think I hear him chuckle.

After that, he hugs and kisses my mother. He kisses her right on the lips! Simon and I both have mouths formed into perfect circles of surprise. We've never seen Mom kiss anyone but Dad.

Simon breaks up their kiss. He throws himself at my uncle and attaches himself around his leg as if my uncle were a tree Simon has decided to climb. That doesn't faze Uncle Theodore in the least. He lifts Simon straight up into the air, tosses him up, and then catches him. When my uncle sets my brother on the ground, Simon's expression is most un-Simon like, and he's unbelievable silent.

Then it's my turn, but I feel shy. When my father introduces me, I walk up to my uncle and stick out my hand, expecting him to shake it, but he doesn't. He grabs me and gives me a great, big bear hug. "You're the one," he says. "I should have known it from the fire in your eyes."

I have no idea what he's talking about. When he frees me, I stare up at him and say, "What?"

Then he laughs, throwing his head back, his mouth to the ceiling. "Simon is a Terran. He takes after his father, but you're different, girl. You've got wanderlust in your eyes."

"Don't you start that," my mother chides him. "Mattie's already star crazy. She doesn't need you to make her worse."

Uncle Theodore laughs again, once more blasting his laughter into the ceiling beams. "That's just what our folks said, isn't it, Matison? Tell Clare how much good it did them. The first moment I was free, I was sailing among the stars. You can't fight wanderlust. Don't you know that?"

Uncle Theodore has instantly won me over. But like a Ping-Pong ball, my eyes bounce back and forth between my father, my mother, and my uncle. Unfortunately, that means I'm not paying any attention to my brother, nor is anyone else, and at that moment, he spots the lady with the flowers.

"There she is, the one who stole your daffodils, Uncle Theodore. Mom brought those from the garden at home and then left them in the restroom. *That woman* took them!"

The man beside the woman is now holding on to our daffodils. He overhears my brother, I'm afraid. His face gets red, and he starts to come toward us, but the woman grabs his sleeve and starts whispering into his ear. It's obvious she doesn't want him to make a scene about the flowers and my brother. The man ignores her.

"Theodore, I should have known you'd be behind something like this. What's going on?" the man blares out, causing everyone in the terminal to turn around and stare at us.

Theodore drops his duffle bag and spreads his feet out like he's about to charge the other man.

Dad sticks his hand on my uncle's chest and says, "Not here, Theodore. You're on Earth, remember?"

My uncle groans and then laughs. "We aren't likely to forget that, are we, Adam? This gravity's killing us."

The other man grins then, and it becomes obvious the two are friends. Introductions take place, and we learn that Adam Chosky is second in command of my uncle's ship.

The woman turns out to be Adam Chosky's sister. She shakes hands with us, but her eyes are very unfriendly, and she and Simon glare darts at each other.

After the handshakes are over, everyone goes into small talk, and I'm thinking that it looks like things are going to be okay after all when Simon brings up the stolen flowers.

"Those are *our* flowers," he declares in a voice that pierces the calm. *She* won't give them back," Simon blurts out, pointing his long, thin finger at the woman.

"Is that right?" Adam Chosky says. "Now, how do you know that, little fellow?"

I can see that Simon resents the title. He wrinkles up his freckled nose in distaste but still answers politely. "Because they're the only daffodils in the world that smell. My dad is a horrorculturist, and he genie-altered them."

"Genetically altered, Simon," my father and I both say at the exact same moment, both of us ignoring the part about the "horrorculturist."

"Is that so? What's different about them?" Adam asked, eyeing the flowers.

"Don't believe anything they say, Adam. I bought those flowers for you at the flower stand. I wanted to have something for you."

"That's a lie," my brother says, in spite of the fact that my parents are trying to smooth the situation over.

Mom pulls Simon over to her side and starts whispering. I keep quiet, but Dad rushes in, saving the day. He tells everyone he's sure it's all a mistake.

In the end, my parents, working together, calm Simon down and allow Adam to keep the daffodils. His sister is smirking over it, acting like that's her due, but I'm pretty sure Mr. Chosky sees the truth. He turns around and winks at me when he walks away.

Chapter Three

At home in Ventura, my uncle is a hero. Everyone wants to come take a look at him. So, even that first night, after spending four hours in sky traffic, we arrive home to see *flybeetles* skimming over our roof as if we had a super big Christmas display in our front yard.

When the passengers see our *F.B.* land, the parade stops, and everyone parks and gets out. The mayor arrives first. He strides over and can hardly wait for my father to get out of our *F.B.* He immediately begins demanding an introduction. Then, after pumping my uncle's hand up and down like an old-time water pump, the mayor asks Uncle Theodore if he'll come downtown on Saturday and speak at the *Happiness Club*.

Uncle Theodore laughs a bit. His eyes flash, and he includes me in the joke, saying, "What do you think, Mattie? Shall we speak before a couple hundred folks and tell them about space travel?"

I know he's joking. It's not really as if my opinion will change anything, but Simon thinks he's really asking us our opinion. My brother blurts out. "Why are you asking *her*? Mattie hasn't been up in space *yet*. Besides, it's *you* they want, not my sister."

That makes me giggle. Mom thinks it's funny, too, but Simon keeps saying, "Please, Uncle Theodore. It would be so cool."

Dad nods that our uncle should do it, and the matter's settled. As we head inside, leaving the mayor to make his announcements to the gathered crowd, Uncle Theodore throws an arm around my mother, and then he scoops me in under the other arm. We walk inside like that, tilting sideways to get through the door.

Almost the moment we enter the house, Simon comes rushing in with a handful of daffodils. "See, Uncle Theodore. I wasn't lying. They were ours."

Aren't little brothers funny?

****

The days unravel with Uncle Theodore there. It's like he can pull them a part and make them go twice as far. I love everything about him, the way he sings while he's shaving in the morning, the way he likes to watch cartoons with Simon, the way he helps Mom with her accounting when she's tired at night. Dad has never seemed so happy, either. He laughs all the time, and the sound of it has changed so much that he laughs exactly like Uncle Theodore.

Uncle Theodore and my father frequently go on walks together, sometimes inviting Simon and sometimes not. Then, when they come back, they arm wrestle at the table until Mom begs them to stop. They tease and kid her, Simon, and me until I almost forget that it's my dad acting silly — a dad grown younger and happier.

More times than not, we turn television off in the evening, and Uncle Theodore entertains us with his stories and, sometimes, with his wacky expressions, like when he crosses his eyes and gives us wild looks. That always sets Simon off. Then my brother rolls around on the floor with his loud-mouthed cackles, and when he's sure the entertainment's over, he goes into the bathroom to practice our uncle's funny faces in the mirror.

I can only imagine what Simon does at school. He must be using what he learns, yet not once while Uncle Theodore's there does Simon get in trouble, and that's quite unusual for him.

I want to glue each of these precious moments together so they don't flow out. If I only knew how, I would do it in a moment, bonding them with the pressure of my hand, cupping them so tightly they'd never come apart. If only . . .

But maybe part of the sweetness is knowing that something can't last, knowing that one day Uncle Theodore will take off into space again, and then I'll only have the memory of the uncle I talk to each night and in my dreams.

But he's here with us now, and every second is a treasure because, as I said, I love everything about my uncle, but especially when he talks with me about space — just the two of us. One night, I finally tell him all about my ship sketches, the ones I've been working on. When he looks at them, he doesn't scan them briefly and say things like "Very nice, Mattie," like my parents do. Uncle Theodore *really* looks at them. Then, he analyzes them. "Mattie," he says, and his eyes grow stern as if he considers me an adult, someone worthy of the truth. "This one's a bit out of proportion," he tells me. "The control room is actually twice this size." We sit together and redefine the dimensions while he talks about each room so vividly I can see it.

On another night, while he's telling me about his visits to alien planets, I tell him about my stories.

"I know they're no good. They ought to be burned," I admit, "but I read them often just to remind me of my dreams because, you see, I'm always in the stories, and I'm always the captain of the ship. Do you think that's silly?"

But he doesn't nod his head or laugh like I was afraid he might. Instead, he turns to me and says, "It really is in your blood, isn't it?"

I feel the truth lying there, shimmering like an ice cube on a hot sidewalk. I'm afraid. I know what happens to the ice cube, but I'm hoping it won't.

Uncle Theodore and I really are alike. He's said that himself. Surely, he will understand. Surely, he'll give me hope.

So, I press forward and answer truthfully. "I want to go to space more than I need food or water, Uncle Theodore. I have to go. I need to explore the new and see what's up there. I can't NOT do it. Do you understand that? I dream about space whenever I'm asleep, and when I'm awake, I know it's my destiny."

There is no one that I would ever have said these things to but Uncle Theodore. I wait breathlessly for his response. But he doesn't say anything. He just nods. I take a long breath of relief. The sun peeks through the clouds. The sky clears. I think everything will be okay from now on because I believe Uncle Theodore will be on my side, but he doesn't smile at me. In fact, his face grows somber.

"I understand, Mattie, but you can't, honey. They won't let you."

They say a magician can pull a tablecloth out from underneath filled dishes of food. I've heard that's true, but I've never actually seen it. Once Simon tried it, but when he did, the food flew every which way. The dishes all broke, and the tablecloth — one of mom's best linens — ripped across the middle.

When Uncle Theodore says that to me, it's just like seeing the magician's trick go all-wrong again. My plans fly off the table. My dreams break, and the part of me that breathes and feels, rips clear across the middle.

"It's all right to dream, Mattie," Uncle Theodore says in a whispery voice, "but you have to know what's possible and what's not. A person can't plan on jumping off a mountain. You won't survive that. And you can't stake your life on something that doesn't have a ghost of a possibility. Do you understand that, sweetheart?"

I hate tears. I despise them, in fact. They always come when you need to be strong. They steal away your grit. But tears attack me at that moment, robbing every drop of spirit. I quiver. I act like a girl, sobbing away at my anguish, hating myself for doing so.

Angrily, I wipe at my eyes, but a sick feeling is welling up inside me. Uncle Theodore has betrayed me. I'm no longer sure whether I need to escape to let the tears out or go throw up in the toilet. I spring up and start to run to my room, but Uncle Theodore grabs my arm.

"Hold it, Mattie. Do you understand why I've said that?"

His words stop me more than his hold on my arm. "Yes, I understand," I yell, raging at my uncle as much as at the injustice. "I know. It's because everyone is prejudiced, but I can't understand. We women have fought so hard for equality, and then mankind takes a step off the Earth, and suddenly, it's back to the caveman days again. Why do you males think you're the only ones who can follow a dream? Why do you think only men can . . . ?"

"It makes us sterile, Mattie," my uncle says, interrupting me. The pain in his voice stops my tirade. "Do you understand what sterile means?" he asks me quietly.

Of course I do. I nod and wipe at a drippy tear.

"We can't have children, Mattie. We give that up, living on the moon. You see, we wear spacesuits, and we stay inside specially constructed housings, but it isn't enough. The radiation takes its due.

It's even worse for a woman. She can still bear children despite the massive doses of solar radiation, but the children are deformed — cruelly. That's why the Academy bans females."

No one has ever told me that. I've combed the Internet. I've read everything INASA allows us to read. Nowhere was it explained. But still, I gather up steam for a new launch of attack.

"But it still isn't fair," I tell my uncle. "There are operations a woman could have. There are solutions . . ."

Uncle Theodore studies me intently. "You're so young, Mattie. How could you decide what will be right twenty years from now? You may say you don't want kids, but how will you feel when you meet a handsome young man? You're very beautiful, Mattie. I haven't figured out why the doorbell isn't ringing steadily with all the young men in Ventura. But that's going to happen soon. Then the Academy will be the last thing on your mind."

My uncle's words completely wipe away my tears. My chin lifts up. My eyes glare. I feel the heat of intense anger pouring from my skin, and I bellow, "How dare you say that to me. I thought you, of all people, would understand."

Then I shake my arm loose and march away to my bedroom.

****

For several days I don't speak to Uncle Theodore. Something's shifted inside me. It's like with the teacher I had a crush on. The door slammed shut, and then all my feelings just evaporated. And now, with Uncle Theodore, the same thing has happened. I don't like him anymore. I don't even respect him.

My mother comes and talks to me. Then my father tries. A few days later even Simon comes in. But I can't change what's inside of me. The magic trick doesn't work. All the dishes — and my soul — are shattered and broken.

Chapter Four

In the weeks that follow, my uncle tries to bring our friendship back alive, but I won't allow it. I eat at the table with the family and watch television with them, but if Uncle Theodore starts in on one of his stories, I get up and leave. I can't bear to see the man I once thought of as *my hero*.

I feel Uncle Theodore's eyes watching me sometimes, but I don't meet them as I would have formerly. I don't exchange smiles, and I avoid conversations. It isn't that I'm still angry with him. How can you be angry with someone who died? The man I thought he was is no longer, and the hope his presence had given me that he would be the one to help me win my dream — that's all gone. I miss him. I miss the belief I had him.

But his turning traitor hasn't stopped my resolution. That's what grit is all about. When something gets tougher, you just have to sink your teeth into it and bite harder. That's what I decide. I pour myself even more into my studies, realizing that academics will have to be my avenue to success. When I'm through with my schoolwork each night, I write a letter to a congresswoman, a senator, a governor — all the females I think that might have the power to change this unfairness.

I am working on one such letter when my uncle knocks and asks if he can come in and talk for a minute.

I have just that evening been lectured again by my mother about being more polite to Uncle Theodore, so, in spite of the fact that I don't want to, I grant him permission to enter.

He sits down in the spare chair and watches me a moment. I'm just closing up another letter, sending this one off to INASA's chief testing pilot — ground division, of course, but I figure that she may be as bitter as I am. Maybe she once had dreams she was forced to cast aside. Maybe she's sorry she settled for something lesser. That's my hope, anyway.

When I seal the envelope and mark off that I've sent a plea to Dr. Stephenson, I turn to look at my uncle. "Yes?" I ask, sighing as if I'm a busy person and he's wasting my time.

"Brrr! Kind of cold in here," Uncle Theodore says, hugging his body with his arms and shivering to show the effect of my attitude. "It's exactly like the general atmosphere I've felt around you all week, isn't that right?"

I know exactly what my uncle means, but I pretend I don't. "I think it's fine in here. I like my room cool. I can get more work done," I tell him.

"I see. Were you studying just now? It looked like you were writing a letter, actually."

I want to tell Uncle Theodore that it's none of his business what I was doing, but I don't quite dare. He's my father's brother, after all. I guess I owe him something.

"I was writing a letter to a Dr. Stephenson," I say, not giving him any more information.

"Dr. Jamie Stephenson?" my uncle asks, leaning forward slightly as if he's made progress forward in our relationship.

I don't elaborate. I just nod, wondering how long politeness requires my uncle's presence in my room.

"She won't be able to help you. She has little power, even at INASA. Now, Dr. Britchford. She'd be a good one to write to."

"I've already written to her," I comment without meaning to.

"How many letters have you written? Who have you written to?"

I eye my uncle distrustfully. Why is he asking? What is it to him?

He sees my hesitation about sharing. "Listen, if you're really as stubborn as all that, and you keep being stubborn every moment of everyday, and you still want to go to the Academy, it *will* happen. The Bible says that even the wall of Jericho fell down from the persistence of *one* fellow. If that man could walk around a stone wall and believe strong enough to make it topple, then I sure don't see why you can't."

Uncle Theodore's words start a small stream of hope trickling through my veins. I don't dare take note of it, yet it's there, tickling, wiggling inside me. I feel it growing. Could it be true that Uncle Theodore …?

"Are you saying that it's *possible* now?" I demand, not quite accepting such a shaky handshake of faith.

He nods. "Look, Mattie. I *had* to test your resolution. I know what your folks said. Your dad's been writing to me for years about your plans, but something like this can't come from outside of you. It has to be inside you, titanium core of such strength that nothing can knock it down. You're resolute, all right. You've shown me that. I think you've got inside you the tenacity it's going to take."

"But I thought you said it was impossible," I say, searching my uncle's face for any indications that he's kidding around or still not taking me seriously.

"You know your mother hates the idea of your going into space, but even she doesn't think you're going to outgrow this obsession of yours. That's the titanium core I said you'd need. But it'll take even more than that. It means boys are off-limits. They're your biggest obstacles, even more so than the rules of the Academy."

I grin. "Boys are no obstacles at all. I don't even have time for them, and I *will* go to the Academy, Uncle Theodore, even if I have to dress up like a boy and sneak in."

I've been brazen to mention that thought, but it's an idea that's been jelling inside in my head. What if…

"Bad idea, Mattie. They'd kick you out for dishonesty before you even had the chance to prove yourself. You've got a perfect heart-shaped face, young lady. Those lashes of yours are too long for a boy — let's just say that it would take a fool not to see your gender."

Uncle Theodore is making me cry again. I sit down on the bed and grab a pillow to hide my face.

My uncle's silent, then. For a moment, he just watches me. Then he heads over to my desk and rips a fresh paper off my pad. "All right, let's see if we can figure this problem out. First of all, you'll have to have an operation. You know that, right? They'll remove your eggs and tie your tubes."

I drop the pillow and come and stand beside him. "I know that. I accept it."

Then I can't hold back anymore. The stream of hope has opened into a river. "Thank you, Uncle Theodore," I tell him, throwing my arms around his neck and hugging him. "I'm so sorry I was such a pain this past week."

He chuckles. "Yeah, you were, weren't you? It really got to me. You and Simon are all the family I'm ever gonna have, you know. I really wouldn't want to leave with you still hating me."

"Leave? You're here for another two weeks, aren't you?"

He shakes his head sadly. "Nope. We loaded up our cargo yesterday, and there's suddenly someone from Fleet we need to cart over to Titan, so I gotta take off the day after tomorrow, Mattie. I'm sorry."

"No!" I cry out, hugging him again. "Just when you've come back to me. Just when everything's going to be okay. It isn't fair. Can't you take me with you? Please?"

He laughs and pats my back, then pushes me up. "Come on. We've got work to do, you and I. Maybe having my signature will speed this process up."

I stay home the next day, and we work on writing letters. We send out over a hundred — one to every person on the board of the Academy, to every graduate, and to anyone who has any influence over changing the rules. The president of the United States even receives a letter before we're done. Next, we start on the media.

"There's a good story here," my uncle explains, "a story about a young woman who's willing to give up motherhood to follow her dreams. Then there's the gender question and the fact that I would bet you're photogenic. Yep, I predict the news will eat this baby up."

****

It was the beginning. After that day, my life was never the same again, and it was Uncle Theodore who set it all in motion. I will always be grateful.

Chapter Five

When the day arrives to take Uncle Theodore back to Space Port, it's almost like the reverse of his arrival. Everyone suddenly becomes strained, super polite, and distanced, as if dealing with the pain has already started.

Simon keeps hugging Uncle Theodore. I just keep sighing. Mom prepares my uncle's favorite breakfast and makes him real orange juice. She wants to pack him a lunch, too, but he tells her he has to eat with his officers, and they'd all be griping about not having what he's having. Mom offers to pack a lunch for all of them, but Dad intercedes. "That's enough, Clare. Let it be."

Uncle Theodore and Dad sit at the table drinking coffee then. For the first time, neither of them brings up arm wrestling, and they don't go off for one of their long walks across the wild parkland fields that border our property.

Breakfast is sad, and no one wants to eat it, but we do. We try, anyway.

The people in town have not been forewarned about Uncle Theodore's leaving. There wasn't time, so the hordes that were there for his arrival aren't present when we head to the *beetleflyer*. Uncle Theodore says he's grateful for that. He really doesn't like a lot of fanfare.

We all climb into the *BF.* and zoom off in the direction of Los Angeles. For a while, the flight is easy, and we talk about the weather and about how Ventura keeps sprawling toward the ocean, filling in the spaces of land with houses. Dad tells his brother about the new settlements out on the ocean coastlines. Piers have been built that people can even drive on, and houses are now being constructed on artificial sea platforms.

Uncle Theodore thinks that's hilarious. "There's a heap of good countryside out in those other planets we're discovering. If I were they, I'd be migrating permanently."

"Isn't that what you do now?" Simon asks.

We all laugh because it's true. Uncle Theodore's ship *is* his home.

Dad tells Simon, "Your uncle is a true nomad, Simon. He carries his home with him as he roams the universe."

Beside us, Mom starts to cry. She tries to hide it. Her tissue starts in blotting, and then she sniffles a bit, attempting to hide her distress by giving a couple of short, brief coughs, but we all know.

We grow silent.

The skies are crowded, as always. The city has too many people, so the *B.F.s* are automatically controlled. When we finally arrive near Space Port, we end up in a holding pattern for about twenty minutes. But Dad has allotted sufficient time, and we make it to the Space Port long before my uncle's departure.

"Listen," Uncle Theodore tells us before we drop out of autopilot. "We need to make this a quick goodbye. I have things to do," he says gruffly. Then he adds, "Besides, I hate tears, and the thought of not getting to see you guys for a couple of years is making me blurry-eyed."

No one argues with him. We all understand, but we've come to see him off. We're not willing to just release him from the side of the *B.F.* landing strip. So we park despite his wishes. Once again, we all have to go through the scans and show our ID cards. They really scrutinize Uncle Theodore's, but he says he's used to it.

"Sugar," he says to the lady, taking his blood, "You can have all the blood you want as long as you let me sit here and admire your pretty eyes."

Dad inhales sharply. Some women would file a report on a man for saying that, but Uncle Theodore gets away with it. The woman just smiles at him as she pokes in the needle.

Then we ride the tram in. Mom starts crying again, and Dad swings his arm around her shoulder and whispers in her ear. I hold onto Simon who keeps leaning out the window, waving to everyone we pass.

Inside the terminal, there are crowds of people. Simon's all wide-eyed by it. He doesn't much care for spaceships, but he loves seeing lots of people. Lately, he's decided he wants to be a clown, and as we walk, he's busy making faces at everyone. He does get some strange looks, but nobody laughs.

We walk Uncle Theodore to his gate, and then we stop. End of the line. For a moment, we stare at each other as if we're not sure what comes next, but Uncle Theodore does. He grabs Mom and kisses her. He doesn't do it very brotherly, and Dad has to pull him away, but it's all in fun. Mom and my uncle are laughing, and we can see that Dad isn't the least bit upset, although he punches his brother on the shoulder for good measure.

Simon is next, but when it comes time for Uncle Theodore to hug my brother, my uncle claps Simon on the shoulder very gently and says, "You're pretty incredible kiddo. You take care." Then they hug, and Simon pulls out a dried daffodil, which he tells his uncle is a souvenir of the visit.

"Spacers don't need souvenirs, Simon. We collect pictures in our mind. And this one's a good one. I'll always remember you giving me a dead flower."

Simon gasps and looks up. He sees that Uncle Theodore is just kidding, so they hug again, and Mom pulls Simon away because he won't let go.

It's my turn then. I step close. "If you took me with you, I could study on the ship and still graduate with honors," I tell him, knowing already that he can't take me with him.

He shakes his head. "I don't know where you get this space craziness, Mattie, but there's no question that you and I are related. You're gonna make a heck of a good captain. I know it."

We hug, and then it's Dad's turn. I turn away to stare out at the ship. *The Jolly Roger* is what Uncle Theodore calls her. That was the name of a famous pirate's ship, the kind of ship that floated on water, he explained to both Simon and me one evening. I understand now because both ships are rigged with sails. My uncle's spaceship floats on solar currents — at least, that's one of its power sources. Uncle Theodore says it's also fueled by fission and anti-grav.

I sigh. The ship stands more than a hundred feet high— the height of a huge building. The morning's sun is shining on the titanium finish, making it glow liked mirrors. The name *Jolly Roger* is etched on its side. They've used copper fluking, so some of it is still copper-colored, but other parts are turning green. I like the green parts best.

Already, men and robots are working on getting the *Jolly Roger* ready for its flight. They've added some high booster rocket fuels to the starter burner, but mostly, the lift-off uses anti-grav. Uncle Theodore says that it pushes itself away from the Earth's magnetic core.

Dad and Mom tell him that we'll stay and watch him lift-off. I don't want to see my uncle leave, but my body is trembling already from the vibration of the other ships prepping for flight. Most of them are just hopping over to Beijing or Sydney, but some of them are probably heading for Mars or the moon. Dad announces that there's now even a weekly trip to the Space Station. He promises to take me up for my eighteenth birthday if I'm still Earthbound.

"I doubt that," Uncle Theodore says to Mattie. She'll be in space by then. I know it. Then he turns. "I love you all," he calls back over his shoulder as he walks through the corridor leading out into the Space Docks. We think he's gone, but he stops and looks back at us. "Mattie, I'll do what I can from space to help you. There are a few contacts that I can lean on, but you keep up your end of the bargain. Okay?"

I nod. Tears are attacking again. I brush at my cheeks. Uncle Theodore blows us all a final kiss, and then he walks away.

It takes another two hours before lift-off. During that time, we explore Space Port, check out their shops, and eat at one of the restaurants. We see the daffodil lady at one point — Adam Chosky's sister. She glares at us and thumbs her nose at Simon, making him so angry he doesn't even see the Captain Jetstream exhibit until we direct his eyes to it. Luckily, that makes him forget the daffodil woman, but I keep my eyes on her. She's strange.

The announcer calls out the name *Jolly Roger*, and we rush toward the windows to watch lift-off. We see the shimmering air spreading out beneath it, then the whole building vibrates, and beneath our feet, we feel the power amassing. I decide that the ship is like a wild cougar, bunching up his haunches, waiting for the moment to spring up into the air.

Simon holds onto the window rail, but I don't. I want to feel the ship's power, to taste it in my mouth. I breathe in deeply and imagine the smells outside — the odor of fire and the fuel mixing with hot air. I reach out and touch the window, placing my palms on its pseudo glass to absorb every sensation. I feel, then, like I'm part of the lift-off. As the *Jolly Roger* rises, in my mind, I lift, too, and I hurl myself into the sky, shooting up faster and faster, heading for space.

The after burner separates and dissolves itself into a mist of spent chemicals. Then the ship, a glowing metal cylinder, heaves itself into true anti-grav and cuts through the sky, leaving behind only a streak of white flame.

When it's all over when we can't see even the glow left behind, I realize I'm still clutching at the window, my face pressed against it, as close as I can possibly come to actually joining in.

Chapter Six

With Uncle Theodore gone, the days grow strange. The very first day, Simon complains that he's lost half his new popularity. For weeks, he walks around, his face all somber. Then he tells us he doesn't want to be a clown anymore because the kids say his faces are stupid — not funny.

Dad stops laughing, too. I won't say he gets all gloomy like Simon, but dinners are not the fun occasions they used to be. Dad and Simon start taking evening walks together, but I can see that isn't the answer. Uncle Theodore was just magical, and now the magic is leaking out.

Mom has to deal with her bookkeeping all alone again since Dad doesn't do figures well. She's cranky as a treed cat. When she sits down to run the figures, Simon and I tiptoe up to our rooms. We stay there, too, until she's done.

At first, I attempt to cheer everyone up, but sometimes the negative flow is so great it pushes me under. So, I try to ignore the gloom around me. With my heavy class-load, I really don't have a lot of time for family, anyway. I'm trying to shave off a couple of years of high school, and I've just received permission to test out of several classes. Needless to say, I have some heavy studying to do.

I've started getting responses to my mailings now. Most are just quick e-mails thanking me for my feedback — meaning that nobody even read the letters. Dr. Stephenson replied, too, but I don't think she read my letter either. She just reaffirms that the Academy policy forbids females, and she hopes I'll consider working at INASA after I graduate from college.

When I get her letter, at first I storm around my room, throwing my pillows and a couple of my stuffed animals. But then I decide to write her again and explain more fully how I feel. I include a copy of the letter that Uncle Theodore sent to the media and to the high-ranking officials.

Then, I shrug. Uncle Theodore said there'd be lots of downbeat letters. He said the vetoes might keep coming for years. I sigh loudly and dramatically (since no one can hear me), pull back my shoulders, pick up my stuffed animals, and get started with my homework.

One night, aware that Jimmy's coming over after supper so we can work on our science project, I buckle down and get to work on my homework right away. I'm bent over my algebra, solving linear equations, when the doorbell rings. I look up, check the clock, and continue. But then Mom calls me to come downstairs.

A local newsman has arrived in response to one of the letters Uncle Theodore and I sent out. He follows my mom and me into the living room, where we sit down. Then he begins to question us.

At first, everything's centered on my uncle — who he is, what ship he captains, how long he's been doing that . . . But then the reporter starts asking about me. I'm very happy to explain. I pour out my story and lay it in his lap.

"I believe the exclusion of women from the Space Academy violates our principles of equality. There's a statute I looked up. It's from 1972, which I know is a long time ago, but it hasn't yet been overturned. I found it under the Educational Amendments – Section 1681. It states: *No person in the United States shall, on the basis of sex, be excluded from participation in, be denied the benefits of, or be subjected to discrimination under any education program or activity receiving Federal financial assistance.*

"The Space Academy on the moon receives funding from the Federal Government. I am sure that's in direct violation of this ruling," I tell the newsman.

He scribbles it all down and then asks me why I want to go to the Academy. "Because of your uncle, right?" he says, with a big smile plastered across his surly face.

I look him straight in the eye and counter with, "I want to captain a spacecraft. Is there any reason I shouldn't be allowed to do so? I am fully willing to undergo the seizure of my eggs. I realize and accept that I will be operated on so I can't ever get pregnant, so I really don't see why I shouldn't have as much right to choose my profession as anyone else. Academically, I'm a prime candidate."

That takes Mr. Flenders aback. At first his face reddens, and he shoots a look at Mom, but she's sitting very quietly in the huge wooden rocker. Her face is calm, and her eyes reflect no embarrassment.

"How do you feel about this, Mrs. Smith? Mattie isn't of age and won't be for some time. Would you be willing to allow her to do . . . ah . . . those things she mentioned?"

The man's red face has paled. I think he'd planned to mention the eggs and pregnancy but chickened out. I don't understand his embarrassment. It's simply a fact of life.

Mom sighs. I figure she's going to give me the usual lecture, but she looks me in the eyes and says, "I would love Mattie to choose to stay here, but she wouldn't be happy, Mr. Flenders. She's a very special girl. I always knew that, but it took my husband's brother to explain *why* she's so special.

"You see, Mr. Flenders, Mattie has a remarkable mind, tenacity enough for two people, and a will just as strong. She needs to do what is right for her, whether I want it or not."

The reporter takes that down, flashes his camera at me a couple of times, and then leaves. I hug my mother and thank her. I'm thrilled that I won't have to fight her about it anymore.

As I head back upstairs, I whisper, "Thank you, Uncle Theodore, thanks for talking to Mom."

Jimmy comes over as planned, and we work several hours on our science project, the designing of a wheelchair that works on snow and ice. Jimmy tries to fool around a bit, and I have to speak sharply to him, but then he settles down, and we get all our research done, discuss our design, sketch out what it would look like, and talk about materials. The evening goes quickly. As usual, when Jimmy asks if he can kiss me goodnight, I ignore him.

The following week, the local paper finally gets around to printing a small blurb about my interview. It's placed on the back page, right next to a large ad for kidney stone medicine. On top of it is an article about what happened at the local PTA meeting. That article is bigger.

Still, it's a beginning. My eyes scan and then widen in horror. Mr. Flenders has gotten half the story wrong. He even misquoted my mother, stating that she'd be extremely happy to see me follow in the footsteps of my famous uncle.

When I show it to my parents, they're furious. Dad calls the paper and rampages for an hour. Then he makes them run a retraction, which gets buried somewhere down at the bottom of page seven (sandwiched in between official name changes and court proceedings) a few days later.

I understand Dad's fury. It isn't fair when a newsman completely changes everything, but it's not the inaccuracies that matter so much to me; it's the fact that Mr. Flenders didn't even mention the Education Amendments or my quote about equal education under the law. What a jerk!

About two weeks after that, when I'm busy cramming for my AP test on Saturday — the first of my challenges for skipping high school classes, I get a call from the local news station. They want me to go in and have an interview for a spot on their show. The only problem is that they want me on *that* Saturday.

Anyone who has ever signed up for AP tests knows that there's no choice in the testing date. The time is scheduled down to the minute, and if the student doesn't appear at that exact given moment, he or she loses all opportunity to test.

So, I have to tell the station I can't come to their interview. Then I hang up and cry because I know such opportunities are very rare. (They'd just offered me that one because of a cancellation and admit they have no other openings for months.)

However, unbeknownst to me, while I'm taking the test, the news station has arrived at the testing site, and when I come out, they interview me LIVE. Try to picture that: I've worn my scruffy jeans and a comfortable, old, faded pink sweatshirt that says, "Think!" My hair is pulled back into a loose braid, which I've probably pulled out during my ordeal since I, unfortunately, have a bad habit of playing with my hair during stressful times.

I've been sitting on a cramped, wooden student's chair, and my butt is stiff, and I desperately need to use the john, and to top all that, I'm "brain dead" from five hours of test-taking.

After the first shock of the photos going off and the bright lights forcing my eyes to blink and tear, I beg to use the bathroom and then scurry inside. A crowd has developed, and there are at least six people from the TV station waiting, so after doing what I urgently needed to do, I take only a second to smooth back my hair and then step back out.

A man named Jim Strager, tells me that they decided to do the show LIVE so they could demonstrate to everyone how "special" I am. "What other student would give up her Saturday to spend all day taking tests?"

Lots of students are dribbling out of rooms, having just finished their essays and multiple choice tests. I wonder if Mr. Strager doesn't see any of them, but I don't argue. I need him on my side.

Someone hands me a bottle of water. I appreciate that immensely. I sip at it and wait for the real questions. Mr. Strager slips them in so smoothly I'm almost unprepared when they come. But the part that surprises me the most — besides their presence — is that when the last student has left from the room, the head of testing company that processes the tests appears and AGREES to correct my test on the spot!

That never happens. In fact, it usually takes months before results are known, and then finally, when they're sent out, the results are on a slip of paper, all computerized and cold.

However, this time, due to the power of the press, I find out I've passed World History, U. S. History, and Civics — the last, something I felt rather shaky on. I whisper a prayer of thanks that I was able to write one of my essays on the Education Amendments, which obviously enabled my pass.

Anyway, the coverage I get from that interview sends the media calling in full force. A week later, I get scheduled for a talk show during the day, and a month after that, I get three late night radio spots. It's scary, but I'm that determined. Besides, it's the start down that long tunnel of my dreams. I whisper about it nightly to my uncle, take lots of deep breaths, and nervously tread forward.

That's the good news. The bad news is that the interviews start the "crazies" calling. One woman begins to leave daily messages on our computer-recorder. She repeatedly tells us that women should "stay home." Mom laughs about the never-ending barrage of calls, but Dad gets angry.

He orders the computer not to record those kinds of calls anymore, but Mom later rescinds that. She thinks it's better to allow someone to have a safe outlet for anger. I don't think Dad changes his mind about the situation, but he doesn't argue further. It's rare for him to ever argue with Mom about anything.

Dr. Stephenson answers my letter. I should be thrilled. I know she's an important woman, and for her to take the time to write me should be quite exciting. When my hands tear open the envelope, they're shaking. At first, I don't even want to read the letter. I throw it down on my desk and walk off. But after dinner, I find that I can't concentrate on my homework until I see what she's said. Giving in, I open the folded sheet and start to read.

Firstly, she tells me she understands the nature of my dissatisfaction but repeats that such rules are for the best. She informs me that she'd love to have me interview for INASA. Angrily, I start to tear the letter up, but I don't. Instead, I sit down at my desk and write to her again. This time, I explain about my media coverage and the interviews I'm scheduled to give. I don't know if it will open her eyes, but I hope it will. Things will change. They must. I have to hold onto those convictions. I have to continue to believe.

Other people are starting to dribble in responses, too. Every board member of the Academy responds using a form letter restating the policies. Not a one of them addresses the equality issue. I write each member another letter, providing them with the same information I sent to Dr. Stephenson. If only one of them will stop and think . . .

On Monday, I sign up for more tests, despite my father lecturing me about taking life a little easier. I don't tell him the truth — that I'm too restless *not* to push. Nor do I tell my father how the ground makes me feel like a prisoner. He'd think I was mentally ill if I explained how I feel claustrophobic whenever I stare up at the stars.

Sometimes, I can recall the vibration of the Jolly Roger's blast off — like I'm there, still witnessing it. If I shut my eyes, I feel the excitement of it, that feeling of going home, as if space is where I *really* belong. At times, I feel like I'll die if I don't get up there. I can't wait for the day I go into space, so I press forward, signing up for Algebra II, biology, and Level I World Literature, and I study incessantly.

Jimmy asks me to go the movies with him. I don't really want to. Nothing interesting is playing. He invites me to go ice-skating, too, but I turn that down flat. Then he offers me a lesson in hang-gliding. To that, I agree. Hang gliding would be worth the loss of study time.

Needless to say, when I bring it up, my mother has a fit. Dad shakes his head "no," but Jimmy, sweet Jimmy, the best friend a girl ever had, comes over and talks to my folks. He shows them a brochure, points out the instructor's qualifications, goes over the safety precautions, and suggests that my dad come with us. Finally, it's agreed that I can go.

Our lesson is not for another two weeks, but for some reason, the thought of hang gliding perks up, not only me, but my father. For a while, dinners are joyful once more, and we laugh and tell stories. It's almost like when Uncle Theodore was there. Almost.

My next set of interviews goes okay. The first one is the worst because I don't know what to expect from them. At the studio, they apply makeup that I don't like, rouge my cheeks, add eyeliner and lash enhancer, then powder my face. Then they stick a microphone on my blouse lapel.

I walk into the room and have to sit there all alone, waiting for my turn to come out onto the stage. Honestly, the waiting is the worst part, for there are lots of people in the audience, and my legs quiver like two tied sticks in a steady current. Even when I finally am called and walk into the area to sit down, my knees continue their vibration. But then the hostess starts asking me questions, and I forget about the spectators. I tell my story, quote the law, and try to convince Ms. Beachum that I should be allowed to enter the Academy.

Ms. Beachum questions me about what I'd be giving up, and I look into the camera and forget everyone is there. "It's not really about what I'll be giving up," I tell her. "Don't you see that? It's what I'll gain. I can still have children if that becomes important later. My eggs will be stored.

And when they do that, the eggs are still viable, maybe even better than if they hadn't been removed — better because they've been examined for genetic mutations. So, you see, that point is trivial. It isn't really an issue as to why the Academy won't allow women to attend. It's an excuse to hide their prejudice.

"And what I'll gain from going to the Academy is the chance to journey through space, to visit other worlds, to explore and to make a difference to humanity. I want that more than anything else. I want to captain a ship that discovers something that will benefit our world, and just because I'm female, I don't believe it's right to forbid me from doing that, do you?"

Poor Ms. Beachum has to cut me off. I've run into commercial time, and she doesn't get all her questions in. But I also have won over the audience. Each time a guest comes on the show after he or she is done speaking, the audience takes a vote. In my case, the decision is unanimous. On public T.V., the audience declares that I should be admitted to the Academy.

Chapter Seven

The day *finally* arrives when Jimmy, his father, my father, and I drive out to the hang-gliding school. The first thing we find out is that to become proficient, we need to take at least a five-day course. Our fathers shrug off that suggestion and insist we're there only for the introductory lesson.

That discussion over, we are then introduced to Tim Zonert, our beginning instructor. He makes us sign all kinds of insurance forms. Both dads raise their eyebrows at that. The forms are rather ominous, filled with warnings about the dangers of the sport. Repeatedly, Jimmy and I have to reassure our fathers that we'll be careful. With heavy sighs, our dad's finally sign, and our freebie lesson begins.

First, Tim gives us a flip chart demonstration, showing us the steps and what not to do when hang-gliding. Then we see a video. My dad's face lights up like Disneyland at night. I can tell he wants to sign up for the full five-day class. I hope that means he'll let me do it, too.

Then Tim gives us some theory about the principles of flight. That's basic stuff for me, but I listen politely and hope nothing about it makes Dad lose his nerve. After that's over, we walk to the beginner's hill, where we get the equipment. Our glider is red, white, and blue. It's the prettiest of all of them — at least, I think so. Tim shows us how to rig the glider. Then we put on our harnesses and helmets.

Jimmy looks really cute in his. He smiles at me when I tell him that, but he's turned pretty pale. I wonder if he's going to make it. Jimmy isn't an enthusiast of tree climbing or anything that involves heights. But he's a trooper, always someone you can count on.

Tim shows us how to check over the glider to make sure it's safe to fly. We each practice clipping ourselves onto the glider and make a "hang check," a mandatory safety requirement.

Through all this, it's difficult not to become impatient. I want to fly, not stand around talking about it all day. But unfortunately, it's *still* not our turn. Tim tells us that first, he will demonstrate how it's done. So he goes through all the steps we just practiced. He takes off and does a short flight. Then he lands and takes off a couple of times more, making sure we understand how to do each step. FINALLY, it's our turn.

Jimmy's father gets to go first. We watch as he picks up the glider and balances it on his shoulders. The wind fights him, but he adjusts for it. Tim runs alongside, with a tether rope on the nose of the glider and extra ropes on the wings. The glider doesn't go much higher than a couple of feet. Jimmy pales even more, but he gives me a thumbs up. He's still willing to try it.

My dad goes next. He has trouble landing, forgetting about what the instructor told him. He pushes the A-frame away from him too much, and when Tim pulls the nose back down, the landing is less than perfect. But Dad's fine. He jumps up, laughing.

We've earlier drawn straws about our order to fly. Jimmy's next. He doesn't go very high, and his landing is even worse than my father's, but he does okay. When he takes his helmet off, I see he's grinning, and his father slaps him on the back.

"That's my boy," his father says. I roll my eyes. That kind of male thing really bugs me.

I'm up next. I'm so excited I almost forget to listen to Tim's coaching. The moment my feet leave the ground, my heart begins pumping at supersonic speeds, but not in fear. I'm laughing from the joy of it. I'm soaring, lifting off into the sky, and it feels so incredibly right.

I think Tim allows me to go further than the others and even slightly higher. The air rushes by, the sky is the blue of freedom, and I feel *alive*. In fact, I'm so happy, I feel like singing, shouting out with the joy of it. I don't ever want to come down, but I can see that Tim is winded.

He's been running beside all of us the whole time. I nod to him that I'm ready to land, and then I smoothly slide the A-frame into position, my knees bent, my body slightly forward. I don't fall like the others. I land almost exactly like the instructor did in his demo land.

"Well done," Tim tells me, panting like an exhausted greyhound. "You've got great form already, Mattie. Are you sure you haven't done this before?"

I grin up at Tim. "Only every night in my dreams." Then I throw my arms up in the air and wheel around in circles, giggling like I'm drunk or something.

Dad quiets me down, kisses my cheek, and murmurs something about showing off, but he's laughing, too. I glance back at the others. Jimmy's face is glowing, and he's smiling almost as broadly as I am, but his father just stares at me, wide-eyed with amazement. "Heavens," he says, "That was incredible! Are you part bird, girl?"

As we head back down to the building that houses the school, all four of us are singing the joy of our flight. There's no doubt about our enthusiasm. Tim gets out the paperwork for signing us up for further classes, his mouth curved around its certainty. We crowd the counter, each of us wanting to be the first to write our name down on the schedule.

Then Jimmy and I back away so the two fathers can pull out their credit cards and sign up for the series of classes. Jimmy and I give a quick high-five when that's all settled and deliver numerous grateful thanks to our fathers. (I give mine a kiss, too.)

Then, the four of us sit down with cans of cola and moisten dry throats, meanwhile attempting to recall every moment of the lesson. It's only while sitting that we realize that our bodies are exhausted. "I feel like I've been through a washing machine and dryer cycle," Jimmy says, and we all nod our heads.

But all that's forgotten when Tim stops by to hand us our golden certificates to show that we've actually flown our first hang-glider.

We ooh and aah for a moment, but then I hand mine back. "I don't want mine until I've really soared by myself — I mean, without you hanging on beside me," I tell Tim. Looking very sheepish, the others all agree, and they each hand theirs back, too.

Then, our colas finished, we head for home. What a wondrous day. I can't wait to do it all again. People really are meant to fly!

When I arrive home, there's an e-mail from Dr. Stephenson stating that she's coming to Los Angeles on business and would like to meet me. I check with my parents, and we take a peek at the calendar hanging on the kitchen wall. The date in question is a school holiday, the first day of spring vacation. Dad says he'll be glad to take me to the city, so I e-mail Dr. Stephenson back with a "yes." Then I wonder about what she has to say. I hope she's not going to bring up again that I can work at INASA. I'm not about to give up my dreams.

All week long I travel through the days in a zombie state, doing the schoolwork, studying, and yet knowing that I'll only really come alive during flight. Then, it rains, and the next week's hang-gliding lesson is canceled. Why does fate do that sometimes? Why doesn't it understand that if something is so wondrous, nothing should be allowed to put it off?

But the days sashay by, and then Saturday rolls around again, and our lesson is even more incredible than I could imagine. We get to go without any ropes, and we fly — at least, I do, almost two hundred yards! We do spend most of our lesson practicing our pitch and roll control, but Dad gets a lot better at landings, even though Jimmy doesn't. My best friend lands on his bottom every time. He's starting to look slightly doubtful about the whole thing, but I know he won't stop, not as long as I want to go, and I absolutely love hang-gliding!

The day after the hang-gliding lesson, on a Sunday, a man with several cameras around his neck and a young woman with rose tattoos on her cheek come to our door saying they're from some women's magazine we've never heard of. They tell us they're investigating gender inequality. Mom won't let them in until she sees some I.D. Then she's super cautious and calls Dad to come in and join us.

Unfortunately, Dad's been out gardening and is wearing ragged and filthy clothes. The woman gives him the strangest look. "You're Mattie's father?" she asks several times, and when my father, each time, assures her he is, the cameraman, without asking permission, takes Dad's picture. Now you have to imagine what my father looks like when he's gardening. He always wears an African safari hat on his head and a cook's apron around his middle.

He usually goes barefoot in the garden, but since that day he was working with the rose bushes, he was wearing his heavy boots, long gray socks, and khaki Bermuda shorts, and a long sleeved, gray tee shirt that shows an apple tree heavy with its autumn crop of *red delicious,* and the words "Gardeners plant their way to the future."

To top that off, Dad has long pink rubber gloves that stretch up his arms, clear past his elbows. In other words, I'm afraid he's rather an odd sight to anyone not used to it.

The woman's eyes finally shrink to a more normal size, and she turns her stare away from my father's apparel and starts questioning me. We forget about the photographer then as I start telling Carmen all about the Academy and the Educational Amendments of 1972, I see she's writing it down, and I start to hope that she'll actually print it all, but I remember how the other reporter did that, too. Do I dare have expectations of a fair interview?

The photographer startles me several times with his flashes since I'm not paying attention to him. Each time, it disturbs my concentration, but I'm too involved with my story to worry about it. Each time, Carmen almost immediately asks me another question, and again, I forget the camera is watching me.

Then when the flash comes, I remember and stop again. I'm sure it makes my words disjointed. I know it makes it harder to be coherent. I probably glare at the man some, but I'm so hopeful that Carmen will actually use what I'm telling her that I just keep going. I'm determined to keep talking as long she's listening.

But after no more than twenty minutes, both Carmen and Frances stand up, ask us to sign a release, and then leave.

In the weeks that follow, at first, Mom and I look for the magazine that Carmen and Frances said they wrote for, but it's not a journal anyone seems to carry locally, so eventually, we just forget about it—until a package comes in the mail. Then we realize they were the real thing.

Carmen and Ken have given my words five whole pages, but on the first one, poor Dad with his pink gloves and his pruning shears raised in a salute to Mom because she's just called him inside, introduces my father to all the magazine's readers. Luckily, he has a good sense of humor and just laughs.

The article also has a picture of Mom, too. She looks great. Then we turn the page, and it's me staring back. I've been given a full-page picture. I don't look at all the way I think I look. It makes me seem older somehow. My eyes are open-wide, staring right into the camera, and I have a serious look on my face, "my determined expression," Mom calls it. I think it was the picture Frances took while I was telling Carmen about the Academy's unfair rule against women cadets.

The written part of the article is extremely well done. Carmen got everything correct. She blends my words with her own commentary, reiterating it all perfectly. We turn the page and see the ending. Carmen has somehow gotten a picture of Uncle Theodore in his space uniform and underneath is another picture. I'm hang-gliding.

"Where did they get that?" I blurt out, but Dad and I remember the picture. The Hang-Gliding School has it mounted in their office.

"Will Mattie Masters Smith follow in the footsteps of her famous uncle?" the line says underneath the picture of Uncle Theodore. Then it gives a brief splattering of information about him, including the year he graduated from the Academy.

Underneath the Hang-Gliding picture is a caption that says, "Space Academy, beware. This young woman will keep her feet on the ground for no man."

"Wow," I say, just at the same moment that Simon comes running in. "Quick, turn on the television. Mattie's on the news."

"A local girl has been stirring things up for the United States Spaceship Academy. News at 4:30."

They flash the same picture of me that *Woman's Equality Magazine* has taken. I gasp.

"What time is it?" Dad asks, his face glowing with excitement. But he doesn't wait to hear. He starts flipping from channel to channel to see if any of the other networks have picked up the story. We catch a couple of news programs, but neither of them mentions me — at least not in the two minutes that Dad allows us to watch.

"Darn. Theodore told me this would happen, but it's too soon. Mattie's not even out of high school yet," Dad complains.

"Calm down, Matison. This is good news. It's what you wanted for her. Isn't it?" Mom asks, plopping down beside him so she can soothe his worry.

Simon glances at me. "Are you famous now? Do you think this will make me popular again?"

I shake my head. "I'm afraid not, Simon. It's not fame I'm looking for. I just want to go to the Academy."

The doorbell rings, and Simon runs to open it, ignoring Mom's, "Find out who it is first."

No danger. It's only our slightly batty next-door neighbor, Barbara. "Did you see that?" she asks, looking pointedly at the television set. They showed Mattie's picture on the news. I'm sure of it. Did you go and do something bad, child?"

Mom stands up, sighing. "She didn't do anything bad, Barbara. Mattie just wants to go to the Space Academy, and they won't let her."

That doesn't appease the neighbor. She's a worrywart who's constantly berating the way things are. One might think that would mean that she'd be on my side, but the way she thinks things should go are usually pretty old-fashioned — as in about two hundred years ago.

"Well then, dear, go somewhere else," she tells me. "There are lots of good schools. Why, my Charlie went to the University of Santa Barbara. He was very happy there."

Meanwhile, she's wagging her finger at me and, for some reason, scolding Simon as well, even though he's obviously years and years away from attending *any* college.

"Yes, we know, Barbara," Mother tells her as she moves the neighbor back toward the front door. "But Mattie wants to go to a special school. She wants to be a spaceship captain."

The neighbor halts, turns around, and stares at me as if I've suddenly spouted green hair and antennae. "That's ridiculous. Haven't you outgrown that foolishness yet, Mattie?"

Without giving me a chance to respond, Barbara continues, ignoring Mom's hand on her arm. "I don't know why anyone would want to go up there anyway. Did you know you can't breathe in space? You have to wear a spacesuit, too, and eat from a tube of toothpaste. It's not a nice place for a sweet girl to go. Tell her that, Clare."

Mom throws an arm around Barbara's shoulder and tries to scoop her further out of the room. She knows better than to argue and nods her head at each of the neighbor's statements. "Thank you, Barbara," my mom tells her. "I'll tell Mattie those things. However, I'm pretty sure she knows about the spacesuits and the food tubes, but thank you for stopping by."

Mom is good at that. She is kind to everyone. She gets lots of practice with Barbara, though, because our neighbor wanders over to our house quite often and then repeatedly goes off on tangents, lecturing us about avoiding homegrown mushrooms or cutting the lawn when it might be too wet or once, even about spraying our rose bushes. The latter really set Dad off because he prides himself on his mildew-free roses, but Mom saved that calamity as well, assuring Barbara that we would be careful.

As the door shuts, Barbara heading off down the driveway, we all pitch in and start dinner. Simon shreds cheese. I start the tomato sauce, and Dad boils the water for the noodles while Mom begins to wash the homegrown lettuce for our usual dinner salad. The news is still on in the other room, though, and all of us continue to listen with one ear. When we hear the teaser mentioning me, we go running in to hear what they're about to say.

We've come too early. We have to sit through two car commercials and a dog food ad before the news returns. Then, the weather report is given, and they discuss which of the two main football teams in our state will go to the finals.

Then finally — "Mattie Masters Smith may look like any other high school girl," they say, accompanying their words by showing my high school photo. "She gets good grades, never causes any trouble, and spends her weekends hang-gliding with her father. (They show the picture of me hanging gliding) but she's also leading a secret life that few in the community know about.

"Mattie Masters Smith has decided to challenge the United States Spaceship Academy for the right to become a cadet. (They show one of my interview pictures, the broadcast with Ms. Beachum.) Yes, you heard me right. This beautiful girl (They show the picture that the photographer for *Woman's Equality Magazine* took) is bound and determined to become the first woman space captain.

"We wish you the best of luck, Mattie. You make us proud."

"That's great," says my father, and he beams at me. "That will stir them up. Bad publicity is what INASA doesn't want."

I sigh. Then I remember the spaghetti sauce and run back into the kitchen. Luckily, Mom remembered to turn it off, so it's fine. Figuring that we've heard everything, we turn off the TV and get back to our dinner preparations.

"We'll have to send a copy of that magazine to Theodore. He'll get a real kick out of . . ." my dad begins as the phone rings. He picks it up, then his eyes slide to mine. "Sure, she's here."

"It's some news station I've never heard of," Dad tells me, smirking slightly.

I almost drop the phone when I hear that it's the main Los Angeles television station.

"Dad!" I scream. "They want me to go on Charlene Finch's HipTalk LA."

I check with my parents, and they study the refrigerator calendar. The interview falls on the same weekend when I meet with Dr. Stephenson. I groan, thinking I can't do both, but it turns out that it works admirably.

I return to the phone to tell the studio that it's a go. However, since I'm a minor, they won't accept my word and insist on talking with my parents. I put Dad back on because he's standing there, half tearing the phone out of my hand.

"Sure, we can do that. That will be fine," he says. "We'll be in the city on that day, speaking with a woman from INASA. She's meeting Mattie at the Hilton. Oh, you will? At the Hilton? Wonderful. That's super!"

Dad hangs up the phone and then turns around to look at us. "Guess who's going to *spend* the night at the Hilton?"

Everyone except Simon starts cheering. But Simon sits down at the table, perches on his elbows, and says, "What about me? What I do while you're there?"

Have you ever seen unhappy green eyes in the middle of a freckle garden? I forget how my brother torments me all the time and go sit down beside him. "I need you there with me. Please, Simon?"

Simon's smile connects all the dots.

We think we'll get to finish our dinner without further interruptions, but just as we sit down with our scoops of ice cream, the phone rings again. Dad disconnects it.

That night when I look at Uncle Theodore's picture, I tell him all about the things that are happening. Sure, I know he can't hear me, but it's a habit from all the years when I used to believe he could. It feels good to talk to him. It feels just like he's there.

When I finish my tale, I check my messages, brush my teeth, and slip into bed. "Night, Uncle Theodore. Thanks for everything."

Chapter Eight

In minutes sleep settles in, and I dream I'm on the *Jolly Roger*. I can see the huge window into space and all the men sitting at their positions, manning the ship. I can even hear the conversation between the two pilots as they discuss the curvature of space. Then, suddenly, the ship begins to roll. I can't understand that. Why would a spaceship be pitching about? Is it solar winds or an uncharted asteroid belt?

"Get up, Sleepy Head," my father says, rocking my bed from side to side. I open my eyes to find that night has turned to morning.

"It can't be time to get up," I protest as I stretch and yawn, but Dad's already gone — off to waken Simon, no doubt.

It's the morning we're going to Los Angeles. My sleepiness dissipates instantly. I spring out of bed. Then I stop and bite my lip. I'm nervous about seeing Dr. Stephenson. What does she want? Why does the INASA need to meet with me? Why couldn't she just have told me whatever it was by e-mail?

I've already packed for our overnighter. All I have to do is dress. I selected what I plan to wear the night before. I step into the revitalizer to freshen up and then tug on a new pair of pants, blouse, and a matching jacket. The cranberry color supposedly suits me — at least, that's what my mother said when we purchased the clothes. I always have doubts, and the truth is that I'd be far happier in a pair of jeans and a tee.

At the table downstairs, Simon is still yawning. His hair's uncombed, and he looks like he's about to fall back asleep. I'm sure he'll do so on our flight to Los Angeles. He does manage to inhale a couple of pieces of Mom's cinnamon toast, however. I just nibble at a breakfast bar and sip some orange juice.

Mom wants to "drive" to the city, so she slides in first. She usually prefers to let Dad do the flying. I raise my eyebrow and look at him. He shrugs. "She wants the practice," he whispers.

The truth is that Mom has been acting kind of funny since she saw the picture of me hang-gliding. I was up in the air when that photo was taken, and I'm laughing, my face all lit up with the joy of it. Mom keeps looking at that picture. I think she's trying to talk herself into taking some hang-gliding lessons with us. Of course, it's possible that has nothing to do with Mom's wanting to fly us into the city, but she's never felt the need to "practice" before.

Really, there's nothing to flying the *beetleflyers*. If I were of age, I'd be able to do it with no problem. In the city, they're all automated, anyway.

Before we even lift up, Simon is contentedly snoozing. He can sleep anywhere. I lean my head against the side of the *B.F.* and eventually nod off a little, too. When I open my eyes, Mom's just taking the flyer off autopilot and is searching for our parking spot. Luckily, the Hilton has reserved us one.

We've arrived early since the traffic was light that morning — a real novelty for the city, Dad tells us. I wake up Simon, and then we step out and stroll into the fancy hotel. Dad and Mom head for the coffee shop, Mom yawningly telling us it's time for her "caffeine fix."

Simon and I aren't interested in eating anything, and we don't need that "fix" since we both napped, so we decide to explore a bit.

We wander around the hotel's gift shops and dart in and out of the fancy ballrooms. I guess we take longer than we thought because Dad has us paged.

At lunchtime, I meet Dr. Stephenson. She's very tall and slender and wears her hair in a neatly trimmed and fashionable style. She's not at all like I pictured her. I thought she'd be dowdy and plain, but she's pretty in a rather stiff way. She invited the whole family for lunch, but Dad's taking Simon off to see dinosaurs at some museum nearby. So, it's just Mom, Dr. Stephenson, and me.

The restaurant is very classy. I'm glad I'm not wearing my jeans. Mom was right. My suit is perfect.

A handsomely suited businessman eyes Dr. Stephenson. He's interested, but she ignores him. I wonder if she's married. I like the way she ignores the man. She's very professional and poised.

We wait until after we've ordered to talk about INASA. Then Dr. Stephenson, Jamie, she tells us to call her, starts explaining why she'd asked for the meeting.

"I'm so glad you could come, Mattie and Clare," she tells us, scooping our interest with a broad smile. "I am delighted to finally meet you after our frequent notes, Mattie. I wanted to talk to you about your campaign to change the rules. You've been stirring up a lot of attention, and it concerns me that you're going to get hurt. You see, INASA's not going to change regulations just to allow one very determined young lady into their Academy. And their reasons are sound.

"Clare," she stays, turning to my mother. "I'm not sure you understand clearly the rationale for the Academy forbidding women in their program. It isn't because of discrimination. It's because . . ."

"I know why," I blurt in. "I've told Mom, too. The radiation from the sun causes mutations in an unborn fetus."

"Mattie, you're being rude," my mother scolds, her eyes stern and disapproving. "Let the doctor finish."

Dr. Stephenson just waves her right hand vaguely. Then she studies each of us a moment. "That's all right. I understand. Don't worry, Clare. I know Mattie only wanted to tell me she understands the dangers."

Then Dr. Stephenson sighs, picks up her goblet of ice water, sips, and, after a moment, returns it to its slightly damp place on the white linen tablecloth. She pauses to wipe her mouth with the cloth napkin. "You know all that about the radiation and the mutations, Mattie, and yet you still want to go?"

My stomach is growling. I ignore it. I forget everything except my need to make Dr. Stephenson see my side of it. "First of all," I tell her, thinking I sound very clear and grown-up. "I don't care if I ever have children. I'm going to have my eggs removed and my tubes tied. Then, when I get up into space, which I'm going to do no matter what INASA decides, there won't be any risk involved — not for my unborn children, I mean."

Our food arrives just then, and Dr. Stephenson waits for our server robot to leave.

"Even so," she starts in again when it rolls away. "Do you understand the precedent you'd be making? You'd force all women to undergo that same operation."

Mom and I haven't really eaten much that morning, so we've chosen from the breakfast menu. The pancakes set in front of us are steaming, the butter melting into huge pools of fat. I scrape it off onto the saucer beside my plate. Then, I reach for the maple syrup.

"I don't require anyone to do anything, Dr. Stephenson, except allow me to go to the Academy. No one has to follow in my footsteps. But what I'm asking for is just to be treated like your other applicants. It should be my right under the Educational Amendments of 1972 to be given equal opportunity under the law."

"You are being unreasonable, Mattie," Dr. Stephenson says. She has ordered a fruit salad with an unbuttered English muffin. My pancakes make me feel childish in comparison, but they're too delicious to wish I'd ordered differently.

"Of course, what you do determines the fate of all those who follow," Dr. Stephenson tells me.

I swallow another bite of pancake, drink some orange juice, and continue my argument. "Other women can choose what they believe is right," I tell her. "But they should be entitled to decide, not have the decision made by someone in the government who unfairly declares that women can't follow their dreams because we're women. That's discrimination, plain and simple."

"And you're only sixteen?" Dr. Stephenson murmurs, raising her eyebrows. She turns to view my mother. "Have you ever had Mattie IQ tested?"

"We don't believe in that," my mom states briskly.

Mom is eating pancakes, too, but she doesn't use maple syrup as I do. Instead, she spreads applesauce across the top and then nibbles at the stack as if she's already full. In a moment, although she's only eaten about one pancake, she slides her plate away and scoots her coffee forward. That's her signal that she's finished eating.

"Every individual has unlimited potential," Mom says, heading into one of her longish lectures. "Mattie just utilizes more of that potential than some, and she's only fifteen still. She won't be sixteen until August."

Dr. Stephenson knows how to deal with impending lectures. She waves her hand again, and for some reason, that distracts Mom, who suddenly stops and picks up her coffee.

"Is that right?" Dr. Stephenson murmurs. "Of course, I agree, Clare. However, I think you must admit that Mattie is very special. In fact, she's so special that I've been sent here by INASA to offer her a junior apprenticeship."

"That's ridiculous. I told you, she's far too young," my mother interrupts again.

"I only have another year of high school," I tell them both. "I've shaved off a year and a half — well, I mean, I will have by the next set of tests, but …"

"Relax. That's not what I mean. INASA's willing to wait for you, Mattie."

Mom slams her coffee cup down into the saucer. Faces turn in our direction. My mother blushes.

"But are they willing to accept me at the Academy?" I ask, leaning forward, unsure exactly what Dr. Stephenson is saying. My blood is racing, full of hope. I feel dizzy, excited . . . scared.

Dr. Stephenson sighs loudly. She lays the unfinished second half of her English muffin back on the plate, wipes her face again, and scoots her chair back slightly, indicating that she's through eating. "I've told you, Mattie. The Space Academy is out of the question. They do *not* now or ever have any plans to accept female cadets."

"Then this is an utter waste of my time," I tell her, bolting up. My unfinished pancakes no longer draw my attention. I couldn't eat another bite. In fact, I feel slightly ill with what I've already consumed.

Yet, the fact that I'm feeling nauseated doesn't keep me silent. The words spill out of me in a rush of anger . . . "I *am* going to the Academy. INASA is wrong to try to bar women. You can go back to them and tell them that. They can't offer me a carrot that sends me off in a whole other direction. I'm going into space with or without them."

"Be polite, Mattie," my mother scolds, catching my sleeve. "I'm sure Dr. Stephenson is just trying to help you."

I look down at my mother, who's still sitting in her chair. I'm so angry I want to snap at her, too, but I don't. "I *am* being polite, Mother," I say frostily. "I didn't throw anything at Dr. Stephenson or walk off without speaking to her about what I really feel. In fact, I haven't even slammed a door or yelled."

Mom reads something in my eyes. Maybe she sees I can't be pressed. She lets go of my sleeve, sighs, and says "Mattie" with that voice that condemns me as *argumentative*.

I shake my head and correct the rest of her statement. "Is Dr. Stephenson *really* trying to help me? I think she's only trying to bribe me so I won't cause trouble."

It's plain to me that brunch is over. I, at least, am ready to leave. "Anything else, Dr. Stephenson? I have an interview to do later for Channel 19. I'd like to rest up for it."

Dr. Stephenson stands. Her eyes stare into mine. "You do understand what I'm offering you, Mattie? We would sponsor your college. That means we would pay *all* expenses."

Beside me, still sitting at the table, Mom gasps. "All expenses? Mattie, do you realize . . .?"

"No, Mom. It's a bribe. I'm going to the Academy. I won't settle for less, not like Dr. Stephenson did. I want to explore planets, not just read about them."

My mother looks stunned. She sputters, but she can't figure out exactly what to say. Dr. Stephenson saves the day. She hands my mother a business card. "A little bit of publicity can make an impressionable young person forget about doing what's best for the future," she tells my mother.

"Call me in a few days. I won't tell INASA that Mattie doesn't want to accept their offer. I'll keep it open so you have some time to talk with her about it. Right now, it's possible Mattie doesn't understand enough about finances to see the whole picture."

I'd promised my mother that I would be polite, but it's getting harder. The kickback she's offering my parents could set them against me. I don't like that.

"Thank you, Dr. Stephenson," I say, my anger barely controlled so that my voice is shaky and higher pitched. "Thank you for your chat. It helps me to see how far INASA will go in their attempts to quiet me."

My mother doesn't like that. Her eyes narrow, and she nibbles at her lip. I hold out my hand to the INASA doctor, thank her, and without waiting for my mother, walk away.

Chapter Nine

Which means that after writing in this diary, I have the rest of the day to do as I please. At first, I turn on TV, but as usual, there are only a couple of soap operas, a talk show about bad daughters, two channels with cartoons where one animal is chasing the other around in circles, and an old Western. I tell it to "shove off," which it recognizes as a valid command, and then I change into my bathing suit, deciding I'll go down to the pool and swim some laps.

Mom walks in just as I'm grabbing a towel. "You could have been more polite, Mattie," she says with a frown that turns her face into one giant mask of disapproval.

"You know what she wants, Mom," I snap back. "She thinks I should drop the whole thing. They're not offering me anything at INASA. They just want me to be quiet."

"You can catch more flies with honey than with vinegar," Mom offers.

That's the oddest of my mother's many such expressions. I can't understand why anyone would want to catch flies. Besides, is she comparing INASA to a bunch of irksome insects? Wisely, I keep quiet. I actually do understand the expression's meaning, but I don't want to think about it at the moment.

Then my mom's eyes take in my swimsuit. "Oh, that's a great idea, Mattie. Wait a minute, and I'll join you."

Downstairs in the basement pool, the sun is delightfully warm as it streams in through the translucent covering overhead. A couple of hotel guest are scattered about on the plastometal chaise lounges. Their bodies are drinking in the filtered sun.

I walk over to the pool. Mom hangs back, checking to see if the sunbathers are looking at her. She always worries that she's getting fat, although she can still fit in the gowns she wore when she first met Dad. Anyway, nobody's looking at her.

I dip my toe into the water. "It's perfect, Mom," I say, and I throw my towel onto a vacant chair and dive in.

I suppose I may have splashed a bit, but Mom doesn't complain. She just follows me in and starts swimming laps. When I come up from my dive, I watch the graceful way her arms cut through the water. I remember how she once told me she was on the swim team in high school. We don't get to swim often, but it must be that those kinds of skills stick with you, for Mom still looks like she's a pro.

I wait until she's back in the shallow end of the pool where I'm standing, and then I launch myself into the water. Soon, I fall into the same routine as Mom's — liquid pacing.

We swim companionably for a long time until Mom gives out. I dog paddle a moment to watch her climb up the ladder. She's no longer concerned about the sunbathers. She's holding onto the plastometal of the ladder bars, gripping them as if she needs help standing up. She lingers there a moment, huffing a bit, and then she makes her way to the chaise and drops down. "Go on, Mattie. I just need to rest a minute."

I fold back into the water and reestablish my robotic strokes — back and forth, back and forth.

I love to swim. I always think that swimming is pretty much like being in space. The body is weightless, floating languidly unless set in motion in one direction or another. I let my mind picture the black emptiness, the peace that comes from feeling such openness all around me. That openness terrifies some people, I've heard. But for me, it's the joy of total, unrestrained freedom.

It surprises me when I feel the impact of a body diving into the water. I figure it's my mother on her second wind, but when I take a breath, my eyes open and see her still stretched out, looking drowsy from the sun.

I continue my laps, but I peek at the invader. It's a woman, one wearing a flowered purple swim cap. She matches my strokes and swims along beside me. I feel as if my freedom has been invaded, and resent her presence, but I'm caught up in my routine and can't stop. Back and forth, back and forth. It hypnotizes me into the rhythm of its flow.

Suddenly, a hand reaches out, and I struggle back into the now. My first thought is that it's my mother grabbing me. Then I paddle backward and push away with my feet, my heart heaving from the touch of a stranger.

"Your mother's calling you," the woman says, and I start to glance at my mother to see what she wants when the voice registers, and I realize I've been swimming with Dr. Stephenson.

"What are you doing here?" I say before I realize how unreasonable that sounds. I try to think of something intelligent to save face from the rudeness of my outburst, but my mind is numbed from the chlorine and the abruptness of being jerked out of weightlessness.

We've drifted into the shallow. I touch the bottom of the pool. "I'm sorry. I didn't mean it to sound like that. I was just surprised to see you, is all."

"I followed you, I'm afraid. You see . . ."

"You followed me? Why?"

I've done it again. I lock my lips and wonder if chlorine is harmful to brain cells.

Dr. Stephenson merely laughs. "It's all right. I've invaded your free time. I respect that normally. You see, I have the same problem. I get very snippy when I'm riding horses, and someone attempts to talk business. That's my time. I do understand, Mattie.

"However, I've been in contact with INASA again. They want you to be their teen spokeswoman at the space agency."

That is the last straw. I fall backwards into the water, trying to cool down my temper. When I come back up, I'm still pretty upset, but I attempt to be cordial.

"You want me to convince females that INASA is a great place to work? Ha! That's totally wrong. INASA discriminates against us women. Why would I want to be a spokesperson for that?"

"We're working on the problem, Mattie. We've been working on it for forty years, ever since we discovered the dangers. It wasn't evident at first. The first women in space didn't stay up there that long. So there weren't any problems. But when they stayed longer, and we discovered what resulted from that — well, we couldn't do anything else but to ban women from the Space Station and from living on the moon."

I sigh and roll my eyes. "I know all that, but it isn't fair for you to just end it as if there aren't any alternatives. We have options. If a woman can't get pregnant, then what does it matter to you?"

"Think, Mattie. Do you believe we can tell women that mandatory sterility is the only route to attend the Space Academy? What law would substantiate that? There would be more disputes over that resolution than over the current ban.

"We want you on our side, Mattie. We want your potential, your dreams, your ability. The day when you decide that we are *not* the enemy, I hope you accept our offer. INASA is the right place for you if you love astronomy as much as you say. You can guide the future. You can see it first-hand. You can live your life and still have it all."

"I will have it all. I'm going to the Academy," I reaffirm.

Dr. Stephenson sighs heavily, shakes her head, and climbs out of the pool. I watch her grab up her hotel towel, wrap it around her, then pull off the swimmer's cap. Her hair flows down her back, much longer than I'd assumed it would be. Her figure is good, too. It's obvious she works out. For a moment, I wonder about her life. Is she happy? Did she become what she really wanted?

Then I shrug and lie back in the water. As I allow my body to drift freely in the warmth of the heated pool, my thoughts float back into space. I sigh happily. Once again, I feel weightless.

Chapter Ten

Later that day, after Dad and Simon return from the museum, we all get ready for the television show interview. At the appointed time, a real chauffeur shows up in an old-fashioned limousine. The man is wearing a uniform in crimson velvet, trimmed with white silk.

Simon whispers that he's dressed like Santa, but he really isn't — more like an elegant spy from long, long ago. His dark skin glows with health, and his smile reveals teeth whiter than Mom's chinaware. He opens the doors for us, clicks his heals together, bows slightly, and we pile in, Simon first.

Mom and I are wearing dresses, so we act lady-like, but Simon is not intimidated by anything. He jumps inside and then starts pouncing around the vehicle's backseat, exploring every button and knob.

A moment passes as the chauffeur walks around the vehicle and slides into the front seat. Then, a window opens between the front seat and back. "Should you care to address me, my name is Eufredrick. Would you care for some beverages?"

"What a lovely name," my mother cries out before Simon can respond to ask about food sources.

"Thank you, ma'am," he says stiffly and nods again. "Which one of you is Mattie Smith?" he asks.

I open my mouth to answer him, but my brother blurts out. "It isn't Smith," he says. "We're Masters Smith. This is my sister, Mattie. She's really Matilda, but no one is supposed to know that."

"I see," the chauffeur says. "Masters Smith?"

"Dad says that's because smiths used to make jewelry, and the master was a smith that did it very well. That's what he thinks, anyway."

"Enough, Simon," my dad says, laughing. "I am sure Mr. Eufredrick doesn't want to hear our whole history."

"Just Eufredrick, Mr. Masters Smith," the chauffeur says, starting up the engine but still managing to throw us an eye-stopping grin full of teeth.

"What about the drinks?" Simon complains to his father.

Without turning around to look at us, Eufredrick replies, "You will find a supply in the refrigerator on the right. There are several fine wines for the adults and a variety of soft drinks and fruit juices for the young people. Please help yourself to whatever you like. There are snacks there, too. Is there anything else I can be of service with?" he asks as he pulls out into the ground traffic.

"No, thank you. This is quite . . ."

"Wowsers! This is the ultimate," Simon exclaims after hurtling himself across the seat so he could be the first to inspect the contents.

"Just one, Simon," Mom says, but Simon is so engrossed I doubt he even hears her at that moment. Meanwhile, the window is sliding back up, just as Simon starts calling off the varieties of candy bars and chips in the side compartments.

Dad laughs and glances at Mom. "Care for anything?" he asks. It's obvious that Mom is getting nervous about the interview. She's been stewing all that morning about what to say and do in front of the camera. I'm glad she's the one who's nervous. It keeps me from being scared.

My mother sighs and shakes her head. Then she calls out that she'll take a water. I ask for one, too. Simon tosses them to us and waits for Dad's order. Just then, the limo stops. We see nothing but a solid carpet of cars.

"What's going on?" Dad asks the chauffeur, buzzing him with the button he's been told to use.

The window slides back down, and the driver says, "This is normal. Nothing to worry about. We'll be there in plenty of time."

Eufredrick doesn't seem to be bothered, but as the window slides up, we all glance at our watches. Only Simon seems oblivious, munching on three candy bars at the same time, something Dad never would have allowed if he were paying attention. Dad gulps down his soda, staring out at the cars all around us. Then he glances at his watch again and shakes his head. "Not going to make it, Mattie. I'm sorry, honey."

I laugh. "I'm not worried about that. Even if I get there too late, I can still talk to them about what INASA's trying to pull. It doesn't really matter, Dad."

"You be careful about what you say now, Mattie. You certainly don't want to make anyone angry with you," Mom scolds. I can tell from the look that she gives Dad that they've discussed what happened with Mrs. Stephenson and her offer of a scholarship.

I sigh. "Mom, that's exactly what I'm *trying* to do. Don't you see? I have to rock the boat to get them to modernize their rules. Of course, they're going to get mad at me. That's the deal. Didn't Uncle Theodore explain that?"

"Calm down," my father attempts to soothe either me — or my mom. "Save your fire for the interview, Mattie. You don't have to convince us. It's just hard to say no to a full scholarship . . . but you have to do what you have to do. We understand that, honey. We do understand."

Looking at his face, I see that he does. It's only Mom who still has a big question right on her pursed lips. Dad gives her a quick kiss to chase away whatever words she might have added.

The limo slides us through traffic with several honks, a couple of forced entries between cars, and a smooth left turn into the iron gates that hold the TV studio. Even Simon stops chewing to look around. "Wow!" he says. "This is really supero!

Inside the studio it's not nearly as exciting as on the outside, but there are cameras everywhere and scaffolding like someone's about to paint. People are talking and laughing. No one notices us as we head past the guard who checks our ID.

We're really appreciative that the limo driver is escorting us to the right place because the studio is enormous. Eufredrick steers us in and out of maze after maze until I begin to feel like a mouse searching for food — or a way out.

"Where's Captain Jetstream?" my brother asks Eufredrick. Simon's eyes are whirling and flitting all about. It's a wonder he doesn't trip over something.

The chauffeur gives an amused smile. "I'm afraid the Captain doesn't work out of this studio. He's with ApplePie Studio."

"What about *CosmoDog* and *Stoufer and Lexion* and *BatCat*?" Simon probes, listing all his favorites.

I tune Simon out and practice deep breathing to still my racing heart.

"You okay?" Dad asks.

I slide closer. "What if I say something I shouldn't, Dad? What if I embarrass everyone?"

Dad stops right in the middle of the long hall, cups my face in his large hands, and, staring down at me, says, "Mattie." Then he gives me of those long, deep-down looks. "I have never been disappointed in anything you've ever said or done. I can't imagine being embarrassed by you. I know you too well to worry about anything, and you must have the confidence in yourself to know that you're going to do an excellent job of presenting your case.

"After all, you are talking about things that are felt from your heart — how it feels to be locked out of something *just* because you're female, how you know you have the gumption, the brains, and the skills to be a top student at the Space Academy, and how following what is right may not always be the easiest thing in the world, but it's what each person must do no matter how difficult or how many times INASA's has to be stepped on to do it. These are the words I know you'll use, Mattie, because they're the same words you've been saying to me, to all of us, for years."

I wipe a tear. Dad can be so sweet. Then, on tiptoes, I fling my arms around his neck and hug him. "Thank you, Dad. I needed to hear that."

Eufredrick is waiting for us, but instead of getting mad about our stopping to talk, he only gives us another flash of a smile and says as we catch up, "It's around the corner here. Are you ready?"

I nod and gulp. So does the rest of the family. Then we walk forward, following our chauffeur.

We've come to a wooden door, one stained in dark mahogany with an elegant doorknob and gold brass decorations.

"Here we go," Eufredrick says. Then he opens it.

Dad gives my shoulder a squeeze as I pass through the doorway. I return his gesture with a brief smile. That's all we have time for since a six-foot-two slender woman clothed in a tight-fitted, red *Slinky-Dress* comes rushing forward to grab my hand.

"You must be Mattie," she says. "I am so happy to finally meet you. I've been watching your struggle for weeks, trying to get permission to have you on the show. I'm so glad you're here. Welcome, welcome, everyone," she says before any of us can get a word out.

She introduces herself as Dana and tugs me forward into her office. I still haven't had a chance to introduce my parents and brother.

Dana pauses a moment to indicate the chairs we should sit in, and I start to present everyone, but she cuts me off. "Of course, these are your parents. I'm so happy to meet you. You must be so very, very proud of your daughter. I think what she's doing for women will be another great stride forward for our gender. It's as big as the vote, as big as owning property. It's like she's opening up the stars and, in fact, the whole universe.

"Imagine this — one high school girl bridging us across the spans of the future . . ."

"Yes, we're quite proud of Mattie," Dad says. "I'd like you to meet our son, Simon. He's going to be a paleontologist — at least, I think that's his latest ambition."

I smile. Good old Dad. I'm glad he's introduced Simon into the conversation. The kid may be a brat sometimes, but he's a nice brat. I wouldn't hurt him for the world.

Dana finally takes a breath and drops down in her chair. "Oh, I've been monopolizing the conversation again, haven't I? Well, we can't have that.

"Nice to meet you, Simon. A paleontologist, is it? Is that a kind of doctor? A foot doctor or — I know, a baby doctor, right?"

Simon opens his mouth to try to explain that it's a dinosaur specialist, but Dana has gotten her second wind.

She cracks a smile and says, "Just kidding, Simon. I really do know. Dinosaurs, right?"

Simon nods, relieved. Then Dana turns to me. "Now, Mattie, you must tell me. Why did you decide you wanted to go to the Space Academy in the first place? Have they actually out and out denied your application?"

My mind is still stuck on the paleontologist mix-up. I'm not ready for the abrupt change of conversation. I stare at Dana a minute, waiting for her to rev up again.

Then, when I realize that she's ready for me to speak, I take a deep breath and say, "I can't apply. I'm not old enough. Or rather I haven't graduated from high school yet. I have to do that first."

"I see," Dana says, nodding her head as if she already knew that. "And how do you know that there will be a problem in getting accepted?" She reaches over to pick up her pen and starts jiggling the side of it back and forth. Fascinated, I blink and dive back in.

"I already have one of INASA's applications. It says pointblank that no females will be accepted. I brought a copy. Would you like to see it?"

Dana stretches out a long, thin hand. The tips of her fingernails are cherry-colored and sharp as ice picks.

"May I?" she says, removing the paper from my hand.

It only takes her a minute to see the part disallowing female applicants. For one thing, I've bolded it with a heavy yellow marker.

"Why this is outrageous," she growls as if it's the first time she's ever heard of the situation. "We can't allow this to go on. We have to fight it. They can't be allowed to get away with this. It *is* pure and simple discrimination!"

"They do have reasons," my rather timid mother inserts and then looks around as if someone will be angry that she's interrupted."

"Yeah," says Simon. "Like girls don't belong in space."

"Simon!" barks my father. "Simon," cries my mother, both of them looking affronted their son would ever say such a thing.

"Well, there's no girls on Captain Jetstream's ship, and that's 'cause they don't belong in space."

I laugh. "There's the android."

Dana surveys our family for a moment and looks thoughtfully at Simon. "That's perfect. I want your whole family to go on the show with you, and Simon, I want you to say *exactly* what you just said. Okay?"

Mom, Dad, and I all turn to stare at Dana, but I think we figure it out about the same time. Dana wants to use Simon's prejudice as an example of what women are facing.

"That's a good idea," I applaud her.

"And I don't argue with Simon then like I usually would. I just tussle his head and laugh. Suddenly, I'm looking forward to the show. Dana's right, if that's what boys Simon's age are thinking, then it's even more important that females attend the Space Academy.

Chapter Eleven

Dana takes us over to the canteen, the name of the place that has sandwiches and drinks. Unbelievably, Simon fills up again, eating two hot dogs, two bags of yam chips, and three chocolate brownies, which he washes down with at least three big sodas. All that's after eating *three* candy bars in the limo.

My folks and I just have salads, as does Dana, and they're not too bad, but the person who made them needs to lighten up on the onions. I take most of mine off, as does everyone around me.

Dad eats one of the brownies and talks the rest of us into sampling one. Forget the salad. The brownies are the highlight of "dinner."

After, we head back to the taping room. Dana tells us that since Simon and I are minors we can't go on the program live but must be taped ahead so they can patch up whatever needs fixing. That's a relief for me. I was wondering if I should tell her that Simon isn't quite what I'd call reliable.

Upstairs, a makeup lady applies some blusher and eyelash enhancer on each of us. I'm really pleased about the effect, but Simon and Dad aren't. Dad says it makes him look like a clown. Simon seconds the notion.

After makeup, we return to the same room I've seen on the show so many times. I sit in a comfortable black couch with my mother on one side and Dad on the other. Simon sits in the chair across from us.

Then Dana, with her make-up and wardrobe all finished, walks into the room. Wow! Her hair has been brushed up into a stylish head-hugging swirl, and she's added a neat-looking jacket and pearls, which set off her business-like but very feminine style. Simon whistles (and gets scolded by Mom.)

Another lady hooks each of us to a microphone, and then Dana begins.

"Well, good evening to all of you watching. We have a great night planned. But when you hear the policy of our government about females, I promise you, your blood will burn, your indignation will boil, and your anger will incite a flood of letters. I know you're going to be writing to INASA because what I'm going to tell you this evening is extremely upsetting.

"Stay tuned to the commercial. Coming right back, a look at the young lady who, with your help, is going to challenge INASA."

"That was great," I tell Dana during the commercial.

She smiles at me and, while the makeup lady is still patting her face with powder, says, "You ready to go to war now, Mattie? I'm going to hand it to you on a plate. Think you can carry it?"

"I don't know," I tell her honestly. "Aren't you going to ask me questions?"

She smiles broadly. "You bet I am, young lady. I have lots of them, too. But it's up to you to sell your mission. Can you do that?"

I glance at Dad. He's giving me a thumbs-up. Mother is smiling, and Simon — well, he's just being Simon, making faces at the cameraman.

Seeing my look, Dana turns around and gives him a very schoolteacher look. Simon sits up straighter. The ugly faces disappear.

The man beside the camera waves his hand and starts counting backwards, fingers in the air. "Okay, here it goes," Dana tells us. The camera light goes on, and Dana smiles. It has begun.

"Today, we are fortunate to have Mattie Masters Smith and her family. This brilliant and courageous young lady is here to tell you about the injustice she's stumbled up against. Can you explain, Mattie, just why you're bucking INASA?"

"It's not that I want to do that, Dana. I'm not a rebel. It's just that I desperately want to go into space, and the only training facility for that is the Space Academy."

"I don't understand, Mattie. Why can't you go to the Academy? Lots of young people do."

I look at her like I can't believe she's saying that, even though I know it's staged for my benefit. "I would love to go to the Academy, but even though I'm in all honor's classes with a perfect grade point average, I'm excluded solely because of my gender."

I hadn't stopped, but Dana interrupts me with an exclamation of disbelief. "You can't go to the Space Academy just because you're *female*? In today's world? Are you talking about *now*?"

"Yes, I'm afraid so," I say, looking straight into the camera. "Would you like me to read the current INASA application exclusion?"

Dana, prepared for this, still asks, slightly disbelieving. "Yes, please do," she says. "I just can't believe that the International Space Academy wouldn't be delighted to accept someone like you, Mattie

Masters Smith. Wasn't your uncle the captain of the United Nation's Argonaut 3?"

I nod my head. "Yes, he understands my need to be in space. We've talked considerably about the hardships and sacrifices. He's on my side, Dana."

(A picture of the ship Uncle Theodore formerly captained flashes over the monitor, followed by a photo of him, resplendent in his official dress uniform.)

I hold up my application to show its authenticity, clear my voice, and begin. "All applicants must be *male*, of sound health and body physique, and between the ages of seventeen and twenty-eight . . . "

"Well, there it is," Dana says as the cameras flashes the lines up on the screen for the at home audience. "All applicants must be *male* . . ."

"How does that make you feel, Mattie?" Dana asks.

"The first time I read it, I cried," I say, and my eyes suddenly fill up with tears. I brush them away and continue. "I couldn't imagine *not* being free to explore other planets. It was as if someone had labeled me defective, not good enough, *not* up to their standards. I've been reading about space since I was five. My parents didn't encourage it. In fact, my mother would really prefer that I do something else . . ."

(The camera narrows in on the face of my mother. She sighs heavily but nods her head. A tear slides down her right cheek. She brushes it away, unaware that the camera is doing a close-up.)

"Did your feelings ever change?" Dana asks.

I turn to look at her. I'm not aware of it, but the camera shows the lights in my eyes, flaring with anger. My chin juts up (most unbecomingly), and my posture straightens. I'm staring into the camera as I say, "Yes, Dana, because then I got angry. Why shouldn't I be allowed to do what is so important to me? Why should I be labeled as a second-class citizen?

"I have the grades to support my ambition. I have the background I need. I'm strong in leadership. I've passed the language bar, having mastered the universal three. I've majored in the sciences, scoring 98.6 % in all areas on the finals. I have taken college courses in biophysics, astrophysics, and geophysics, and I have the highest rating in my psychoanalysis profiles.

"You see, in every way, I have fulfilled all their markers of qualifications, except in that one, the one thing that I can't change, the one that is so clearly sexual discrimination and contrary to the Educational Amendments – Section 1681 which states, 'No person in the United States shall, on the basis of sex, be excluded from participation in, be denied the benefits of, or be subjected to discrimination under any education program or activity receiving Federal financial assistance.'

"Wait a minute, Mattie. Are you saying that INASA's exclusion of females is illegal?"

"I'm not a lawyer, Dana, but I do question it. It appears to me to be a case of illegal discrimination, wouldn't you agree?"

Dana turns to stare into the camera. "This is one smart girl, INASA. She declines to accuse you directly of illegal discrimination and hopes that I will do so." Dana laughs. "It sure looks like it to me, Mattie. That's my non-legal opinion.

"Tell me, Mattie. Do you have any idea *why* INASA forbids women from applying to the Space Academy? Have you questioned them?"

I draw in a breath. "Yes, my uncle explained it."

"Captain Theodore, formerly of the United Nation's Argonaut 3?" Dana restates.

I nod my head and then dive into the rough part of the interview. I'm fully aware that this is the part that is controversial. There will be many people who think what I'm proposing is a sin. Dana even warned me about the hate mail that will probably bombard the station, but it's time to lay the facts down on the table. This is what I'm going to do. It's what I have to convince the world of. I have to win them to my side.

"Yes, Dana," I begin. "There is a reason why INASA bans females from the Space Academy. It isn't a fair reason, for there are alternatives, but you see, space radiation causes sterility in males.

Those living at the Space Academy will probably be unable to pass on their genes to future generations. The students know that when they sign up. They give up the right to father children, or they make provisions ahead of time by depositing their genes in a sperm bank."

I take a breath and look away from the camera, glancing at Dana. She winks at me, encouraging me to go on.

"Men have that option. They can still go to space and follow their dreams. But the radiation of space doesn't, apparently, cause a woman to become sterile. It causes her eggs to mutate. That is why INASA disallows women from their program.

"But that isn't necessary. Women can do the same as men do. They can make provisions ahead of time. They can leave their eggs behind for the future. They can be made sterile, so there are no complications."

"I see," says Dana. "Are you willing to make that sacrifice, Mattie? Are you willing to have that surgery?"

I glance over at my mother. Her face has whitened. She's wiping at several more tears. I straighten my shoulders and turn back to Dana. "Absolutely. But it's not really a sacrifice. I don't want children — I want a life in space. But even if I should change my mind, the other option still exists. My eggs will be waiting for me on Earth. Just like for the men who choose to journey to new worlds, I will have the same freedom to choose."

"You do realize what you've just said, Mattie."

I'm not sure what she means. I've told her nothing new. I pause to search her face.

She sees my expression and laughs. "It's not "if" anymore, Mattie. It's "when." You said, and I quote you, 'Just like the men who choose to journey to new worlds, I *will* have the same freedom to choose.'

"INASA, I hope you're listening because this is one determined young lady, and she's not just wishing on a star. She's making it happen."

I smile then, understanding. I'm just about to comment on it, but the light switches to orange, and I see we're going into another commercial.

"I want you to call into Station 32," Dana tells the watching viewers. "The number for you to call is 818-366-4567. Let us know what you think about Mattie's attending the Space Academy. Is it a good idea? Is it fair to women to be deprived of this career in space? Let us know your thoughts. Call 818-366-4567."

The moment the light turns red, a young man comes running onto the stage with ice water for all of us. Simon doesn't want one, neither does Mom.

"Hey, when do I get to speak?" Simon yells out.

Dana is having her makeup and hair touched up, but she still takes the time to say, "You're on next, Simon. Do you remember what you said before?"

He nods. Then he reaches for Dad's water. "Okay. I got it. I remember."

"Won't it look funny that no one calls in?" I ask, remembering that this is not a live show.

Dana laughs. "We've already taken care of that — this time. We ran that question at another session. The callers will be arguing about the issue. We'll just plug it in and let you respond to a couple. Don't worry if you can't answer someone. We can always edit that out. Just do the best you can. And relax. You're doing great."

"Ready?" the cameraman asks. Dana scans our faces. "Yeah, we're set."

The light turns green, and Dana says, "Mattie, tell me what your parents think about this plan of yours."

I smile and glance at them. Dad's nodding approval. I'm happy to see that Mom's not crying anymore. "They're very supportive," I answer. "They know how important this is to me."

Dana looks directly into the camera. "How many of you would be supportive of your daughter wanting to go into space?"

"You're positive about how they feel, Mattie? Let's ask them. I'd like to introduce Mattie's parents and her little brother, Simon."

"Mrs. Masters Smith, "Is that true? Are you ready to allow your daughter to go to the Space Academy, even if that means she must be operated on?"

Mom swallows, but she's wiped up her tears. Her eyes aren't red anymore. She takes a quick breath and then says, "Mattie deserves to follow her dream. She has so much potential. I'm proud of her."

"Yes, I can see that you would be. She's an amazing young woman. Didn't I hear that she was in all honor's classes at her high school?"

Mother's face glows. She smiles even broader. "Yes, and she makes me proud each and every day to be her mother."

Someone out in the studio says, "Ahhh…" I peer into the lights but can't see them. I flash my mother a smile and move my lips to form a thank you.

Dana's eyes travel to my father. "How about you, Mr. Masters Smith?"

My father uncrosses his legs and leans forward. "Mattie is just like my brother. She's a go-getter. There's no holding her back. Even the sky can't contain her."

"So you have no hesitation, Mr. Masters Smith, in sending her off to the Space Academy?"

"Hesitation? The Academy should be begging my daughter to come. In a week, she'll be their top student. In two weeks, she'll be in charge of half a dozen committees. In three, why, they'll probably vote her student of the year." Dad laughs.

Then he sobers. "Sure, like my wife, I wish Mattie would be content to stay on the ground. Several universities have already indicated an interest in her. And we certainly don't want her to go so far away. We kind of wish, like all parents, that she'd stay home forever, but that can't happen, you know. Kids grow up, and they must fly their own path. Mattie's path takes her to the stars. We can't stand in the way of that. We have to let her go."

"Well, you certainly do have supportive parents, Mattie," Dana says, glancing back at me.

I smile. I know the camera's doing a close-up, but it doesn't matter. My smile is for my parents, telling them more than thank you, telling them I love them,

"Well, there's one member of the family we haven't heard from — Mattie's little brother. "Simon, what do you think about all this? Should Mattie be allowed to go to the Space Academy?"

Simon perks up. You can tell he's delighted that he finally gets his chance to speak. This waiting has been very hard on him, forcing him not only to sit still for a very long time, but to behave. All that suppressed energy comes into play with his chance to answer Dana. He pops up, bolting out of the chair.

"No way," he says. "Only boys should go to the Academy. That's the way it is in Captain Jetstream. Girls don't belong in space — not unless they're robots, anyway."

Dana smiles into the camera. "Captain Jetstream is from the ApplePie Studio, not ours, of course. I've never watched it."

Dana glances away from the camera to regard Simon. "Do you mean that in Captain Jetstream, there are no females?"

Simon stares at her. "What does that mean?" he questions without a blink of embarrassment.

Dana restates the question. "Do you mean there are no *girls* in Captain Jetstream?"

"Well, not real ones. Only except when Captain goes home to Earth. Then, sometimes, we see some. But they don't go up to space. They're fixing dinner and stuff."

Dana laughs bitterly. "I think we've gone back in time, Simon, back to the days when a woman's role was housework."

"No, they can do other things. My best friend, Petey — his mom's a police officer."

"That's right, Simon. Women *can* do other things. They can even go into space if they have the determination and the tenacity of your sister."

"Well, not on Captain Jetstream," Simon retorts.

Dana smiles. "No, not on programs like Captain Jetstream. Maybe that needs to change, Simon. Maybe your sister is the one who's going to change that."

The light indicates that it's time for a commercial break, and the water boy comes forward. Simon grabs at a bottle this time, and Mom takes one, too. I still have most of my water, so I wave the guy away, but he stands there a moment.

"You have my vote, Mattie," he says. "Besides, I don't understand why all those guys want to go into space if there aren't any females up there. Talking with pretty girls is half the fun of life."

Only after he leaves do I realize that the cameraman was filming the exchange. I wonder why.

Dana stands up then and rolls her shoulders. "You might want to do this, too," she tells me. "How are you standing up to this? You okay, Mattie — everyone?"

We all nod that we're fine. Dana sits back down. "Okay," she says. "We're ready for the next segment."

She does another quick introduction about who I am and who my parents and brother are. Then she nods for the first caller.

I know these are "packaged calls" as Dana has informed me. No one is sitting on the phone waiting for an answer, but still, my hands grow sweaty, and I feel slightly sick, wondering what it is they'll ask me.

"Isn't it true that Mattie is only a minor? How can she make a decision to undergo such a radical operation?"

"Good question," Dana says, swiveling her chair to look at me. "Well, Mattie?"

"My parents *will* have to sign for me, but they've agreed."

"Is that true?" Dana asks, turning to face my folks.

"As long as her eggs are set aside just in case," my mother answers.

"Caller number two. You're on now."

"Mattie, did you ever think that maybe God doesn't want women in space? Maybe this is His sign."

I start to answer, but Mom cuts me off. "Caller number two, it is not God who sets limits on mankind. He gifted us with free choice." Then Mom kind of sputters, embarrassed that she's taken my question. "I'm sorry, Mattie. I shouldn't have spoken.

I . . ."

"Of course, you should, dear. That's why Dana has included all of us, right?" my dad inserts smoothly.

"Absolutely," Dana chuckles. "Anyone else care to address this question?"

Dad can't resist. I can see the twinkle in his eyes as he raises his hand. "Well, this may be a bit controversial, but I believe that God is both male and female — all encompassing. Therefore, he would not, to use a Biblical expression here, smite his right eye to aid his left one."

"And where was that exactly in the Bible?" my mother teases.

We all laugh at Dad's expression but then suddenly remember that this is all being filmed. Apparently, our consternation is visible to Dana. "Don't worry," she tells us. "I loved your explanation, Mr. Masters Smith."

"Let's go to caller number three," she calls out to whomever's in charge of the recordings.

"This question is for the little boy."

"All right," Dana inserts in the pause. "This one's for you, Simon. Are you listening?"

Simon nods and sits up straighter. For a moment, he even stops kicking the chair to make sure he can hear. In that second, seeing his freckled face with the light shining on it, I realize that when I do go away, I'll miss the brat. The thought amazes me so much I almost miss hearing caller number three's question.

"Why do you watch trash like that show? You ought to be outside playing soccer or baseball. Don't you do any team sports?"

Simon sighs. "I hate soccer and baseball. What I like is field hockey. I play that every day after school. But I still watch Captain Jetstream, and it's not trash. It's a cool show."

Dana laughs. "Good job, Simon. I'm sure ApplePie Studio will be happy to hear that their sex-biased cartoon has at least one fan."

Simon opens and closes his mouth. He knows she's said something to demean his show, but he can't figure out what it is. In the end, he just shrugs and goes back to swinging his legs, incidentally beating the chair with his heels.

"Caller number four?" Dana nudges the soundman.

"Yes, this question is for Mattie's mother. "How can you allow your daughter to expose herself to such danger? Don't you know that the odds are that she will die in space?"

I can't help myself. I bust in with a statistic. "Caller number four, this is Mattie Masters Smith speaking. I just want to reassure you. There is only a 16.789 percent chance of dying from an accident in space. The state's statistics concerning *beetleflyer* accidents list fatalities at over 256,500 a year. That means that the percent of people dying in a *B.F.* accident is 21.5%, making it much more dangerous to remain on Earth than to leave it."

"Thank you, Mattie," Dana laughs. "And Mrs. Masters Smith, do you have a response to caller number four's question?"

Mom clears her throat and looks at me. "Danger is all around us, as Mattie pointed out. I've heard that the odds are higher that a person will be hurt in their own home than elsewhere. I don't have all the answers. I don't even have most of them.

"But I do know that when your child talks about nothing but space and stars and astronomy from the time she can barely walk, one finally becomes resigned to it. Mattie was born with a mission. She's going to space no matter what I say or do.

"I look into my daughter's eyes, and I know what I must say. INASA is wrong. Mattie belongs at their Space Academy, and no matter what their beliefs or reasons for barring her from it, I think they're going to have to modernize their application form. They must admit females to their program. They must undo this grievous wrong."

"I think we'll end our segment here," Dana announces. "That is a wonderful conclusion. Is that okay with you, Mattie?"

I nod, and Dana wraps it up with the smoothest of endings: "Thank you, Mr. and Mrs. Masters Smith, Simon, and Mattie, the girl who has started it all with her demand for equal rights in space.

"I wish you all the best of luck in your campaign, Mattie. You certainly have my vote. I want to look up at the moon and know that you've made it up there, Mattie. The world needs you at the Space Academy."

****

After we are finished with the session, Dana asks us if we can come back the following weekend after the segment has aired. She tells us that she wants to do another session with new questions.

I'm delighted and agree right off, but Dad frowns. "Don't you have a game that day, Simon?" he asks.

"Yeah, but the game's on Sunday, not Saturday," Simon tell us. He's smiling hugely because Dana has just given Dad free tickets to visit the studio where Captain Jetstream is made.

Dad remarks that he's not sure the ApplePie Studios will be very happy about the things our family said about their show.

"Are you kidding?" Dana laughs. "ApplePie Studios will be delighted by it. Negative publicity or not, the more time a studio gets their name batted about, the happier they are. Besides, remember they won't have seen this show. It doesn't air for another week."

So it's set. We leave immediately and head over to Apple Studios. Inside, there are rides and lots of interesting things to see, but Simon is enamored by the displays concerning his favorite show. He spends all his money on their junk. It's money that is Simon's to spend, but it still brings frowns and short lectures from my folks.

I sneak off and buy several things Simon has admired but can't afford. His birthday is only two weeks away. I figure they'll make great presents.

We have a wonderful time inside ApplePie Studios, learn a lot about making cartoons, and bring home a heap of souvenirs, but despite what Dana has told us, I notice that we all keep very quiet about the interview we've just been involved in. Not even Simon mentions it, and for Simon, that's a real miracle.

Chapter Twelve

We spend the night in the hotel and then head home the next day. Dad flies this time since Mom's coming down with one of her bad headaches. Simon and I get really quiet then. He starts reading the pamphlets from ApplePie Studios, and I study for a test I have in leadership.

We arrive at the house before ten a.m. Poor Mom slips off into her bedroom while Dad hits the roses out back, acting positive that a stray aphid might have alit on one of his blooms while we were gone. I make a fresh pot of coffee and continue studying while Simon goes outside to search for his best friend, who lives three doors down.

When the phone rings, therefore, it's I who take the call. Strangely, it's an agent from INASA who asks to speak with my parents. For some reason, I assume the call is connected to the interview we just did, and my heart speeds up, ready to defend our words, but then I realize that no one has even viewed it yet. Then I remember telling Mrs. Stephenson about it. "Is this concerning my discussion with Mrs. Stephenson?" I ask.

"I cannot discuss the subject of this call," the man says coldly. "I must speak to your parents, preferably your father. Please inform them of the call.

"My mother's not feeling well. She's lying down. Dad's out in the backyard, probably layered in dirt. Can't I just take a message?"

"Tell your father that we will be stopping by within the hour. We must talk to him in person."

Most people have phones they can carry everywhere with them. My parents don't believe in that. They say that phones monopolize one's life if permitted. Thus, I walk out to the backyard and hunt down my father. He's bending over his apricot rose, the one he calls a Tropicana.

"Dad, INASA is on the phone, and they're not only demanding to talk with you right this minute, but they say that they'll be dropping by to speak to you in person within the hour. It's really weird. They wouldn't tell me what it was all about, and they won't talk to me."

"It's really bad, Mattie. Do you see that touch of black rot? If I hadn't discovered that right away, the next thing you know, it would have taken over the whole bush. It's very contagious. I don't have time to waste. I've got to get my sprayer out and take care of this."

He stops and turns to look at me. "Who did you say is on the phone? Couldn't you just take down a message? Is it about the Space Academy? Why do they need to talk with me about that? I don't understand."

I shrug. Once Dad's in his "worry over the roses syndrome," it's really hard to get through to him.

He sees my look, apparently runs my words back through his mind, and stands up. "Well, I really don't understand why they won't talk to you. It's not like I can change your mind about anything."

Then he sighs again and inspects the top leaves of the plant.

"Dad, the caller is still waiting," I remind him.

"Oh, all right, but it better be a quick chat. I have to get to work on this right away. "

Dad's already walking with me back into the kitchen, so I don't comment. I do understand the significance of black rot. It's hard to get rid of, but it isn't all that uncommon. When you live in an area with a lot of fog, it's what happens whenever it mists or drizzles all day long.

Dad smells the coffee the moment he's inside. "Pour me a cup, would you honey?"

I smile and get his mug out. As I fill it up and doctor it the way Dad likes with ¼ cup of nonfat milk and two packages of sweetener, I listen. Apparently, Dad isn't getting any more information than I did about the purpose of the upcoming visit. He keeps telling them not to come since he has work to do, but I guess INASA is used to getting their own way. When Dad hangs up the phone and takes a big sip of coffee, he has a look on his face that tells me he lost the argument.

"That was strange," he says. "The man wouldn't tell me what INASA wanted, either."

It's almost time for lunch. I start making some tuna mix for sandwiches, stirring in the mayonnaise, some celery, water chestnuts, pepper, and dill. I like mine with lettuce and pickles. Simon always wants chopped black olives on his. Mom uses a sprinkling of cilantro, and Dad demands a slice of cheese and chopped onions. I get all the fixings together and slice up a salad of oranges, shredded carrots, and coconut. Just as I'm getting down a fresh box of raisin oatmeal cookies, Simon comes in, slamming the front door behind him.

"Hey, what's for lunch?" he calls out.

Dad returns with Mom, and we slide into our seats, each making our individualistic sandwiches, and are happily munching away when INASA shows up.

Two hard knocks pound at the door, followed by the ringing of the doorbell. Simon jumps up first and runs to open it.

"Hey, it's the cops," he says.

That stops us all. We put down our sandwiches and make our way to the door. "Yes, may I help you?" Dad asks.

Simon's wrong about them being cops. They're military police, and their faces look like doomsday.

Mom invites them to come into the living room. Two step forward. The others stand at the door, guarding it like we're important people or something. What's going on? Could all this be about one silly interview?

"It would be better if the children were not here," the man with the gold stars on his uniform tells my father.

"Anything you have to tell my wife and me needs to be heard by the kids. What is this about? Are we in trouble for something? Should I be contacting a lawyer?"

"I am sure an attorney will be in touch with you later," the other one says, "but for right now, all we can say is how sorry we are."

"Sorry?" my mother says. "Sorry for what?"

"What is this about?" my father repeats, getting irritated.

"It's about your brother, I'm afraid."

"Theodore?" Dad blurts out, looking even more mystified. "What's he done now?"

"I'm sorry. I'm not doing this very well, I'm afraid. There's been an accident. It's tragic. We don't understand what happened. But, you see, your brother was killed. Please accept my condolences."

"What do you mean — killed? Who killed him? What are you talking about?" Dad demands.

Simon and I are suddenly clinging to each other. I don't know how that happens, but the same moment I realize it, Simon turns to me and buries his face in my arm and starts to cry.

Mom is gripping Dad's arm. She's crying, too, but Dad is just looking puzzled still. It hasn't sunk in yet that his brother is dead.

I stare at the officers' uniforms and wonder why it is they're the ones informing us of this. Uncle Theodore wasn't in the military any longer. Why would the military be telling us this?

Dad must have had the same thought. He suddenly straightens up and demands with a voice angrier than sorrowful. "Why are *you* telling us this? Not to be rude or anything, but how the heck are you involved?"

"Uncle Theodore was a spy, wasn't he?" Simon yells out, suddenly jerking away from me

"Be quiet, Simon. This is real. This isn't one of your imaginative little games. This is real, son," Dad says, wiping a tear.

The man's face has no emotions in it, for all his declarations of being sorry. He is as emotive as an android. I can't stand having him in our house. I hate him, hate the news he's told us, and hate everything about the day. I want to scream at him to leave, to go away and never return, but I can't speak. It's almost as if I've swallowed a rock, a scratchy, heavy rock.

"I'm afraid, actually, that your son is right, Mr. Masters Smith," the officer says. "Your brother worked for the United States government. He was on a mission when his ship blew up. We have reason to suspect it was sabotage."

The man clears his throat. A ripple in his cheek tells me he's thinking about retreating. I can't bear the thought of that either. If he leaves, we'll all explode in grief. We'll all sink into the ground, weeping tears of horror.

"He would have told us," I blurt out, unable to be silent anymore. I cover my mouth, surprised I've spoken. I hadn't meant to. I hadn't known I could. I'd thought my throat had closed, my jaw locked. Oh, Uncle Theodore, how could this be true? How could you be dead?

Dad doesn't say anything. He holds out his arms and says, "Come here, Simon, Mattie. We need each other right now. We need our family to be strong."

We cry then. All of us. Even Dad. The two officers and, I suppose, the ones at the door stand there, waiting. We only break down for a minute. It isn't long enough to grieve fully. It's only long enough to let the grief filter down inside. I suppose, in a way, that crying bonds us as a family. We have each other. Our grief is shared.

"We need to sit down and hear what else these officers have to tell us," Dad says after a moment, the tears running down his face. He doesn't seem to mind them. He doesn't even wipe them away. "Is there more you have to tell us?" he asks the officers.

The man with all the stars shakes his head. "That's the main part, sir. We'd prefer you keep what we've told you about your brother, your uncle," he says, looking at us kids, a secret. He was a good man. He served his country well. We want you to know that.

We'll leave now to allow you to mourn. But there will be a public ceremony. Theodore Masters Smith will receive a purple heart and full honors. This paper here has the date and time for his recognition," the officer says as he hands over an unwrinkled and stiff notification. "As you can see, you will be escorted there and flown to Washington D. C. I assume you and your family will wish to attend?"

Dad nods for all of us. Then, the officers walk away, shutting the door behind them.

I retreat into my bedroom and get Uncle Theodore's picture off the wall. I bring it into the living room and find that Mom has done the same thing. Simon stands up and goes to retrieve his. We line the three pictures up on the fireplace mantel. Then we sit down on the couch and mourn.

Poor Uncle Theodore. We loved you so much. We will always miss you. Always.

Chapter Thirteen

The days that follow are not good days. I stay home, even though I have a big test, but I just can't stop crying. I keep thinking there's a mistake. I'm sure Uncle Theodore will call and tell us he's fine. Then we'll laugh, and he'll tell us more stories about government foul-ups. But he doesn't call. We get his death certificate in the mail the next day. It's registered, and Dad has to sign for it like it's something valuable.

Simon stays home, too, but I don't see him cry. He just kicks the wall and storms at his toys. Dad goes to work on Monday, but he comes back home a couple of hours later. Then he mopes around the house, his face bloodless and sallow.

Only Mom continues as normal. She leaves for work and arrives home at the usual time, and she's patient as a seed waiting for life.

This goes on for several days. Simon's the first one to return to our usual schedule. On Wednesday morning he declares he's going to school. I sigh and say, "I guess I will, too." So we head off. Dad's still sitting around in his pajamas, acting like he's never going to work again.

I last the full day and arrive back home with a boxful of homework. That's when I find out that Simon got expelled for fighting. Yet despite that, Dad and he are busy assembling a plastic pirate ship from a kit that Uncle Theodore once gave my brother. I don't have the heart to say anything about the strange way Dad is treating someone in trouble at school.

I climb the stairs and start my piles of work. However, when Mom arrives home, the calm ends. For the first time I hear her raise her voice. I go down a couple of steps to hear what she's saying. Unbelievably, she's not even mentioning Simon's unsuitable punishment. She's yelling because the roses have black rot!

I edge down a couple of steps and try to figure out why Mom should be so upset about roses.

But Dad is so lethargic he doesn't seem to care about his precious roses. In fact, he doesn't even look up. "Who cares?" he says. "Spraying them won't bring back Theodore, will it?"

My mother drags Dad outside. He's not willing. He resists her pulling him outside, but I guess he loves her too much to protest too much. When they step out into the backyard, I creep down the rest of the way and watch. Simon does, too.

"That was not cool about your getting expelled," I whisper to him. "Don't you think Mom and Dad have enough problems right now?"

"Go jump in a lake," my brother says nastily. But he doesn't want Mom and Dad to catch us spying on them, so he whispers just like I did.

I don't reply. Angry words won't help him. I know that. I crack the door open to hear what Mom and Dad are saying.

Dad is crying. "My poor roses," he's saying as the tears flow down his cheeks.

Mom is holding him. "It's all right, dear. It's not too late. We'll spray them together. They'll be fine again."

I back up. The drama's over. I know that Mom has just miraculously healed our father. The sight of it is something I'll remember forever. I quietly close the door and turn to go back to my homework.

"I'm sorry, Mattie. I shouldn't have said that," Simon whispers. "I don't really want you to jump in a lake,"

Simon's head is bowed halfway down his chest. For the second time, I throw my arms around him and pull him close. "It hurts, doesn't it, Simon? I do understand, you know. I really do."

That's all it takes for him to let go. He sobs, just like my father did. Then, when he's finished crying, I lead him up to my room and say, "I have something for you. I was saving it for next week, but I think you need it now. Okay?"

Simon's not looking at me, but I see his eyes light up when he sees the package wrapped in dinosaur paper.

"Cool, man," he says. "Can I really open it now?"

I gesture for him to sit on my bed, something he's not usually allowed to do since I keep my room shipshape. Simon doesn't even notice the honor. He flops down, pulls his shoes up onto the spread (making me wince), and tears at the paper.

"The ship? It's Captain Jetstream's ship! You bought it. I wanted this so bad, but I didn't have enough money. I can't believe you got it for me."

He jumps up and hugs me. Then, without taking his eyes off the present, he starts ripping into the box. Of course, it's disassembled. The pieces fall all over my bed.

"Will you help me put them together, please?" Simon begs his eyes like shiny marbles, magnified huge.

I push my homework aside and sit down on the bed. Together, we start working, me reading the directions Simon attempting to follow them.

Mom peeks in a few minutes later. She observes what we're doing, her eyes taking in the ribbon and wrapping paper all torn. Then she gives me a thumbs-up and walks off. Simon doesn't even notice. He's too busy inserting part 9-A into part 9-B.

It's my turn to cook dinner that night, but Mom doesn't call me downstairs. Instead, she does it herself, allowing me to continue soothing my brother's soul.

That night we eat dinner together with heartier appetites and even try out a couple of smiles.

"I was just thinking," my mom says as she passes out some store-bought ice cream sandwiches. "Do you think that Simon and I could go with you for your next hang-gliding lesson?"

Dad and I exchange a look. The truth is we've already finished our lessons, but Dad nods and says. "That's a great idea. How about tomorrow?"

Mom frowns. Her son has just been expelled from school. She has work to finish, and I unquestionably have bundles of homework to catch up on, but she pauses to consider. "Do you think you could, Mattie?" she asks me.

I think about all the work upstairs waiting for my attention. I think about the tests I have to study for. Then I look at my family. "Sure. Let's do it," I tell them.

We have a wonderful time. The hang-gliding school gives us a lesson that even includes my little brother and Mom. They let Simon fly for a short hop with the instructor. Mom tries it, too, but we soon see she's not quite ready. Her face whitens to the color of her teeth, and when she gets back down on the ground, she sits down under a shade tree and won't get up to participate for the rest of the lesson.

We go to a neat restaurant afterward, one overlooking a pond with baby ducks swimming behind their mothers. There are fish in the pond, too, so Simon is enthralled. After we finish our turkey burgers and salads, Simon insists on getting closer. Of course, he falls in.

It's only two o'clock in the afternoon when we get back. Simon rushes to his room to play with his new Captain Jetstream ship. I buckle down to go through my mountain of homework, and Dad and Mom head out to the roses.

I'd never before played hooky from school before, but, in retrospect, I think that sometimes therapy requires strict measures. It was a day well spent.

On Friday, we journey forth. Dad goes back to the office, Mom off to work, and Simon and I make a beeline for school.

Chapter Fourteen

Friday is the day the special we interviewed for is to be aired. That night, we all sit around the television and wait for it to begin. Dad comments that the timing is super bad since we're probably going to see INASA people at the funeral the next day, but we can't stop the show from airing. The studio has a schedule. Already, since we've had to postpone the follow-up, they've been inconvenienced, although Dana says they fully understand.

So, we're sitting in the living room all set to watch the airing when my best friend, Jimmy, pops in. "Okay, if I watch with you?" he asks.

Dad frowns but shrugs. Jimmy's actually part of the family since he's at our house so often. That's why Jimmy grabs a big handful of popcorn, plops himself down on the floor, and begins to tell Simon about the new dinosaur movie he saw advertised.

"Sh!" Dad says, even though they're only showing advertisements. But Jimmy knows when to be quiet. He flashes me a smile and leans against the couch, his head between my mom's legs and mine.

Now, before you're wondering about Jimmy and any romance between us, there absolutely isn't any. Jimmy is my best friend and has been since we were six years old, but he's not my boyfriend. That's been our policy all along. Sometimes, we go to dances together or to the movies, but we've never once taken it beyond the friend bit. We just don't think of each other that way. Jimmy's like a brother.

Anyway, the commercial ends and Dad turns up the volume. Dana comes on, and Simon cheers. He's still crazy about her for giving us the tickets to the ApplePie Studio.

Then the camera shows us! We're sitting there all stiff and awkward. I cry out, commenting that I look horrible. Dad and Jimmy both disagree vehemently. Mom shushes them, but I smile, somewhat relieved.

The commercial comes on, and we still haven't said anything. Dana's just had time to do the introductions and has filled in the audience about what INASA's Academy rule says.

"There, that's done," Mom jokes. "Now we can watch something else."

Of course, we all boo her, knowing she's only joking.

Jimmy empties the popcorn and so has to be the one to put the next bag into the microwave. He fusses, but scoots. Before the ads are done, he's back with a full bag, dumping it into the heavy wooden bowl.

The moment he's finished, Dana comes back on. "Kind of pretty lady," Jimmy comments. Everyone shouts, "Shush!"

I guess I do an okay job. It's hard to watch yourself on television. For some reason, you don't like how you look or talk. You appear like someone else, only very, very familiar. I listen to my words and wish I'd said things differently. I think of several things I wish I'd added. I groan when I see the face I made at something Dana's said.

Another commercial comes, but this time, we're all silent except Jimmy.

"Wow!" he says. "I can't believe I'm sitting here beside a family of movie stars. You looked so glamorous, my hang-gliding friend. Mostly, I've seen you with dirt smudges and baggy jeans. I never knew you could clean up that good."

I fidget. I don't want Jimmy to talk like that. It bothers me. I change the subject, pointing to the cute dog on the screen. So, then we're all sitting, staring at the commercial as if we've never seen the dog push his bowl across the kitchen floor. The dog's eagerness for dinner suddenly seems new, and we savor it, fascinated by whatever brand of dog food is being peddled.

Jimmy quickly gets the message. He tosses a piece of popcorn at me and says, "Of course, you're not half as cute as that dog."

Simon remarkably argues. "She is too!"

That makes the rest of us speechless, which is just as well because the program comes back on then.

Simon looks adorable during his part. I bet half the girls in his class have crushes on him, but I don't mention that. It's kind of like Jimmy's words. Sometimes, it's better not to notice things — or, at least, not to say them.

We watch the entire show, and then, almost the moment it's over, the phone rings. Dad gets it, figuring it's someone from work since he's asked them all to watch. But it's *Hip Teen Magazine.*

With my parent's permission, I schedule an interview time. The writer and photographer agree to see me after school the following week.

I hang up the phone, but it rings again.

"Hello?" I say before Dad can get there. Whoever it is, it's for my mother. Some woman's magazine that I've never heard of wants the family to pose for pictures and to answer a few questions.

That goes on and on the rest of the evening. Jimmy's wowed, but he has to leave. He's promised to baby sit for his little sister while his parents go bowling. I thank him for coming over and walk him to the door.

"You were super," Jimmy tells me. "I'm proud to be your friend, you know."

What do you do when someone says something like that? You have to kiss them, right? I do, right on the lips. Unfortunately, Simon's watching. Wouldn't you know?

Dana calls later, too. "Well, what did you think?" she asks. We all crowd around the phone and tell her what a great job she did. I can almost hear her smile. She laughs as she disconnects.

What a day, I think, as I head for my bed. Then I hear Dad slamming down the phone. It's that caller again, the one who always says that women should stay at home. Dad's stopped arguing with the woman. He's asked her not to call anymore. He's also threatened to report her to the police, which he already did, but they tell him that the woman hasn't really done anything wrong.

Poor Dad. She doesn't bother anyone else that much — just Dad. I wish *he* hadn't been the one to pick up the phone just then. I wish it had been me. Why does the woman persist, though? Does she really think she'll change my goals? How could she think that by irritating anyone, she could make a difference?

I shake my head and slip into my pajamas. By the time I slide into bed, the caller isn't even on my mind. I'm thinking, instead, about the way Jimmy's lips felt touching mine. Why should I be thinking about that? I sigh, close my eyes, and fall asleep, a smile on my face.

Chapter Fifteen

In the morning, we have to get up at five. It's just like when we flew into the city, except this time, we're flying a lot further. We head to the superport and board a special jet. It's one of the military's, and the guards who accompany us make sure that we don't stand in lines or run into any difficulties.

On board, we find seats that are far more elegant than we're used to. There's actually legroom.

"This is so cool!" Simon tells everyone who'll listen. The guards very politely agree.

The ride is incredibly short. In fact, it's like a miracle. We fly clear across the continental U.S., and it only takes us an hour. Wow!

Then when we walk down the ramp, exiting the jet, we see the same man who came to our house — the one with all the stars on his uniform. Captain Donahue gives us a half-smile and then leads us to a waiting car. A driver takes us directly to the cemetery.

Uncle Theodore is being buried at Arlington National Cemetery with full ceremony. "It is a great honor," Captain Donahue tells us. "Your brother," he explains, "was a full hero."

While we're standing there beside Captain Donahue, we see the caisson carrying Uncle Theodore's casket. We know *he* isn't in it.

Space doesn't give up her own. But we feel like he's inside. The symbolism makes our eyes water.

There is a riderless horse that one of the officers is walking. "Did someone fall off?" Simon asks the captain. Captain Donahue, at that moment, is at full salute and cannot answer, but he explains later that the riderless horse represents the fallen soldier who is Uncle Theodore.

"Oh," says Simon. "Did he used to ride?"

No one answers him. We're all sniffling.

A team of soldiers picks up the casket. It's all very formal, and they do it as if they've practiced many times. Then they march Uncle Theodore's empty casket with its draped flag toward the chaplain. He turns, and we accompany the casket to the prepared gravesite, walking slowly as the soldiers carry the casket by hand.

I suppose the chaplain says nice things about Uncle Theodore. I cry too much to hear them. All the formality and the pomp really bring home the fact that I'll never see my uncle again. That realization fills my hankie with tears. Mom hugs me close to her, and Dad kisses me, but I can't stop crying. It's as if I've just been told he's not coming back.

Some officers raise up their rifles. There are seven rifles, Simon later tells me. I don't remember that, but I do know shots were fired, three volleys worth. Then, a bugler steps forward and plays taps. That's the worst moment. The song hits me inside. I can barely stand, and Dad grabs me, supporting me with his strength.

Afterward, when it's all over, I'm embarrassed at my selfishness. *He* was Dad's brother, and yet I, instead of consoling my father, required his support. I apologize to my father, but Dad, instead of being upset with me, thanks me. He says that because I was so upset, he couldn't be. "You got me through that ceremony without falling apart, Mattie," he tells me gravely. "I am grateful you needed me."

But I've skipped ahead, and I shouldn't. So now, I go back. After Taps, the soldiers march over to fold the flag that was draped over the coffin. The soldiers take a long time and do the folding very neatly. Then they back away and present the flag to the chaplain, who brings it to my father.

"Goodbye," I whisper then as we walk away, even though I know Uncle Theodore isn't there. "But who's to say? Maybe he did come back to watch. Maybe he saw us all grieving for his loss. I hope so because then he'll know how much we loved him. I hope he was able to do that.

"I love you, Uncle Theodore," I repeat as I look back to see the lone soldier standing guard, keeping vigil over Uncle Theodore's death.

Chapter Sixteen

That Monday at school, I get some strange looks. It seems that everybody saw the special, but no one comes up to me to comment. They just gather in circles and talk about me. It's the most uncomfortable day I've ever spent at school.

I'm not one of the popular students. My goals are too different from theirs. I'm not saying theirs are less or anything, just different. I don't fall into any of the other groups either — the radicals, the computer geeks, the jocks, the immature. I just don't fit anywhere. Or rather, I fit with myself and not with groups.

I have friends, sure — quiet-voiced intellectuals who want to learn about life through books. I have lots of those kinds of friends, but no one that I'm particularly close with except Jimmy. He and I spend more time together than I do with anyone else. It will be lonely without him. He plans to go to Stanford next year, and I'm sure they'll accept him. I've applied there too, but I really have no intention of attending a college on terra firma.

I think I've finally caught up with all the missed work, but that day, my instructors pile on more to make up for my absence on Friday. I sigh lots. I suppose it's a good thing I don't know how much worse it will get before the sunshine comes out again.

I begin work on a term paper assigned on the preceding Friday. The teacher told the class that we could write about anything we wanted, but when I submit my ideas, she negates every one of them. "I want you to write something different, Mattie," she tells me. "I want nothing scientific or mathematical from you. You can write about *almost* anything else."

With her words, she's taken away everything I'm really interested in. I stare at her, coming up blank. Sammy, one of the girls in the class, and my chemistry partner from last year, butts in. "Why don't you write about horseback riding or about cats. Or — I know, you could investigate the presidency or someplace far away — Morocco, for heaven's sake."

Mrs. Blomefield is smiling at her, so I know it would be inappropriate to ask Sammy to back off. "That's an excellent idea, "Mrs. Blomefield tells my sometimes friend. "How about Morocco, Mattie?"

I'm really not pleased with Sammy's interference, but the die has been tossed and came up snake eyes. I shrug and nod my head. Then I pick up my notebooks and books and say, "Morocco? What on earth is there to say about Morocco? It's all desert, isn't it?"

Both the teacher and Sammy laugh. "That's what you will unfold," Mrs. Blomefield informs me. "Remember, I want a preliminary outline on Tuesday, and the final term paper will follow the format given and be between twenty pages and twenty-five, including graphs, maps, and pictures."

Again, I nod, and then I flee to the school library, where I pick up a stack of books and seven different magazine articles about the wonders of Morocco.

That happens on Monday. When I get home, there's a long message on the phone computer. That same strange woman has called.

She says she saw me at the cemetery and wanted to slap my face. She says that I'm a Benedict Arnold. Why?

Chills run through me thinking about her being there during the ceremony. Is the strange woman vicious? Would she actually hurt someone? Dad is already worried about her frequent harassments. I don't want him to hear this message. I back it up on a tape, toss that into my desk drawer, and then delete it from the phone computer.

I hope I'm doing the right thing, but the fact that the woman mentioned certain details about where we stood and what we did gives me the willies.

Like my mom says, "There will always be crazies. Some are vocal about it. Some just carry their thoughts in silence, but all of them are to be pitied." I do pity the woman who calls so tirelessly, but the persistence of her fixation fills me with doubts. What if Dad is right that this one is truly dangerous?

I look at the tape throughout the evening. I think about sharing it with Mom, but I know she'd tell Dad, and the woman never actually threatened us. The police would still not be interested, yet . . .

I fret about it for a while but then forget. I'm too busy nosing through travel books, note taking my way through my explorations of the exotic country that I formerly knew nothing about.

On Friday night, I'm still working on my report and find myself unable to proceed because I start agonizing over how I'm going to spend all Saturday taping a second show and still finish my outline by the due date. I know that stressing over it is not the way to get it done. Sighing long and hard, I open my laptop, take a sip from my water bottle, and set to work composing the necessary outline.

An hour later, my mother calls me. It isn't my night to prepare dinner. I glance at the clock and wonder what Mom wants me for. I've completely forgotten the magazine photos for *Family Life*.

I scream, run back upstairs, and change into something presentable. Then I pose with Simon, Dad, and Mom and separately for some single pictures. I answer the same questions I've gone over at least twenty times, wondering if I should just type out my answers and hand them to reporters on future interviews. But I need the articles. Anything that puts pressure on INASA is a plus. So I smile pretty and pretend that their questions are new and different and that I'm thrilled to be offered the chance to explain.

When that's over, it's time for dinner, and then Dad insists that I watch the news with him, reminding me that it's important to keep up with current events. He's right, of course, but the moment it's over, I run up to my room and resume my research.

I work until ten when Mom calls, "Lights out." Then I move into my bed and try to work by flashlight. Dad comes in and takes away the laptop. I get a lecture, then, about pushing too hard. Dad really doesn't understand what school is like, but I don't argue with him. I figure I'll just have to write my notes in long hand. But almost as she suspects I'll do that, Mom drops by and warns, "You're going to have black shadows under your eyes. Then what will INASA say about you being unable to withstand the pressure?"

That clicks. Mom's right. I puff up my pillows and close my eyes.

I can't understand why she's suddenly waking me up, saying, "It's morning, Mattie. We leave in thirty minutes."

I prop my eyes open, jump into the shower, slip into a dress, and go running down the stairs. I pour a cup of coffee, grab a nutribar, and manage to beat Simon into the *beetleflyer*. He gives me a grin and hands me a pillow. "This is what made me late," he says. "I took it from your room. I figured you might want it."

Is it possible that a troublesome pest can sometimes be an okay person? I start to ruffle his hair, but he dodges my hand. "Don't mess with the air, Mattie. It's perfect."

I laugh. His hair looks like dropped pick-up sticks — if one could play a three dimensional game. I smile, close down my insulated cup of coffee and, place it in its holder, slam my head on the pillow, and shut my eyes.

We've decided *not* to spend the night in a hotel, although the studio offered to put us up again. Instead, we fly directly into the studio's lot, land on the strip we have a code for, and meet our greeter. A young lady named Bonnie leads us into the correct building and through the maze.

Dana is there, waiting for us. She yells out as if we're her long lost family, which is kind of nice, except it makes everyone inside the room turn to look at us. Then they all stand up and clap like we're someone important. Dana nods her head at them and leads us into her office.

"What was that about?" my dad asks.

"You're getting famous," she quips. "Sit down. What would you like to drink? Simon, are you hungry?"

We laugh. She's really gotten to know us well. However the truth is that this time we're all hungry, so Dana takes us to the canteen for breakfast. While we're reacquainting ourselves with the wonders of the cook, Dana hands me the letter she got from INASA. I scan it and look up at her.

"There's nothing new here. It's all just a repetition of what I said."

She smiles. "Yes, but isn't it interesting that they felt they needed to readdress this issue? That means someone *was* watching your interview. INASA is starting to feel threatened, Mattie."

I laugh. "They already were. They offered me a job even before the interview. I wonder what they'll offer me now."

Dana laughs, but her eyes are examining me. "Late night?" she asks.

Mom shoves her elbow into my ribs. Dad gives me a look.

Dana, seeing them, smiles even broader. "Don't worry about it, Mattie. Make-up will take care of that. Today, we want to make sure that you are as fresh and full of fortitude as possible. The studio president likes this issue. He wants us to ride it hard."

"You mean until INASA caves in?" Mom asks.

Dana shakes her head. "I wish I could promise that, but we ride numbers, not results. As long as the populace likes this issue and watches Mattie, we'll continue with the tapings. However, I must warn you that audiences are fickle, Mattie. One day, we'll call and say, 'No more tapings.' Do you understand that? It won't be because we've changed our mind or anything. It just means that the viewing public is bored.

Right now, they like watching you. You're a pretty girl. Your family is real. The audience identifies. They want to see you beat the system. This has all the elements for instant popularity. Simon even has some fan mail. So do all the rest of you. Mattie, you have a room full of it with more coming every day since the taping was picked up by a couple of sister networks."

Simon stops chewing a moment to express his amazement. "Wow! Fan mail! Cool. What's it say? Did they send me any money?"

I shake my head at him, but it reminds Dana to tell me that money has been sent. She checks her messages. "Yep, here it is. Your account now has $2,653 dollars."

"But why? Why would anyone send that? I didn't ask for it."

"Whenever there's a good cause, people write checks for it, Mattie. These donations are to see that you get where you're going. Money does speak, even if INASA isn't yet listening, yet."

After breakfast, we head for the taping session. We sit in the same seats. Then Dana does another introduction and asks me to explain my problem. She checks with Simon to see if he still feels that girls shouldn't go into space.

"Well, there aren't any girls in Captain Jetstream, but maybe Mattie should be a 'ception. She's awfully smart, you know. My uncle was a real space captain, and he said she should go."

"Thank you, Simon," Dana says, chuckling. Then she meets my eyes. "It looks like you've won over your brother, if not Captain Jetstream,"

Dana turns to the camera again and says, "I'm sorry to say that the Masters Smiths have been dealing with a heavy tragedy. Last Saturday, they attended the funeral of Mattie's uncle, who was killed in space. A hero, Theodore Masters Smith, was buried in Arlington National Cemetery, where he was laid to rest with the other brave men and women who died serving our country."

While Dana's speaking, the monitor shows several clips of the actual funeral. I'm embarrassed to see myself sobbing into my father's chest while his face appears ancient and lined with grief.

A tear makes its way down my cheek. I'm not prepared for it. I wipe my eye and sniffle, letting out a sob of pain over the throbbing ache of our loss.

"Are you okay?" Dana inquires, and the camera swings to me. I nod my head, uncertain if I can speak, until Dana asks, "I'm sorry to have to ask you this, Mattie. I can see the tears in your eyes, and I know you're still grieving, but are you sure, after all that just happened — your beloved uncle dying out there among the stars — are you positive you still want to go to the Space Academy?"

I take in a steadying breath. I wipe another tear, but then I answer. "I want it even more. You see, my uncle made a difference to all of us. He was a real hero, not just for my family but also for our country. I don't know if I can ever follow in his footsteps. I don't think I'll ever be anyone's hero, but I know that my uncle believed in what he was doing. He was fulfilled by it. He was in the place and the position he wanted to be — in space, the captain of a ship, exploring the outer reaches.

"That's where I belong, too. My whole life has been in preparation for that destiny. I have to go to the Space Academy. I must. Uncle Theodore saw that. He said he read it in my eyes. He told me that the fire burning inside me reflected my need to explore other worlds, to see what no one has ever seen. 'Wanderlust,' Uncle Theodore called it. He said some of us are born with it.

"So you see, I have to go to the Space Academy, Dana, because it's the only way I can hope to become an officer on a space ship, and that's something I must and will do — no matter what INASA says. I'm going to fight until they cave in until they finally admit that females have just as much right as males to attend the Academy. And I'll do it in my uncle's name and for the women who want this just as much as I do, so they, too, can explore new worlds."

"Mattie, you make me want to quit my job and jump on the bandwagon, and I get claustrophobia from being in too small a bathroom," Dana laughs.

I laugh, too, just to share the moment with her, but I've poured out my heart and tapped into my emotions, and my heart is beating such a tom-tom I'm feeling the need to jump up and run around in circles. I'm all twisted up inside, too, with unshed tears. I breathe a heavy sigh when Dana gives the usual patter just before a commercial. The moment the camera light turns red, I sag down in my chair.

"You were wonderful, Mattie," Dana tells me. "I bet there's not a dry eye left in the audience. Wouldn't you agree?" she asks, turning to check my parents. Dad is staring at the wall, his eyes red, his skin beaded with sweat. Mom has given into it. Her hankie is filling with tears. Even Simon is subdued, staring down at his feet.

"Give us ten," Dana calls out. "Water," she yells, and then she unhooks herself and strides over, grabbing a tissue box on the way.

The same make-up lady comes over a moment later to repair what she's applied earlier. I'm glad, figuring my face is a mess. "Blow," the woman orders, and then she mists me with water and puts drops in my eyes, which sting like a thousand needles.

"Eat this," the woman orders, handing me a small wrapped parcel of food.

"What is it?" I counter, hoping she's not offering me drugs.

She laughs, reading my suspicion. Then she glances over at my parents and at Dana. "Tell her it's okay. It's only a piece of chocolate. You need something to perk you back up. This usually helps."

So I nibble and drink as my face gets restored.

Then, all too soon, the light turns green, and we start up again. Thankfully, the rest of the taping slides by quickly. I answer the questions taped after the first interview. None of it shocks me. I glide through it without blinking until the last one.

"Do you think it's right to set a precedence that other women must follow?"

That stops me cold. It reminds me of something Dr. Stephenson said. I can't remember my answer to her, but I take a deep breath and format my thinking.

"I'm not declaring that other women should follow in my footsteps. I'm only saying that we should have the right to pursue our dreams.

"Long ago, women weren't allowed to be firemen. They weren't at one time permitted to patrol our streets like their male counterparts. Women weren't acceptable as CEO's, or senators, or even presidents. But we as a country have grown to understand that women can handle those careers. In fact, women make fine firemen, policemen, CEO's, senators, and presidents, and they will make outstanding space officers, crewmen, and captains."

Again I sag back against the chair, slightly uncomfortable with the passion of my speech.

Dana smiles. "Thank you, Mattie. You've answered all these questions with the skill, not of a sixteen-year-old high school student, but with the fortitude of the worthiest of candidates for any high-level institute — especially that of the Space Academy." Then Dana twists her chair and, stares into the third of the cameras, and says, "Let's give Mattie Masters Smith a hand and wish her well."

As if the audience were clapping loudly, Dana uses her hands to wave them silent. "I'm delighted to tell everyone that Mattie has agreed to be with us again. She will be back next week to answer more of your questions. Please write, e-mail, or fax your questions to the numbers on the screen. As always, we look forward to hearing from each one of you in our beloved audience.

"And INASA, if you are listening to this broadcast, we would like to invite you to the station to discuss your side of the situation. Please let us know if there is anyone who can still defend this refusal of INASA to allow women at the Space Academy. We would be happy to accommodate your spokesman on the show, and I know the public is dying to hear from you.

"In fact, let's all write to INASA and urge them either to appear on the show and air their position or to modernize their application form, bringing INASA into the present by allowing women to attend the Space Academy.

"Oh, I see that it's time to say my goodbye. This is Dana, wishing you a happy, healthy, and productive week."

Chapter Seventeen

With the taping over, we fly home, and I return to my Morocco report. I don't know what the rest of the family does. Seriously determined to finish my outline, I ostracize myself from them, nibble my sandwich, polish off three cookies, and drink down both bottles of water I've carried up from the kitchen.

I guess I would have worked until dinnertime, but Jimmy arrives, knocking at my door. "Hey, guess what just came into town?" he teases.

I eye him with blurred vision and blink a couple of times. "What?" I ask, suffering from mental fatigue.

"Eyes to the Stars" is finally at the theatre," Jimmy tells me, grinning like a dancing Halloween skeleton I once saw. "Do you want to go? You know how they never keep science fiction here very long. It's tonight or never."

I drop my pencil. "Eyes to the Stars?" The sequel? I've gotta go," I say. Then I look down at my still unfinished outline.

"Look, if you go with me tonight, I'll even pay," Jimmy offers.

"You? Pay for me? That's a novelty," I kid. "All right. You've got a deal. Go downstairs, and I'll be there in a minute, okay?"

"You're going to primp for me?" Jimmy laughs. "Since when?"

I toss a stuffed animal at him as he darts for the door. Then I search for the right shirt and jeans, put on socks and shoes, and grab a jacket.

When I get downstairs, Mom and Dad are talking with Jimmy about the movie. "Okay to go?" I ask.

Dad smiles. "It's not only okay. I insist. You've been working too hard. Here's a couple of twenties. I want you guys to grab a pizza afterwards. The treat's on me."

I kiss them both good night and scoot out the door. "Wow," Jimmy says, sounding just like my brother. "What cool parents you have. Does this mean I'm off the hook about paying your way in?"

"Yeah, you really lucked out. You owe me next time," I laugh.

I can't describe how wonderful the movie is, or how Jimmy sits with his arm around me the whole time, and how it feels really nice. Just accept that I had a good time — movie, pizza, and the kiss that came at the end of our time together. Ah.

****

The next day I finish my outline and start the term paper, even though my head is still spinning over aliens and space. It gets turned in on time, I learn all about Morocco and breathe once again.

Then, as always, the weeks fly by. In between homework and term papers, I read the letters that my "fans" have sent. The studio says that I should answer as many as I can, but there are hundreds. Mainly I write thank you's to the people who sent me money.

Dad has warned me not to give my address or even hints about where I live. I think that's silly because everyone sounds so nice, but I've heard enough in the news about how strange some people can be.

I'm cautious in my replies. I can't even mail them from our town. I have to take them all to the studio.

Dana calls us Thursday night to remind us to watch the show on Friday. Like we'd forget! She says there's still no contact from INASA. That disappoints me. I was hoping they'd at least attempt to argue their side. That would mean I was getting to them. The silence is ominous.

I've already sent in my application to the Space Academy as if I couldn't read their note about males only. I included my recommendations and a copy of my scholastic records. I also crossed my fingers and said a prayer. What if I've been wasting my time? What if they don't accept me after all this? I choose not to dwell on it. I must believe that miracles happen.

On Wednesday, I receive my preliminary acceptance to UC Berkeley. The other colleges will soon be letting me know if I'm in — Stanford, MIT, and UCLA. Then I'll have to decide what to do. I can't drag my feet forever. I'll need to choose someplace if I don't hear from the Academy.

"Oh, Uncle Theodore, what if they still won't accept me? What then?"

On Saturday morning, we're up early again, repeating the week before. Dana meets us and takes us directly to the canteen. Over breakfast, I find that my account has escalated to $22,567.

"What do I do with that money if INASA still won't listen?" I ask her.

She laughs. "You just keep doing what you're doing. You're beating INASA, Mattie. They've got to cave in. Right now, you're the hottest thing in the news. Everyone's talking about it — everyone but INASA."

I sigh because that's not going to get me into the Academy. Is INASA even listening?

The taping goes well. The questions are more or less the same, except now people want to know more about *who* I am than *why* I want to go to the Academy. It's like they've accepted that part of me, and now they're curious what makes me tick.

Dana shows us the boxes and boxes of letters that have come for me. She shows them to the viewers and even has me read some of them. There's no correlation between the writers. Some are housewives. Some are professionals. Some are children. I read one letter from a writer in Detroit who's sent me $20. She's a college student who says that she just babysat and earned the money. She's sending it to me because she's studying to be a fireman and says without people like me, she wouldn't have that opportunity.

Another writer, a young girl, has sent me her entire allowance — a dollar. She says that I'm her idol, and she wants to go to the Space Academy too someday. It goes on and on like that. Even men write, telling me INASA is not being fair — that equality means the freedom to choose one's profession, no matter the dangers.

I look into the camera and thank those people, not just the ones who have sent me money, but all of them because they care, because they feel like I do that females should have the choice.

That day, Dana doesn't involve my family in the taping. It's just me. I answer the questions, and I talk. It's gotten so easy I hardly notice the cameras now. I just babble on and on about how I feel and why it's important. I even tell Dana (and all America) about how INASA offered me a job if I were willing to stay on the ground.

"I just can't do that, Dana. It would be giving in to something wrong, something unfair — this gender prejudice and inequality. It no longer exists in other areas, not anymore. In fact, there's a law about equality in education. I don't understand why INASA ignores it."

Dana smiles. "We'd like to invite you back next week, Mattie. I've lined up a physician to talk about the dangers of space on the human body and an attorney who will discuss the Educational Amendments of 1972, which pertain to equal opportunity under the law."

"What about INASA?" I ask Dana in front of the viewers. "Didn't they want to come onto the show and present their side?"

Dana looks into the camera. "I'll invite them once again, Mattie. INASA, America wants to know why you persist in ignoring the rights of women. We at the studio will be glad to find you a spot on the show anytime you want to come here to discuss your side. Why are you silent about this issue? Are you avoiding the truth? Aren't you listening to America, INASA?"

It was the perfect touch. Dana is really good. She attacks without attacking and always covers herself perfectly from stating something which might cause legal jeopardy for the network.

After the light on the camera goes out, I compliment her again. "You're so good at that," I tell her. "Thank you for your constant pricks at them."

Dad and Mom rush forward, telling me what a good job I did. Simon just smiles. He's playing with his new alien station, the other present I bought him for his birthday.

We take Dana out for dinner that night and have a really good time. Then, after we've all celebrated with ice cream sundaes, we drop her back off at the studio and return home.

No sooner do we walk into the house than the phone's ringing. Dana's just heard the best of news. "INASA has agreed to send a representative."

"But they haven't even seen the third show," I remind her.

"They will, won't they? I can't wait until Friday night. Don't forget to watch."

So I'm feeling buoyant that week at school. Things are looking up. On Monday I get a letter from Stanford wanting me to come up for an interview. Jimmy gets one, too. His eyes, which should look ecstatic, are sad when we compare acceptance letters.

"What's wrong?" I ask. "I thought you'd be glad that they're considering me."

He laughs. "They'd be fools not to, Mattie. It's just that I know you won't be going there. You'll be going up there," he says, pointing skyward. "You've always been honest about that. I've known since we were six, it's just that before, it was always a long time away, and now it's just around the corner."

"Well, they haven't accepted me at the Academy, Jimmy. They're still adamant that I can't go. That should make you happy."

"Don't be that way," Jimmy says, reaching out to take my hand. "I want you to be happy. You must know that."

I jerk my hand back quickly. Then I nod. "I know, Jimmy. I know."

He sighs loudly, looking so sad I want to do something about it, but I don't know what.

He sighs again and then says, "Well, at least we can go to the interview together, right?"

I nod. I guess I'll go. But as much as I want to please my friend, Stanford isn't actually my first choice next to the academy — Berkeley is.

I turn in my oral paper on Friday. The teacher is making us do mini presentations on what we've discovered from doing the term papers. I tell the kids about the Erg Chebbi desert dunes, which are the largest in Morocco, explaining that the dunes often tower above the flats as high as 164 feet.

I tell them that according to legend, the dunes were built from a sandstorm, the punishment from God when the townspeople of Merzouga neglected the needs of a homeless mother and child. Then I talk about Ramadan and the soup called harira. As a treat, I pass out a date to each person so they can appreciate the natural candy of the Moroccans.

Of course, I get my usual "A."

If only everything were that simple.

Some of the kids at school have started being malicious. They call me the "Movie Star" and "Space Girl." One of the sophomores called me "that whiner on TV." That name stings. I'll be glad when high school's over. I'm ready to step into a bigger world.

Chapter Eighteen

I'll never forget this evening!

First, Dana called to tell us that Ardis Anderson, the richest woman in the world, wants me to come talk to her. Ms. Anderson's mother was the one who invented AMACS, the antimatter conversion system that permits our space ships faster than light speed capability. Her mother passed on several years ago, but her daughter still runs a multi-billion-dollar company, whose Anti Matter Conversion Company's System still goes on every spaceship. I don't know why Ms. Anderson wants to speak with me, but I can't help being excited. Could she possibly have tie-ins with INASA?

It's too late at night to call, but Mom says she'll call the next day and try to set up an appointment for Friday after school.

Is it any wonder that I can't concentrate on my trig that day? The numbers are gyrating like constellations. Why does Ms. Anderson want to speak to me?

When I get home, I find out the news that Mom has made contact with the woman. We've been invited for dinner! Ms. Anderson says she wants to meet our whole family, so even Simon gets to go. I hug Mom as if she's been the benefactor of this strange miracle. Then I drill her with questions, but she has no answers for me.

No one ever sees Ms. Anderson. She's more or less a recluse. Do I dare hope that she's interested in my situation? Would she be for me or against? Could she be doing INASA a favor? Will she spend the evening trying to talk me out of my dreams, or she is on my side?

Mom only laughs at my questions. She doesn't bother playing a guessing game with me. "Wait and see," she says. "I have no idea what she wants. She didn't say, but if she's working with INASA, it will be a short, fast dinner."

When Dad comes home, we tell him about the call. He's impressed, all right, but our dinner date hardly slows him down. He's too excited about the appointment he's set up that day at Stanford University. I've been scheduled for an interview.

I've already told Dad how I feel, but he tells me again why I should have the opportunity to see Stanford and find out what it is they're offering. Dad says I shouldn't just thumb my nose because I think I'd rather go to Berkeley. I sigh, worrying that Dad has his heart set on Stanford, but then he says, with a twinkle in his eye, that it will, of course, be the perfect occasion to stop afterwards to check out Berkeley's astrophysics lab. That brings a smile on my face — well, at least a little one, since I really don't want to go to Berkeley either. I want to go to the Space Academy.

On Thursday, as if life hasn't suddenly turned into a carousel of bright colors and pleasant surprises, *Fast Time Magazine* calls. They're interested in my story. Everything is happening at once! Is this the start of what Uncle Theodore would have called "the Grand Slam?"

Luckily — or my heart would be doing cartwheels all the time — at school, things are starting to slow down a little. The major tests have already happened, and the extracurricular kinds of things are taking over. I'm involved in the Leadership Group, which means that I work with junior high kids after school two times a week. My little buddy, Lina, is having some problems. She doesn't want to do her schoolwork anymore, which is really hard for me to understand. We talk about her feelings, but I can tell I'm not helping her. She still looks sullen.

"What's going on?" I ask her for the seventh time. Then, finally, she breaks down and tells me that her parents are splitting up. Why hadn't I suspected that? I hug Lina and tell her how sorry I am. Is there anything more one can do under the circumstances?

Mainly, I just let her talk, and I listen. She's crying, and I feel ineffective. I remove a small packet of tissues from my backpack and hand it to her. When I leave, Lina looks a little less unhappy, but I don't see that I've really helped her much. There are some problems a big sister just can't solve.

As I leave with my team, I wave goodbye. "See you next week," I tell her, and she gives me a shaky grin.

That night I start thinking — really thinking — about how lucky I am. My parents aren't about to break up like Lina's are. My parents never even quarrel. Most of the time, they act like they're best friends, except when I stumble on them kissing each other because they think I'm not around. But that's a good thing — their kissing. It makes me sure that they still love each other. It would be awful if they didn't. Really awful.

Speaking of kissing, which everyone at school seems to be doing, it's that part of the year when everyone is talking about the BIG DANCE. This year, I'm a senior, so, of course, I'm supposed to go. I hadn't planned on attending, but then Jimmy starting pleading with me about it. He's been bugging me to go for the past three weeks. Why he wants to go to a dance, I don't have the foggiest.

Frankly, I think school dances are a terrible waste of time, but I don't want to hurt Jimmy's feelings. I can see from looking in his eyes that the Senior Prom, for some reason, is really, really important to him. So, on Thursday, the same day as the *Past Time Magazine* thing, I finally say okay. Jimmy gives such a whoop, it's like he's won the lottery or something.

Sigh. Now I have to go buy a dress — another big waste of time. Why can't people wear jeans to a prom? Why can't they do something interesting there instead of dancing around in circles? As I think about it, I'm sorry I relented. I wish I could back out of it, but I'm stuck because I told Mom I was going, and she's acting like it's the best thing that's happened since Simon, who broke his arm last summer, finally got his cast off.

It's only one night, though. I'll survive. I'll just consider it training for the Space Academy. Uncle Theodore told me once that the Academy has monthly formal dinners where everyone has to wear their best uniforms and show perfect manners. He always laughed about it when he told us, but he also said, looking at me, that the people who have the best manners are the ones picked to be officers. If that's true, then I need to practice a lot.

I sigh again and walk over to my closet to try to figure out what to wear to Mrs. Anderson's mansion — something officer's caliber, I decide.

Chapter Nineteen

Sweet, sweet Friday. All class work is done, all tests taken, and I have no homework for the weekend. Jimmy is excited about the Prom but even more so about our visit to Stanford. His father and mine have agreed to meet in Palo Alto. We're even going to spend the night at the same hotel. Our fathers arranged the interviews to be back-to-back, so we could tour the campus together. Is that a good idea? I'd be feeling really pressured if it weren't for my appointment with Ms. Anderson. If that pans out, I won't have to decide between Stanford and Berkeley. Is there a chance Mrs. Anderson will be on my side? I have my fingers crossed.

The day drags, but when I get home, time rushes by like an express train. I primp a bit, curl my hair and even apply some mascara. I start to put on a hint of shadow, but I don't want to go that far. If Ms. Anderson's seeing me, it's because of what I've said and done, not because of what I look like. Still, I touch up my paleness with a dab of "blushing powder," which is what my mother calls it. I certainly don't want Ms. Anderson to think I'm sickly.

The president of AMACS has sent a *Butterfly* to pick us up. I've never actually seen one. It's a personal jet that the owner must take out a special license for because they're so fast. It's rumored to go from zero to 500 M.P.H. in thirty seconds. Of course, I'm sure this one won't. My mother would flip out if it did.

Not many pilots are certified for them, either. The man who's flying it looks young —in his thirties, I'd say. I'm fascinated.

"May I sit in the front with Mr. Aheed?" I ask Dad.

He glances at the pilot, who smiles and shrugs. Of course, Simon wants to sit in front, too, but Dad shoos him into the back with them. I am so thankful. I have a million questions I want to ask Mr. Aheed if he's at all friendly.

We take off at a considerably slower thrust than the *Butterfly* is capable. But once we're airborne, I launch my questions.

Mr. Aheed proves to be just as pleasant as his gorgeous smile. Almost immediately, I'm engaged in the most satisfying of conversations. Mr. Aheed, who orders me to call him Hakim, although he tells me his full name is Hakim bin Ahmed bin Salman Al-Aheed, is very knowledgeable about the inner propulsion of the *Butterfly* and appears to be quite content to discuss it with me. The flight doesn't last nearly long enough. Long before I've learned what each of the controls does, the abilities of the *Butterfly* and its hang-ups, we are landing in the private airstrip on Ms. Anderson's property.

A car is waiting to transport us to her mansion. I say my goodbyes to Hakim using his given name as he's asked me to do. That raises my father's eyebrows. He frowns at our handsome, young pilot. I take my father's arm and begin to impart some of the jewels of information I gleaned. Dad relaxes then and pats my hand. Thinking I've avoided getting the lecture, his frown indicated, I climb into the limo and scoot back against its leather seat, pushing my feet underneath me, completely forgetting I'm in a dress.

"I hope you weren't sitting like that next to that pilot," my mother says.

With such a simple statement, all my babbling about the *Butterfly*'s marvels is completely erased. My dad frowns again and opens his mouth to deliver lecture number four hundred thirty-three, the one about how I shouldn't be too friendly with strangers.

However, the drive to Ms. Anderson's estate takes no more than five minutes. Dad is left spluttering. "We will discuss this later," he warns me.

I'm in a rather subdued frame of mind when we enter the residence. Dad is glowering, Mom is fretting over that, and Simon is snickering because I got in trouble, something which doesn't happen very often — at least, not as often as it happens to him.

Ms. Anderson steps out from behind a staircase, just as if she's been observing us as we walked down the long hall. "Ah," she says, "Here's the happy family."

None of us says a word. We've all forgotten our polite framework of words. There's something in the look in her eye and in the tone of her voice that makes us think she's been listening in.

My mother is the first to recover. She walks forward and holds out her hand. "Ms. Anderson? Thank you so much for inviting us to your house. It's lovely."

Ms. Anderson holds out her hand and clasps my mother's, but she is watching my father. "I shall see that another pilot flies you home. Will that solve the problem?"

My father's face turns a color somewhat between squashed cherries and mashed grapes. "There are no problems. Mr. Aheed flew us here successfully and seems to have entertained my daughter quite skillfully."

"True — and when Mattie lives at the Space Academy, she will be residing with a vast number of handsome and equally polished young men. Have you thought about that, Mr. Masters Smith?"

Dad sighs loudly. "You're right. It is difficult when daughters grow up. It's hard on the father — and the mother, too. I suppose we have to let go, don't we?"

My eyes are studying Ms. Anderson. She has said *when* — *when* Mattie lives at the Academy. She hasn't said *if.*

"You think I *will* be allowed to go, then?" I burst out the moment my dad and Ms. Anderson have stopped speaking.

Ms. Anderson's eyes move to mine. "You are quick. I expected that after studying your test results, but it still takes me by surprise because you really don't look like . . . No matter. Come."

Her words chase the squirrels around inside my mind. What does she mean — I don't look like…? Like someone who could be good at astrophysics or someone who would buck authority — or did she mean someone who would fight for my rights? Did she mean she found me lacking in some way?

She is walking us forward into an enormous room filled with elegant furniture and statues of Greek gods. It is impressive. I stop and gape. Simon, unfortunately, runs over to touch one. "Wow!" he says, "Is this Icarus, the boy who flew too close to the sun?"

Ms. Anderson, instead of being upset because Simon has interrupted her discussion with my father about her new shimmer windows, pauses and says, "How delightful. Your son, also, is knowledgeable. Good job, Simon. You are perfectly correct. That is Icarus. Notice his expression as he stares up into the sky.

That is my favorite piece because of the look in his eyes. It is how we all must feel as we gaze into our future. We are all like Icarus, just learning to fly. If we do not listen to wisdom, our wings will melt, and we will plunge to the ground, having failed in our aspirations. But if we can find our way, like his father, Daedalus, we can soar into the heavens. Then our future, like the horizon, is unlimited."

"How beautiful," I whisper, not intending to speak but trapped inside the sphere of her words.

"Yes, I was sure that would mean something special to you, my dear. Someday, that statue will be yours. I have written that into my will, but for now, this picture is all that you can take."

She picks up a small photo and holds it out to me. I step closer, taking it from her hands. "Thank you," I say, too amazed to have any other words of gratefulness. "But

Why . . . ?

Ms. Anderson cuts me off as she did before. "Come, sit down. Sergio," she yells out and then plops herself on a large black leather chair.

Of course, we obey, but everything's happening too strangely for us to hold onto our identities. We're moving about like automatons, stiffly and disjointedly. At least, that's how I feel. I struggle to relax.

"Good. Breathe in deeply, Mattie. I know I have the tendency to unnerve people. I've been told that often. It's not just you. In fact, I'd be surprised if you babbled in front of me as freely as you do before the camera."

Does she read thoughts, too? I swallow hard and look down at the photo she's given me. The wistful look in Icarus' eyes, for some reason, fills with unease. He's so innocent, so full of life. He doesn't have any idea of what could happen to him — what is going to occur. He only sees the excitement of it — not the reality of death. I shudder.

"Good. You have common sense, and you're intuitive. These are strong qualities. I wasn't sure if you had them sufficiently, but now I know. You have reacted to the photo brilliantly, my dear. Perfectly."

I look up into her eyes. I can't follow her anymore. I'm lost, but I don't glance at my parents for support. I just stare into Ms. Anderson's face, trying to figure her out.

She laughs openly loudly. "Yes, I'll support you, Mattie. I thought it would take a long, drawn-out dinner to probe the essence of you, but that wasn't necessary. You're too easy to read. We'll have to work on that. But first things first — I shall lean on INASA until they smother in their shortsightedness. I only ask one thing in exchange. Will you join my company? Will you wear the silks of AMACS?"

"What are you asking her? Can you explain?" my father says, leaning forward and shaking his head at me.

"You want Mattie to dress in silk pj's? She wears t-shirts to bed," Simon interrupts.

That freezes all conversation. We gape at him, trying to understand what he's talking about. Mom figures it out first. She's laughing. "Wearing … the silks… of …AMACS…" she giggles. "Oh, dear, Simon. I'm afraid you've got it wrong. The silks are…"

"Simon that is an easy misunderstanding. The "wearing of silks" is an expression that comes from the sport of horseracing. The jockey, the man who rides the horse, dons the colors of the stable that owns the animal. His riding costume is called his *silks*."

"Oh." Simon nods. "Well, then you want Mattie to wear a costume in your colors? What are your colors?"

Again the rest of us chuckle, but we try to do it in a way that we're not hurting Simon's feelings. Ms. Anderson tries again. "I only want Mattie to be an employee, Simon. She doesn't have to wear any particular costume — or rather, she'll soon be wearing the Academy uniform, of course."

"I will? You think they'll let me attend?" I gasp.

Ms. Anderson laughs, this time not at Simon's misunderstandings. "Ah, Mattie, have you given them any choice? They will have to surrender to public opinion. Oh, they'll still kick at the dust a bit more and beat their fists against the necessity of it, but they'll fall in the end. Progress doesn't wait for those who resist change."

She laughs again. "Besides, if I pull all my ships, what will that leave INASA to practice with?"

A young man enters the room then. His eyes flick over us, but they fasten on Ms. Anderson. "You called, ma'am?" he says.

"Sergio, we need drinks and some snacks. Simon, what kind of beverage would you like?"

"A suicide?" he suggests.

Mom rushes in. "He means, can you mix things — a little cola, a little root beer, a little orange? Simon, Ms. Anderson probably doesn't have all those sodas. Why don't you. .?"

"Nonsense. Of course, he may have a suicide if he wants it? Do you understand, Sergio, how to make one?"

He laughs. "I think I can construct one, ma'am. And the others?"

I ask for a cola, and Dad and Mom just want coffee. Ms. Anderson orders white wine.

For a moment, while we wait, we all relax and look each other over. Ms. Anderson is dressed in an expensive pantsuit — very stylish and sharp looking, but the rest of her is just average. She's not particularly tall, about like my mom. She's not fat or thin. Her hair is a curly bob. Her eyes are gray, her mouth is full and wide. Her nose looks slightly flat and rounded. She's attractive, I guess, but not overly.

"Well, what do you think, Mattie? Do I look like you expected?" she laughs.

I feel my face flaring with heat and look down. My mother comes to the rescue. "You look even younger in person," she compliments Ms. Anderson.

I nod, and so does Dad. Simon is too busy staring out the window. We can see the airstrip from the living room vista, and the *Butterfly* is getting a bath.

Ms. Anderson follows our gaze. "I once wanted to go up into space, Mattie. I wanted to attend the Space Academy, but my mother wouldn't support me in it. She said the company needed me. She was right, I suppose, but the *Butterfly* is all that is left of that ambition.

"Your Mattie has the same aspiration. I'm going to sponsor her if you'll let me. I'll see that she gets to follow that dream of hers. Dreams are meant to be lived — regardless of whether the dreamer is a female or the CEO of AMACS."

Sergio returns with our drinks, and the conversation moves in a direction that is more, shall I say, down to Earth. I relax a bit, listening to my parents and Ms. Anderson discuss politics.

Then Sergio calls us into dinner. For dinner, there's fresh salmon, which we find out Ms. Anderson raises on her property. I've never heard of such a thing and am fascinated by it. She promises to show me the hatchery next time I come for a visit.

The dinner is comfortable. All the stiffness has gone. We laugh and talk. Even Simon enters the conversation now and then with his strange views of life. (He tells Ms. Anderson that instead of salmon, she should be breeding Brontosauruses at her fish farm because they have more meat on them.)

When we head home that night, it is already dark, and much later than my parents intended since we have to get up early for the taping out in Los Angeles. But it was a productive dinner and meeting, and everyone had a good time. Hakim flies us home, me sitting in the back, this time beside my father, which is just as well because I fall asleep mid-flight.

The next morning, after five hours of sleep, we head off for the city. Mom is driving, and Dad snoozes — so do Simon and I. But Mom has no trouble. She scoots us right through the studio's entrance gates, flashes a pass at the guard, and lands us in the correct lot.

For the first time, Dana meets us in the landing area. "You're not going to believe it! Do I ever have news for you! You know how I said that INASA was coming today for the taping? Well, the man they'd promised has been exchanged for a higher official. Dr. Nathaniel is arriving in a few minutes, and he's going to be their spokesman. Do you understand the importance of that? He has power, real power. It may be that they've decided to start listening."

Dana pauses, checks us over, and gasps. "What happened to you? You all look exhausted. Were you up late last night? What happened? Did you see Ms. Anderson?"

We're walking forward as she's filling us in with her news. We don't even bother to go to her office first. She knows us too well by now. We go directly to the canteen for coffee and breakfast. Over pancakes, we tell her about our meeting with Ms. Anderson. Then, we all speculate about what Dr. Nathaniel's going to say during the scheduled taping.

"Is the specialist still coming to comment on the operation I'll need?" I ask as I blow on my cup of coffee.

"Yes. She's already in my office, tied up on the phone. Her daughter's having a baby in a couple of months, and they were discussing its arrival when I left. The daughter is painting the room yellow. Her mother, the doctor, thinks it should be a mellower color." Dana rolls her eyes and sighs.

The INASA representative flies in, the doctor hangs up, and we all assembly in the interviewing section's comfortable chairs. Dana begins with the standard review so that anyone who hasn't been following the situation can catch up. A couple of scenes from the previous taping are aired, and then it's on to introductions and a new session.

Dana lets Dr. Nathaniel from INASA speak first. I watch him as a mouse must eye a cat, waiting for the pounce.

He studies me a moment, checking my appearance. I've dressed conservatively that day, but I've worn slacks and a matching jacket, believing that a dress might emphasize my gender even more. After all, I've been told to dress for the position I want. My outfit that day looks as close to the Space Academy uniform as I can get.

I don't know if Dr. Nathaniel is aware of that, but his eyes noticeably rake over me. He pauses on my long hair, which I've tied back into a subdued ponytail. Then, without warning, he tosses a barb. "What does your boyfriend think of your ambition?" he asks.

It's an unfair question. Yet, I let the sting of it brush over me. I raise my head and tell him calmly that I have none, for my interest lies in pursuing my career.

"Have you explained that to your boyfriend, the one who's taking you to the Senior Prom? I bet he doesn't want you to go live on the moon."

So, INASA's been spying on me. I take a deep breath, calm myself, and start to answer. Dana gives the signal for a break.

By the time that I'm back before the camera, my temper has cooled, so I probably do a better job than I would have before. "Jimmy is my *best friend*, not my boyfriend, Dr. Nathaniel. Because of that, he's always known I planned to go to space the moment I graduated. A good friend encourages. He doesn't try to hold you back."

"Yet you and he will be scouting out Stanford University next week? That seems odd."

I wait, wondering if I should answer a non-question. Does it make me look bad that I'm checking out a college? Is that something INASA will use against me?

Apparently not, for then Dr. Nathaniel launches into a full-fledged Academy candidate's interview. By the third question, I recognize its substance from what my uncle told me. The fact that Dr. Nathaniel would ask me these questions over national T.V. surprises me, but I'm ready enough for the grilling. After all, I've been practicing all my life.

"Why do you think you're qualified to be an Academy student?" Dr. Nathaniel begins.

I almost laugh at that one, but I smile instead and plunge into the challenge of it — for me, that comes in summarizing everything I want to say in under a minute. Apparently, I'm successful because I don't get the signal from Dana "to wrap it up."

Then, Dr. Nathaniel asks about my ability to work with others. I explain that I'm president of two school organizations and an active member of several others, giving specific examples of various committees I've worked on.

That is followed by a question about my athletic ability — which, unbelievably, is a major component for going into space. My uncle used to warn me about that one, too. I tell Dr. Nathaniel about my daily routine: one hundred push-ups and sit-ups, as well as several other weight lifting exercises — the same regimen that my uncle formerly practiced.

"Good," Dr. Nathaniel says. "Exemplary health is often achieved through the establishment of such a regime. I hope more youths follow your example."

"Thank you," I tell him, not sure if he's just given me a compliment or is lecturing me about my generation's lack.

Dana breaks it there, but she tells us later that we've gone too long for the segment, and she'll have to do some cutting. I nod and sip the bottled water that's been brought to me.

Dr. Nathaniel does, too, but then he goes down to chat with my father, which makes me even more nervous than before.

When Dana brings us back and reintroduces us, Dr. Nathaniel consults his notes and clears his throat. The man has a very long nose that seems even longer when he's looking down. I glance away. My parents are sitting in the section where the audience would sit if there was one. My father, noticing the direction of my eyes, gives me a thumbs up. I smile at him. Simon, sitting right beside Dad, makes a face at me.

I look back at Dr. Nathaniel and find him watching me. I meet his gaze.

The man is growing bald, although he's younger than my father. His hair is sparse over the front part of his head. As if he feels my thought, he takes a moment to hand brush any strays back into place.

"One could suppose," he says, still eyeing me with a faint look of distaste, "that anyone who would be willing to create an upheaval in our current system might be anti-authoritarian and prone to anarchy. Does that describe you, Miss Masters Smith?"

Again, I have to stop myself from giggling. Me anti-establishment?

I search for the right words. "I believe, as all Americans do, that when a law is wrong, when a system has been corrupted by prejudice, that wrong must be changed. I am not anti-establishment, anti-authoritarian, or in favor of anarchy — merely a proponent of change when that change is necessary to make a wrong right."

"Well said, Miss Masters Smith. But why should INASA change when to do so would create permanent damage to the welfare of our society?"

I can't believe it's time for another commercial. I barely get to speak before Dana's cutting me off. I sip my water, listen to my stomach gurgle that it's hungry, and stand up and stretch.

Dana brings the audience back by showing Dr. Nathaniel issuing the question again.

"What permanent damage, Dr. Nathaniel?" I ask. "Do you mean that the welfare of our society is dependent on excluding females from good jobs?"

He pales visibly, stiffens in his seat, and sits forward. "You are misquoting me, young lady. You know that a stay on the moon longer than two months will harm a female's reproductive system. Do you wish to see malformed babies, mutants who cannot possibly survive beyond a year?"

I sigh — mainly because my anger is bubbling up again. I hate the way he's feeding the audience pseudo lies just to scare them. "Dr. Nathaniel, you and I both know that INASA is hiding behind that belief, but it doesn't . . . "

"Hiding?" he blasts out. "INASA is not hiding behind anything. We have faced reality, unlike some young girls who only see what they want to see and are willing to sacrifice the good of all for their own personal goals."

"May I finish now, Dr. Nathaniel?" I say calmly while the furor inside me is a raging fire.

I don't wait for his answer. I just want it pointed out that his rudeness has cut me off. "As I was saying, INASA is hiding behind the belief that women cannot prevent that from happening when the reality is that it can *easily* be prevented."

Dana jumps in then with a smooth introduction for the reproductive specialist, Dr. Carrie Treadful, and cuts us off with a "Stay tuned for the unfolding of this exciting drama.

Then we head off into a commercial for, of all things — diapers.

"Was that commercial planned?" I ask, sighing because it's the worst possible timing.

Dana laughs. "Don't worry about it, Mattie. You're doing fine. He's punching right and left, and you're not giving an inch."

I grimace and stand up. An assistant comes over to give Dana her usual backrub. Dana orders her to attend to me. That's really bizarre. I've never had anyone rub my back. I feel like a baby and don't know where to look.

"Relax," the masseur says. "You're all tense. Sit down and lean back. This will help you."

I need all the help I can get. I do as she says and let her rub my back sideways and forwards. I'll admit it feels good.

When the commercials are over, I see that Dr. Nathaniel has left, or at least he's not on the stage where Dr. Treadful, Dana, and I are sitting. I look about, but I don't see him. Am I finished? Was that all INASA had to say this time?

Dr. Treadful takes the audience inside the methodology I've been advocating. She discusses the simplicity of having all the eggs removed from a woman's ovaries. Then she explains how they can be stored easily and safely so they're ready for a transplant back into the woman's ovary if she, at some point, should desire a pregnancy.

I've already studied everything Dr. Treadful is telling the audience, but I listen carefully. She's really doing a great job with her explanations.

When her chat with the audience is finished, Dana calls another break. This time, she tells us that we won't be able to continue for an hour since Dr. Nathaniel is tied up.

We all look at each other and wonder what that means. Dr. Treadful, however, interrupts to hand me her card. "I think you'll need this in a couple of months," she says.

It takes a moment to understand what she means, but then my smile broadens and I thank her.

That's one more person on my side. How many more will it take until INASA yields?

Chapter Twenty

We start taping again when Dr. Nathaniel returns. I don't know what his telephone call was about, but the nastiness of the fellow seems to have departed. He asks me how I would be able to live among the Academy's current seven hundred thirty-seven men with no other woman to offer me solace.

That's a question I've thought about a great deal. I wish I could say I have a pat answer, but I don't. I tell him that, and I add that I do not wish to attend the Academy as a social function, but merely to learn. I mention also that my first ship will likewise be devoid of female company. Perhaps having a brother and a best friend who are males will help, I say, smiling because Simon is making another face at me.

"Do you not think the presence of *one* female at the Academy will cause a different sort of problem?"

I am unsure what Dr. Nathaniel is talking about. "Could you clarify what problem you're expecting?" I ask him.

He laughs. "Miss Masters Smith, surely someone has told you that you are beautiful. What kind of complication will that add to the Academy's already difficult regimen? Would you enjoy having men fall in your wake?"

I laugh at that. "Thank you for the compliment, sir, however, I am sure that if the men are as motivated as I am, we will be fine. Should anyone actually fall in my wake —I believe a wake streams behind a passing object — then, it should not be too difficult for me to continue forward.

"Does that sound cold? I hope not. I don't mean it that way. You see, chances are I wouldn't even notice. When I'm studying, as I'll be doing at the Space Academy, my concentration level is pretty high."

"I see," he said. "Yes, that is rather cold. The men would be devastated, and you would merely pass them by, your nose in a book. I wonder if their scores would fall? Would some men forget to test their breathers when they stepped out on the moon? Would rivalries break out? Would some young man take his life when you didn't give him that perfect smile one day?"

"Oh, really, Dr. Nathaniel," Dana laughs. "Aren't you being a bit melodramatic now? You, a man of science, a top field representative from INASA? You act like Mattie will turn the whole Academy on its head when all she wants to do is to have the opportunity to attend classes."

That is Dana's introduction for another break. I stand up and wander down to talk to my parents. I kiss Mom and ask her where Simon's gone. "Stop worrying," she tells me, patting me on the cheek. "He's only gone to the restroom. He'll be back in a moment."

"You let him go by himself?" I ask, worried because I know my brother well.

Dana calls for me to return to the stage, and I scurry back, but I'm also searching for my brother. Why didn't Dad go with him? Why did they let Simon go off by himself?

I forget about my brother, though, the moment Dr. Nathaniel asks me another question. The first one's easy: What if I were to fall in love with one of the Academy students?

I answer that quickly. "I won't. I wouldn't fight so hard just to blow it like that. This means *everything* to me, Dr. Nathaniel. I want to see other worlds. I want that more than anything else. No one is going to interfere with that desire. No one."

"All right, Miss Master Smith, this is my last question at this time. Do you actually think that you will be able to perform all the duties, and physically endure all the hardships as well as a male?"

"Name a duty that you don't think I can perform. Tell me one physical act of endurance the other students would be required to achieve that you think I would be incapable of, Dr. Nathaniel."

He stutters a bit. Then he glances at the camera. "I can't reveal such things, I'm afraid, this publicly. Let's just say I have my doubts that you could keep up at all."

It is a rotten evasion. By leaving it unstated, he has given the audience the supposition that I would not be up to the task.

"That's funny, Dr. Nathaniel," I comment. "My uncle told me that I was well-qualified in all areas. He also told me that I would fly through the Space Academy with the highest marks and a top rating. As you know, my uncle was an American hero who never issued a false word. I know he wouldn't have lied about that. He believed in me. He knew I could do it."

Dr. Nathaniel shifts in his seat. He glances once at the camera, and then says, "Your uncle adored you. Of course, he'd say that."

Dana interrupts then with another commercial. Good thing. I am just about to throw something at Dr. Nathaniel. He's really trying my patience.

I don't try to leave the stage that time. I glance down and see that Simon is back in his seat. I guess my parents were right to have confidence in him. Yet, he has a strange smirk on his face. It's the look he always gets just before he pulls something really awful.

I shut out that thought, sip my water, and glance over at Dr. Nathaniel who's talking with Dana. I'm not sure, but I think he's trying to ask her for a date. I smother a giggle and hope she turns him down.

When the commercial ends, it's question time. The inquiries have all come from the previous airing, but they're still pertinent. Dana even asks the callers to call in some questions for the INASA representative. I look forward to what I hope will be his torment.

"The first question is for Dr. Nathaniel," Dana says. "Caller number one from Chicago, Illinois wants to know why INASA is so resistant to change."

INASA's PR man straightens up, clears his throat, and responds smoothly. "INASA is about space exploration. We move slowly because safety is our first issue. When death is the result of one accidental misstep, believe me, it makes an agency very cautious."

"Thank you. Caller number two is from Bakersfield, California. She wants to know why INASA can't start an Academy for women."

Dr. Nathaniel laughs. "Why would we want to endanger the future population of Earth so gravely? Women cannot live in space, not without doing grave damage to their progeny."

"Thank you. Caller number three, from Boulder, Colorado asks, "Mattie, why can't you do something else with your life? Couldn't you find something that would help humanity and change our world for the better?"

I sigh. "Space exploration has already given us radonians, the small rocks that fuel our *beetleflyers*. It has given us a foundation toward understanding the universe and how we're connected to it. We've been able to plant solar deflectors to avoid meteorite damage. We've colonized the moon and Mars, and now we're working on terra-forming several of the moons of Jupiter.

They have brought and in the future will bring the building blocks for discoveries, for power sources and for precious metals we're lacking. I want to be a part of all that. When someone believes strongly that a specific career is the right choice for her, she must develop it. I will make the world a better place, but I must do it in my own manner, using my God given talents."

"Well answered," Dr. Nathaniel comments. "We have need of young women like you at INASA, Miss Masters Smith. We will be happy to offer you several positions when you're finished with your education."

"Everything except space exploration?" I say, sighing because I realize that I have not won him over in the least. Will the public still be on my side after this? And most importantly, will INASA ever begin to listen?

The taping is not yet finished. One last caller comes on then. From the first word, I start to smile. It's my brother. Just as I suspected, his trip to the bathroom was not without a prank.

"Why are you picking on my sister just because she's a girl? I think you should let Mattie go to the Academy. What are you afraid of?"

Dana inserts that she thinks the caller is addressing the question to Dr. Nathaniel. The man glares out into the seating area, directly at my brother. But after Dana says that, Dr. Nathaniel collects himself, pastes on a fake smile, and stutters through a response.

"We . . . we . . . wa . . . want what is best for your sister, ah . . . Simon, isn't it? You don't want to see her get sick, do you?" He clears his throat again. "I mean, not that being at the Academy would make her sick, but she'd get sick inside, and then if she had any babies they'd all get sick. Do you understand, Simon?"

Simon sees his eyes on him. He shakes his head emphatically.

The camera moves to catch the gesture. A second camera is still centered on Dr. Nathaniel. He gulps again and continues. "You see, Simon, if your sister were to go to the Academy there would be others who would try to do the same thing. All those women would get sick inside, too. And it would be your sister's fault."

Simon shakes his head again. Then he stands up. My dad starts to pull him back down, but Dana gestures to let him come up on stage. So my brother walks forward, someone lifts him up, and he's there with us in front of the main cameras.

Simon tries to speak then, but he's not wired. They bring him a microphone. He grabs at it, blows, and then starts to talk.

"Mattie isn't telling all those women to follow her. That's what you guys keep saying. Mattie just wants to go. She has to go. It's what she needs to do. She's special. When I got into trouble at school, she didn't get mad at me. She gave me a Captain Jetstream toy. She did that even though I wasn't supposed to get it until my birthday. But she knew to give it to me that day.

"You see, Dr. You shouldn't be afraid of Mattie. She's really nice. She'll go to your Academy, and she won't cause you trouble. She never gets in trouble. She's not like me. I get in trouble lots, you see. Mattie studies all the time. She'll pretty soon be the best. She's going to be a space captain like my uncle."

Dr. Nathaniel starts to interrupt, but Simon just keeps talking.

"You need to relax and give in because Mattie never stops. She'll go there even if she has to build herself a spaceship. Well, that's all I got to say, except you need to stop making up stuff."

Simon takes a step back to his seat down below, but Dana stops him. "Wait, Simon. I'm confused. Didn't you tell everyone that girls shouldn't be in space?"

Simon gives her one of his Simon looks, then he looks into the camera. "Yeah, I said there weren't any girls on Captain Jetstream, but I've been thinking about that. It's wrong. I bet there's lots of girls who could do stuff like Captain Jetstream does.

Mattie can hang-glide. I tried it, but I don't like going up high. It made me feel yicky. Mattie likes to do it. She likes to fly. She gets a funny look on her face, too. It's like she sees more than we do. I think when she glides out in the air, she's going into space and she's exploring other planets, or something.

You should see her eyes. You'd believe she should go to the Academy if you watched her hang-gliding. It would be like taking something from her. I don't know, like tearing her arm or leg off. It's that important to her. How come you can't see that, Dr. Nathaniel? How come all you space guys are so blind?"

It is time for a commercial, and the time has already been exceeded, but Dana has tears in her eyes when Simon stops talking. She can't close out the session, so she just waves for a break.

"We'll patch it in later," she says, wiping her eyes. "Or maybe we'll just leave it like that, Simon doing the conclusion. That was wonderful, Simon. Thank you."

"You're going to let a kid have the final word? Where's my chance at rebuttal?" Dr. Nathaniel storms. "You have to let me explain."

"What would you say that you haven't already?" Dana questions him. "How would you answer Simon's words?"

Dr. Nathaniel's face grows dark. He is so angry his hands are shaking, but he doesn't answer Dana. He stands up and storms away.

Chapter Twenty-One

My family and I fly off shortly after that. I'm drained from the taping. From the moment we crawl into our *beetleflyer*, I snooze.

The next day, Dad and I get up late and go hang-gliding. The sky is so blue it's like lake water. The clouds are puffy streaks of wavering froth, and the air is so clear, you can breathe in and hold onto it, feeling high from the richness.

Dad and I have a chance to talk, too. That's really cool. He tells me that listening to Simon and me up on that stage, he's realized finally that he was attempting to meld me into someone else. "You never wanted to go to Stanford, did you? I mean, if something happened and you couldn't go up to the Academy, Stanford's still not where you'd be going, is it?" Dad asks.

I look down and shake my head. "No. My first choice is the Space Academy, Dad. I don't want to go anywhere else or do anything other than that. However, if INASA doesn't relent, my next choice would be Berkeley."

"Do you want me to cancel your interview, then?" Dad asks.

He and Jimmy's father are looking forward to that day. I know that. I remember that Jimmy's excited about it, too. "No, Dad. It will be a good practice for me. I'll go to the interview, but it's nice to hear that you understand how I feel and that you respect that. Thank you."

Dad pats me on the shoulder and says, "Are you ready for another lift-off?"

We fly for two hours and only drag ourselves back to the hangar when we're completely spent. There, Stan, who's in charge that day, takes our rentals back and invites us, as always, to come in for a cup of coffee or a soda. We figure he must understand after all the activity, we can barely keep from collapsing.

While we're sitting at the outside table, pouring a cola down each of our throats, Stan mentions the photographer who was snapping our pictures.

"Photographer?" I gasp, looking down at my old jeans and the t-shirt that has a huge sunflower draped across its front. My hair is probably a mess, too. I reach up to smooth it down, but, of course, now it's too late.

"Who was he or she with? Did you question the person?"

Stan shakes his head. "Sorry, I was busy outfitting someone. I just noticed the equipment, and then the guy asked if you were Mattie Masters Smith. I nodded my head because you were the only two up there so far, and then next time I turned around, he was gone."

I shrug. "Well, I hope he got what he needed. I hope he's on my side. You are, aren't you, Stan?"

Stan, a very small-sized man who is only slightly taller than I am, pulls himself up, looks down into my eyes and says, "If I told you I thought women should always stay on Earth to prevent the destruction of our race, you'd stop coming here, wouldn't you? So, I think I'll just take the fifth and clam up."

So that was that. It's obvious I haven't yet won over the world.

Dad and I fly home, arriving just in time to catch Simon and his friend attempting to shave themselves with a dinner knife and Dad's shaving cream. Mom, busy washing windows in the back, isn't even aware.

After we recover from that calamity, we sit down to eat a massive lunch of waffles and scrambled eggs. We're just finishing up when the phone rings. It's our pest telling us that "women should stay at home." I thank her for her opinion and hang up.

I sit back down just as the phone rings a second time. "Darn it. If it's that crazy woman again, pass the phone to me," Dad demands, his face sliding into the reds of anger.

But it's not. Instead, I hear Jimmy's father announcing that Jimmy has just had an attack of appendicitis and has been taken to the hospital for surgery. He's scheduled for later in the day.

"Poor Jimmy," I say. "I'm so sorry."

His father wants to speak to mine. I watch Dad as he listens. After a moment, Dad quietly hangs up the phone. "We can't see Jimmy today, Mattie. In fact, he can't have visitors until tomorrow. But do you know what bothered Jimmy the most?"

I glance at my mother, puzzled by something I see in my Dad's eyes. Dad starts to explain what should be obvious.

"Jimmy will be in the hospital for at least a week, maybe even longer. Then he'll be at home recuperating. He's not going to be able to take you to the Senior Prom, Mattie. Jimmy's devastated."

I stop my face from breaking into a huge smile. There are some things just not appropriate, but I can't help the fact that my body feels buoyant with relief.

"I understand," I tell my father, attempting to look suitably saddened by the news. "Can we still take the dress back?" I ask my mother.

She peers into my eyes, studying me, then nods. "Yes, we'll take it back tomorrow, just before we stop off and see Jimmy. I hope you'll tell him how crushed you are that you won't get to go to the dance with him?"

"It would be better if she not say that," my father argues, but I can read my mother's eyes. We've talked about the way Jimmy feels about me. We've also discussed how it's not reciprocated, not in that way.

I nod. "I'll tell him I'm crushed, but that I'll make it up to him some other time. We can go to the show together or go surfing. He'd like that. He's been after me to try it. Don't worry, Dad. I'll cheer him up."

I leave the table to go upstairs, glancing at the new dress hanging in my closet. It's black, the current "in" color with an a-line frame and a flaring skirt. It really looked good on me. I have to admit I was pleasingly surprised by that. Mom said it showed off "my graceful, slender neck." I never knew I had graceful neck, another revelation, although it kind of makes me sound a bit like a swan. Dad said he liked the way my legs were displayed with the panels of skirt that shimmered as I moved. I sigh as I zip up the outer covering. The new shoes will go back, too. So will the fake diamond barrette for my hair.

I shrug. It was a waste of money, anyway. I'd rather spend it on … Then I stop. I don't have anything I need. A new telescope? I can't take one with me. Another book? For what purpose? Everything I need, I'll have to buy on my instructor's recommendations.

I lie down on the bed, not quite as pleased about missing the Prom after all. It will be the last of its kind, the final chance to show off my supposedly graceful neck and the legs that, according to Dad, are as shapely as a dancer's.

I think about what it would have been like to go to the dance with Jimmy. He's always so comfortable to be with. We would have had a good time, laughing and dancing, talking about science things. We might even have kissed.

Poor Jimmy, lying in a hospital bed. Would they give him something for the pain? Would he be able to sleep while he waited for the operation? How long would it take? Would he be okay?

"Of course, he will," I say out loud. Then I rise up to go check out "appendix" on the computer. What I find frightens me. What if Jimmy's had burst open? What if the infection had spread all over his body? What if he'd died?

"He's my best friend," I tell myself. "Of course, I care about him."

I pace for a while, thinking about how I'd feel if I never saw Jimmy again. Yet, wasn't that what was going to happen soon? Would we see each other after we went our different directions? Maybe I should go to Stanford. Maybe friendship was too important to lose.

Then I stop and realize what I'm thinking. I remind myself once again exactly what Ms. Anderson has said. She told me that I *will* be going to the Academy. She said she has that kind of faith in me, believing that I can overcome every obstacle.

I drop onto the bed and stare up at the fake stars on my ceiling. Is it really worth it, Uncle Theodore? Is all this trouble, this constant battle, really worth it? Am I doing the right thing?

Uncle Theodore's picture stares down at me. He's smiling, but his eyes aren't looking at the camera. They're gazing out into the stars. I know what Uncle Theodore would say. He's already said it to me.

I sigh and close my eyes, picturing those words, remembering that no matter what, I have just one goal — space.

Chapter Twenty-Two

On Monday, Mom and I return the Prom things. The woman at the counter looks sad for me. "I'm so sorry," she says. "This is such a shame. You must be devastated by the tragedy, and I hope your fellow feels better soon."

"Yes, I'm worried about him. He's the one who's really upset about it," I tell her, but her eyes say she doesn't believe me. Apparently, her long-ago Senior Prom was quite something. The look in her face as she remembers it tells me that she has fond memories.

The hospital is a cold, sterile place. I pass the flower shop and wonder if I should pick up some daisies, but Jimmy's never really cared much for such things. Besides, I've brought him a new magazine, *Telescope and Path Finder*. He doesn't subscribe to it, and he usually buys one the moment it comes out. Since it was new on the shelf today, I figure he won't have had a chance to pick one up yet.

When I walk into his room, I hardly recognize Jimmy. His skin is sallow, and he looks like he's been sick forever instead of for just two days. I'm not exactly sure what to do. I feel all stiff and formal. I hand Jimmy the magazine. He looks down and then back up at me. Then he thanks me and slides it into his lap.

"I'll read it later," he says. "Right now, I just want to enjoy your visit."

I look around his room. There are flowers everywhere. Again I wonder if I should have stopped and bought some. "Wow! What a lot of flowers," I comment.

He grins, looking a tad more like himself. "I wish you'd take them out of here. They make me feel like I'm in a funeral parlor. I suppose it would hurt someone's feelings if they came in and didn't seem them, though."

I smile. "I'm glad I didn't bring you more, then."

Mom interrupts to say how sorry she is about Jimmy's appendicitis. She chats a moment, then tells me she's going down to get a cup of coffee. I know she's just leaving to allow Jimmy and me some time alone. I flash her a smile and watch her leave.

"I'm sorry," Jimmy says quietly the moment Mom closes the door.

My eyes return to his. "You mean about the Prom? It's not your fault, Jimmy. I'm sorry, too. I won't get to go with you now. We would have had fun together."

He nods and then grimaces. "I want you to go with someone else. Byron isn't going with anyone. He'd love to go with you."

I shake my head and give Jimmy a huge smile. "Don't be a silly. You're the one who talked me into it. You know I didn't want to go — at least, not at first. I'd certainly never go with anyone else."

Jimmy smiles then, a pale-looking imitation of his usual broad grin, but it's enough for me. I reach out for his hand, something I've never done before.

He cocks his head. "What's this? You feeling sorry for me? Is this the result of your sympathy? If so, I like it very much," he says, squeezing my hand gently.

"Don't start that. You're my best friend. Of course, I feel sympathy."

"Nothing more?" Jimmy urges, holding my hand more firmly as if he suspects I'll pull away. A wistful look has crept into his eyes. I've been seeing that a lot lately.

"I'm going to the Academy," I tell Jimmy. "I can't afford anything more."

His eyes light up. "Anything more than what?" he asks. "What happened? Were you worrying about me? Were you finally thinking about *us*?"

My mouth opens and closes. I don't know what to say. I've reached the end of firm footing. "You know I can't go there," I say, turning away withdrawing my hand.

A moment of silence passes between us. I can't look at Jimmy. My eyes start to water. I can't stand the feeling.

"Hey, best friend. Come back here," Jimmy whispers suddenly.

I still can't bear to meet his eyes. He seems so knowing as if he's peering down into my soul.

"It's okay, Mattie," he tells me gently. "Look at me."

For some reason, he has the power to command me. I turn. His eyes are shining. I look away again, unsure, afraid. I don't know where this is going, but I sense that it's dangerous.

"I do understand," Jimmy says. "I've always known I was only second."

I don't understand what he means. I need to read what his eyes are saying. "What?" I ask.

He laughs, not like his usual laugh. This one's shallow, almost a caricature of a laugh, and it holds an acid drop of bitterness.

"Space, Mattie. That's always been first with you. You've never tried to hide it. It's who you are. But I'll wait . . ."

I back up, shaking my head. "No, Jimmy. That's not . . ."

"Listen, Mattie. I'm young, but I'm no fool. I know things. Like no matter what INASA says now, you're going to that Academy. I've never doubted that. Anyone who really knows you couldn't doubt it. I'd never try to interfere with that. But there will be a time when you're finished with all your training, Mattie. Someday, and I'll be at your side that day. You can count on it."

"Jimmy, you don't understand. I have four years to go at the Academy, and then, if I really make it that far, I'll be struggling to rise through the officer's corps. That will take me years, Jimmy. Maybe even my whole life. Don't you see that? I won't give it up, not ever."

Jimmy tries to lift himself up, but he can't. He falls back and groans.

I turn toward him. "Jimmy, what can I do to help? Do you want a drink? Another pillow?"

His eyes are full of pain, not like a moment ago, but this time, ragged, physical pain. "It hurts, Mattie, but the pain of the incision will go away soon. I'll recover from that, but not from you.

Listen, this is probably bad timing. But it's always bad timing with you. Just remember that I said all this. Maybe I'm telling you now because they've got me all pumped up with medicine. I don't know. Maybe it's just time for you to know. But I'll be waiting, Mattie. No matter what. No matter how many years. I'll still wait."

A nurse walks in then. She lectures me with her finger. "You've be in here too long, young lady. Your young man needs some rest now. Look at his face. He's all tuckered out. Shoo, now. Come back tomorrow."

I glance back at Jimmy. He's trying to hide the pain, but he's not succeeding very well. I run over to him and kiss him on the lips. "I do care for you," I whisper in his ears. Then before the heavy-set nurse with the massive finger can wag it at me again, I rush out the door.

When I find my mom in the waiting room, she stands up, takes one look at my face, and hugs me. "Sometimes life's pretty tough, isn't it?" she says.

I nod, and we walk out of the hospital without speaking.

"How about I make dinner tonight?" Mom asks when we arrive at the house.

I nod again, but I still can't say anything. My eyes are tearing, and my throat is raw. I'm feeling sick at my stomach. Upstairs, I climb into bed. No one wakes me for supper. Mom lets me sleep through the night.

Chapter Twenty-Three

Ms. Anderson calls on Wednesday, which is good because the daily doses of Jimmy's wistful eyes are breaking me down into a teary-eyed wreck.

I've been talking with Ms. Anderson on the phone, but that's not what she wants. She asks if we can come to dinner. We suggest Friday again, but she says it must be sooner. "The news can't wait," she tells us.

I look at my parents and nod. "Please?" I mouth.

Once again, Hakim does the ferrying. Dad doesn't even ask where I want to sit. He more or less pushes me into the back. I sigh. Hakim is no danger to my stability. Dad should look closer to home.

Ms. Anderson greets us at the airstrip, not bothering to wait for our arrival at the house. She offers me a kiss on the cheek, saying, "I've been taken with your daughter, Mrs. Masters Smith. I find her quite refreshing."

That makes me sound like a soft drink, but I smile. Ms. Anderson's attentions make me a little uneasy. She flits from subject to subject, which often leaves me lost in the breeze of her passage. I wish she were calmer and easier to understand, but as she walks forward down the moss and stone path, I stay besides her, lapping up each word.

"I've already spoken to INASA. They're still being incredibly stubborn, but I saw the tape of last Friday's show. INASA's stuck in a rut. They don't have any idea how Simon's appeal is going to affect the public. Simon, you were wonderful."

Although I'm puzzled how Ms. Anderson could have seen the taping since it hasn't been broadcast yet, I don't want to interrupt. Yet when she says that about Simon, I can't help but speak.

"He was fantastic, wasn't he?" I agree, nodding my head and giving his hair a fond pat.

Ms. Anderson smiles at me and then squats down to look into Simon's eyes. "You won your sister's battle, you know. You're quite a hero."

Simon beams and looks around at his parents. The looks on their faces are equally proud. "I didn't get in trouble for it, either," he says, and we all laugh.

"Your sister is lucky to have you on her team. What are you going to be when you grow up, Simon? Maybe I'd better find you a position, too."

That sets him off. It's always dangerous to praise Simon too much.

"I'm going to be a clown, a fireman, a paleontologist, a baker because I like cookies, and a plumber to make my mom happy."

Again, we laugh. Each time I hear the list of Simon's ambitions, it gets longer and longer. Last year, he only wanted to be a paleontologist. The plumber is the newest, based on dad's bad experiences with reworking the sprinkler system out back, I imagine.

We've reached a large building. Ms. Anderson tells us it's the salmon farm. As we walk inside, we're assaulted by fishy odors as well as the sound of water running. The poor salmon are leaping from the man-made rivers, swimming steadily against the current. "Here you see my pride and joy," Ms. Anderson says. "Life is like this. To get somewhere different, we must all swim against the current. That's what you're doing, Mattie."

"Let's hope her story has a better ending than the salmon's," Dad jokes.

Ms. Anderson regards him without laughing, and we all sober, wondering why she takes such a comment so seriously. "We all die. It's the law of nature. The salmon know that. They fight the current to reach their destination. Then they die. It is the achievement that counts, not the length of time spent traveling against the current."

Ms. Anderson can be a bit abrupt at times. I stir the conversation into a lighter tone by thanking her for showing us her salmon factory.

Her eyes light as she gazes at me. "She has diplomacy skills, as well. Lovely. You are perfect, child. Those at INASA are idiots."

Without another word, we head for the main house, on the way, discussing nothing more important than the flower gardens that surround the mansion. Ms. Anderson perks up at that. My father, seeing a patch of daffodils, starts telling her about his hybrids, the all season and fragrant yellow, pink, and violet daffodils.

"You're mistaken," Ms. Anderson tells Dad sharply. "Daffodils don't come in colors."

So, Dad whips out his pictures. He carries them everywhere. By the time we get to the house, Ms. Anderson is begging him to sell her some.

That continues all through our dinner of white asparagus, baby Brussels sprouts, salmon and homegrown tomato slices. Simon, not fond of such food, interrupts the horticulture lecture my father's giving Ms. Anderson to ask for a piece of bread.

Ms. Anderson's face turns red. "Bread?" she chuckles. "All this, and you want bread?" Then she calls out to Sergio. "Bring a platter of bread, please. Oh, and some honey and jam. I think little Simon has a marvelous idea. I'd like a piece, too."

I don't think her cooks are prepared for the request. It takes several minutes for the bread to arrive, and then when it does, we see it's the tasteless, white kind. It doesn't matter. We all grab a piece and lavish the orange clover honey butter onto it. The salmon is delicious and we all enjoy that, but that bread with fresh honey butter is the highlight.

When we slide away from the table, Ms. Anderson once more starts laughing. "I haven't been so stuffed in ages. What a delightful feeling. Thank you, Simon. I can see that you will make an excellent — ah, whatever you decide to be."

"Ms. Anderson, what was the news that you wanted to tell us?" I ask.

Again, she laughs. "What delightful children you have, Mr. and Mrs. Masters Smith. I would love to adopt them both."

My parents look at each other, not quite understanding what she means, but that only makes Ms. Anderson laugh harder. "I won't steal them away from you. You have nothing to fear," she says, touching my mother's arm.

"The news, Mattie, is that I have given INASA a final warning. They have until this Friday at nine o'clock, our time, to resolve this issue about your attending the Academy. If they should be idiotic enough to refuse your application, they will find themselves without AMACS in their ships.

They would sue me, of course, but they wouldn't win. I'm sure they're intelligent enough to realize that. That's why I am reasonably positive that tomorrow night, immediately following the broadcast of your interview, INASA will make their official announcement. We must cross our fingers that it will be the correct one."

Chapter Twenty-Four

So it is needles and pins until Friday evening. Still, my day flies by. I see my junior high little buddy that afternoon and am relieved to hear that she is doing better. Her parents are seeing a marriage counselor, which is super news, and the radiance in Lina's eyes gives no doubt that she is happy about that.

She tells me she is catching up on her homework, too, and has hopes to repair all the damage her earlier neglect caused. I speak with her teachers and put in a good word. I have my fingers crossed that my support will do Lina some good. My time with her is almost over.

That evening, I go home via the hospital. Jimmy's getting out the next day, sometime late in the afternoon. He looks better. His complexion is back to normal, and his smile is full of mischief once again.

"Remember all that stuff I told you when I was pumped full of meds," he asks. I nod and look away, still nervous about it. "Well, I'm off the meds now, Mattie."

I look up and see his grin. I smile back. Then he takes my hand. "Do you remember how you held my hand while I was sick?"

I nod. I know something's coming. It feels like the punch line.

"Yeah, well, as I said, there's no meds inside me now, and I feel exactly the same way."

I try to withdraw my hand, but his strength has come back. "Mattie, wait," he says, and I stop jerking.

"Listen, I know you're not ready. That's okay. This has been uncomfortable for you, and I can see it in your eyes that you don't want to talk about it. I'm not going to bring it up again. Not for a couple of years, anyway — or at least not unless I have to have my appendix removed again."

I bounce a smile off him with that because he sounds like he's back to his normal self.

"I just want to remind you that if anything goes wrong, I'll be there for you. Not up at the Academy, of course, but down here waiting. Will you remember that?"

I nod, and I try to pull away.

"Mattie, one more thing, and then I let you go."

I look up into his eyes. Big mistake. His eyes are the green of lichen. Except they're full of love and hope — and are brilliantly distracting.

"Mattie, at the Academy . . . "

"I might not be going, you know," I interrupt.

"Sh! I know you will. Now listen. At the Academy, there's going to be hundreds of men, and they're all going to want you. Don't give in, Mattie. Remember how much I love you. Remember that and don't say "yes" to any of them, not unless . . . .not unless you really . . . "

"I won't, Jimmy. I'll promise you that. I couldn't. Do you know how much trouble that would make? They'd probably kick me out. I'll never even be best friends with any of them or go on a single date."

Jimmy bends forward slightly and taps my forehead with a kiss. "You'll never go to the Senior Prom with any of them? Do you promise me?"

It's the perfect thing for him to say. He's turned the seriousness of the moment into something I can handle. I kiss him back, a firm one, right on the lips. I think that might have developed into something truly nice, but the heavyweight nurse comes in at that moment to wag her finger at me again.

"Ah, you young people," she scolds. "Never miss a moment, do you? That's enough of that now. Off with you, young lady. He'll be out tomorrow."

I look at Jimmy and as our eyes meet, we laugh, and it's okay between us again. In fact more than okay. For I've made a promise, and Jimmy is feeling confident again. For the moment, the wistfulness in his eyes is gone, and he's once more my best friend, Jimmy.

At home that evening, we all gather round the TV. Dad's made popcorn, but even Simon is too keyed up to eat it.

"Do you think INASA's going to announce it tonight?" he asks again and again until I want to scream at him, but I don't, remembering the sweetness of his words in front of the camera.

I'm lying on the floor with my back against the sofa, Simon beside me. Mom and Dad are sitting on the couch. We're all sipping iced tea, clinking the ice to make it cooler. Simon starts in again.

"Why don't you go get the lemon slices for us, dear?" Mom suggests, and Simon slowly gets up and ambles into the kitchen.

"If he says that one more time . . ." I threaten.

"Yes?" Mom says, "What will you say to him?" She's laughing, just as if she can read my mind.

In come the lemons, and we all grab one, but before Simon can start in with THE QUESTION, Dana comes on.

Simon drops a lemon into my glass, and I take advantage of his proximity and hug him. He pulls back, of course, but then he sets the bowl of lemons on the sofa table and drops down beside me again. His eyes are glued to the TV, and his skin looks as pale as when I first saw Jimmy in the hospital.

"Are you okay?" I whisper, but he doesn't answer me except to say, "sh!"

So we watch the whole program through. Everything is just as we remember. Dana didn't cut anything. In fact, she's apparently gotten extra minutes because the program goes beyond its normal time. Then, at the final moment, when Dana's bidding us goodnight, she says, "Stay tuned for an official announcement from INASA right after the commercial."

"Yippee!" yells Simon, bursting up from the floor like a rocket, spilling lemons, popcorn, and two bowls full of kernels all over the floor.

"Calm down, son, and clean up the mess, please," Dad orders. "We don't know what they're going to say, remember. They could just say they're thinking about it. They could say they've decided to stand by their former decision, or . . ."

"Or that they're going to let Mattie go!" yells Simon. "That's what it means. Ms. Anderson told us that. They're going to let Mattie go!"

It was the longest set of commercials I've ever watched. I am sure they threw in a couple more than usual. My family and I all sat staring at the screen like we were fixated with the detergent, the cat food, the diapers being advertised, and the newest pill that solved incontinency.

"This is torture," Simon yells out.

"Have some popcorn," Mom tells him, and we all look down at the kernels still scattered across the carpeting.

"I'll clean it up after they tell us," Simon promises.

Mom sighs. "Good thing there's no butter on . . ."

Then Dana's back on, telling the audience that INASA has an announcement to make. We wait while Dana catches up the audience that just tuned in, obviously ad-libbing to fill time.

Then the station plunks in one of the earlier tapings where I'm telling everyone about why it's so important for me to go to the Academy. They show Simon's speech again. Finally, Dana comes back on. "What do you think this announcement from INASA can mean? Will they tell Mattie Masters Smith she can be the first female to attend the INASA Academy on the moon?"

Suddenly the station blurs and kind of burps. Then we see it, the INASA symbol, in the background, and unbelievably, in the foreground, getting ready to speak is the president of the United States, Jerome M. Washington.

"Ladies and Gentleman, I interrupt this broadcast now to make an announcement that will change the path of INASA forever. With due consideration for the dangers entailed, but after discussion, analysis, and consultation, it has been determined that Mattie Masters Smith *will* be admitted in the fall to the INASA Academy as a full-fledged member of the International team of candidates for space.

"Thank you for your time. This is the President of the United States wishing you all a good night and a great weekend."

"Wow!" Simon yells out. "The president knows you! Wow!"

Mom and Dad, and I are all hugging. But we can do that only for a minute because almost immediately, the phone starts to ring.

Jimmy's first to give me congratulations. "See, I knew it," he tells me. "Remember, I love you." Wide mouthed, I stand there staring at the phone even though he's already hung up.

Mom takes it from me. "Jimmy?" she asks as she sets the receiver back down.

The moment it makes contact, it's ringing again. But I back away, not bothering to see who it is. I turn and run up to my room. I have too much to think about, and I'm suddenly on overload.

Chapter Twenty-Five

So it's going to happen. I'm really going to the Space Academy. I'm almost numb with the concept. It's been so long getting me to that point. I don't know what to do next. "I've been accepted at the Academy," I say, just to test out the sound of it.

"Mattie," my father calls.

I go to my door and peer down. Of course, I can't see anything, but I listen. "Yeah?" I say.

"Get down here, Mattie."

That sounds like I'm in trouble. I take the stairs two by two, jogging. Then I stop at the bottom. There's a stranger in our house, one with a uniform.

I walk the last few steps in a more sedate manner.

"Mattie Masters Smith?" the man says, saluting.

Having returned the salute with my uncle so many times, I automatically salute back. A flash goes off, and I see the photographer wedged over to the side.

The officer steps forward. "I am here to offer you your acceptance letter to the INASA Space Academy. Are you willing to accept it?"

"Yes," I say, holding out my hand for the miracle.

He places it on my palm. It's sealed. I tear it open. "Oh, my God," I say as I read the lines I've been longing to see. "It's really true. I've been accepted. Thank you so much."

"You're welcome, ma'am. You are asked to report on August 12th in Washington, D.C., for transfer to the moon. Will you comply?"

"Yes, sir," I say, saluting him again.

"You will find all pertinent information in the letters beneath your acceptance. Please read that over and follow the orders. Any carelessness on your part will be severely dealt with. Do you understand?"

"Yes, sir," I tell him, dazed but saluting properly.

He turns on a dime, facing the door, and my father lets him out. The photographer, walking behind him, first grabs a couple more close-ups, then follows behind without a word to either of us.

"Did you see that, Dad? It's happened. It's really happened."

Dad laughs. "Did you have any doubts? The dripping sprinkler always brings out a bloom."

"What?" I laugh.

"The big question is — is this what you still want, Mattie," my mother says, coming up behind Dad.

"Mom! How can you say that? You know this is what I want."

Mom walks closer and puts her arm around me. "Your father's right. You're like a bloom just opening up. Something happened this week. It opened your eyes to other possibilities. Are you going to ignore them? Do you *want* to ignore him?"

"What on earth are you talking about?" Dad questions, looking as puzzled as Simon, who's just come into the room.

But I know. Mom is talking about Jimmy. "Yes, I still want to go to the Academy, Mom, more than anything. Nothing's going to stop me now. Not Jimmy, not anything."

"Why would Jimmy . . .?" Dad is slow, but then he gets it. "So my little girl is growing up? That's not all bad, although the timing's off a bit. However, it may be for the best. It won't make you as susceptible to all those others. We need to talk about that, Mattie. A whole school full of males — all guys with smiles and uniforms like that soldier had. Think you can handle that?"

I smile. "Sure," I say. "I promised Jimmy I wouldn't allow a single one of them to take me to the prom. I mean it, too."

"The Prom?" Simon butts in. "Why would they take you to the prom? That's a high school thing. You're graduating."

"Exactly, Simon. I'm graduating into the Space Academy, where my nose is going to be tucked into every book someone recommends. You see, I'm not just going to attend the Academy. I've got to do high honors. I want to be a spaceship captain like Uncle Theodore. I won't have time for anything else."

"I sure hope it works out like that," Dad says, meeting Mom's eyes. "I really hope so, baby. I'd like to see you achieve your dreams."

But Mom isn't ready to let it go so easily. "What did Jimmy say on the phone to you? What did he say that upset you so?"

"Oh, Mom. Nothing."

The nothing pains her. I see it flash across her eyes. I can't bear that. "He just congratulated me, Mom."

"And?"

"Now, maybe that's personal, honey," Dad offers, defending me from Mom's probing.

But her eyes are still demanding. I turn away and look at Simon. The phone rings. Mom goes to answer it. Freed from her look, I run upstairs.

I throw myself on the bed and spend a moment looking around my room. Soon, I'll be leaving it. I want to remember it exactly as it is, for I'm never coming back, not to live here. My new home is space.

My eyes study the dark mahogany of the dresser and the little bear atop it that Jimmy gave me long ago. I memorize the rest of it — the color of the drapes, the way the sunlight streams through them. My eyes scan the bedposts, examining them as if I were about to take a test on their composition. Everything is the same as it's been for years, yet tonight, it's new and impermanent.

"I made it, Uncle Theodore. What do you think of that? I'm going to be like you now. I'm finally going to feel the end of gravity. I'll see the Earth from up there, too. I'll look down and watch it turning. It's going to be wonderful, won't it, Uncle Theodore?"

But he can't answer me. He died up there. Parts of him are still drifting. "I miss you," I whisper. "I wish you could have been here today. I really need to talk to you."

I'm being silly. It's the happiest day of my life. I've just taken a step toward my dreams. I look down at the paper in my hand. Then I open it and read it again. On the next page I find a list.

There's nothing surprising on it. The uniforms are supplied by the Academy. I only have to take care of my underwear and sleeping needs. A short list of things like sonar brushes for my teeth, combs, shaving gear . . . . Most of that is commonsense. I read it over again, anyway, double-checking that I understand everything.

Then I flip to the next page at the address of the place where I'm supposed to meet my lift-up group. We're assembling at the White House. My uncle never said anything about that. I scratch my head and ponder it.

At the bottom is the coupon for tuition. I gasp, even though I've been forewarned about the amount. But the part I'm not expecting is that mine says that it's been paid in full.

"Dad," I call out and go running down the stairs.

He's on the phone, but he sees me and waves me over. "Here she is now. I'll put her on."

It's Ms. Anderson. She congratulates me, and I thank her for all her help.

"Have you read over your acceptance package?" she asks.

"I was just doing that, but I can't understand it. I was just checking out the tuition, and it says that it's been paid — all four years! I don't under . . . "

"I paid it, Mattie. I believe in you. I want to see you achieve your goal. Accept this as my personal gift to you. I won't force you to sign onto my company. I know your ambition is to become a space captain. That's what I wanted, too. We're alike that way, except you get to live your dreams, and all I can do is watch. Live that dream for me, Mattie. Will you do that for me?"

I don't know what to answer. My throat is all choked up. "What's wrong, Mattie?" my mother says, grabbing the phone away from me.

"What did you say to her?" Mom demands. Then, I guess Ms. Anderson explains about the tuition being paid. I hear my mother thanking her. I want to, too. In a moment, I get my chance.

"Will you come to dinner next Friday night?" Ms. Anderson asks, and I share the invitation with the others.

My father nods and smiles at my mother, so she nods, too.

"Yes, we'd love to come. Thank you. Thank you for everything."

We don't go to bed until very late that night. The phone keeps ringing with neighbors and friends and the usual news reporters. The pestilence calls, telling us again that women should stay at home, but this time, she only makes us laugh. Even Dad bends over in spasms. Finally, only when we're yawning and Simon's already snoring away on the floor, we head upstairs, thankful that, for once, there's no taping the next day.

Chapter Twenty-Six

Lovely Saturday! When I wake up, it's almost eleven o'clock. My window is slightly open. I hear sounds coming from the lawn. I peek out and see that our front yard is full of people. Cameras are everywhere, as are reporters with microphones, video flyers, and strange machines I've never seen before and have no idea what they do.

I get dressed and head downstairs. Mom and Dad are both at the table eating breakfast. "Where's Simon?" I ask first thing.

"Right behind you," he tells me, clumping into the kitchen in his bare feet and pajamas.

"What's going on? Are aliens invading?" he asks. He's grinning, so it's obvious he's looked out the window, too, and knows all about the situation.

Mom hands me a cup of coffee and hands Simon a glass of already-poured orange juice. "The lawn was covered with them when we got up. They woke me at six, fighting over their positions. I just can't believe it. I called the police, but they said there was nothing that they could do except move the horde back. They're on their way."

The moment Mom says that we hear sirens. Simon and I rush to the kitchen window to watch. We're just in time to see the police flyers dropping out of the sky. They can't land since there's no place for them, but their loud speakers blare warnings to the crowd to move back.

"Can I go outside and watch?" Simon asks.

Mom and Dad almost drop their coffee mugs. "Absolutely not, Simon. Don't you step anywhere near that group of locusts," Mom orders fiercely.

Dad grins. "I figured they might come around today, but I sure never thought they'd drop by in such mass. You're a real star now, Mattie. You, too, Simon. Everyone will want your autograph."

Simon jumps up. "Really? Will they pay for it?"

Mom gives Dad one of those looks. "Don't encourage him. You know he believes everything you say."

Dad winks at Simon, and my brother winks back. I shake my head. "Mom, they're just kidding you," I tell her. "Simon's smarter than that. He knows they'd pluck out each of his hairs for souvenirs."

"My hair?" he yelps. "Would they really?"

"They might," Dad says. "Fans do strange things."

The phone rings. I'm the first one to pick it up. I don't speak until I hear who it is. It's only Jimmy calling to ask me why the whole street is filled with cars. I laugh and explain what's going on.

"How are you feeling now that you're home?" I want to know, but Jimmy doesn't want to talk about that. He wants to know if I'm going to change now that I'm famous.

We're just arguing about it when Dad tells me to get off the phone.

"Did you hear my Dad?" I ask. "I gotta' hang up."

I return to the table, but as soon as I sit down, the phone rings again. This time, it's Ms. Anderson. "You okay with this?" she asks. I tell her we're all fine. She curtly orders me to get my father.

He gets up and starts to talk, but his eyes get big, and he stops suddenly and yells at us. "Go upstairs and pack a bag. We're leaving for the week. Do it. Now. Quickly."

My mom starts to argue, but Simon and I don't. We run upstairs and throw jeans and tees, and other essentials into our duffle bags. We're downstairs in less than five minutes. Mom is, too. Dad's already off the phone and cleaning the kitchen mess we left.

"Okay," he says. "There's been a bomb threat. Someone doesn't want females on the moon, apparently. The moment Hakim lowers down into our front yard, we make a run for it. Got that?"

"A bomb in our house?" Mom cries. Then she covers her mouth, and her eyes bulge with fear.

Dad runs out to the backyard, checks the automatic watering system, and then joins us at the front door.

Hakim lowers down in the *butterfly*, Dad opens the front door, and we all step out. The crowd surges forward, but the police are still there to restrain them. Hakim lowers a hook, which we hang the duffle bags on. It recoils, and a ladder slides down, and one by one, we climb up into the *Butterfly*.

Simon's talking a mile a minute, telling everyone that this is most exciting thing that's ever happened to him. Mom is looking white-faced and worried. Dad's not showing a thing on his face, but I'm pretty sure he's worrying about his daffodils and roses.

Hakim takes us up at about forty miles an hour. It's the first time he's demonstrated what the *Butterfly* can do. I wonder if it's loaded with defensive mechanisms. I start to ask, but Dad pulls me back.

"Let Hakim fly without any distractions. Okay, Mattie?" Dad snaps at me.

"Are you still worried about him?" I rib him, hoping to put Dad into a better mood, but he isn't in a teasing mode. He's looking back at our house as if he expects it to blow up while he's watching. I pat his hand.

"I'm sure it's just a false alarm, Dad. Lots of people say they're going to do things, but they don't really."

"Yeah, I know that, Mattie. I'm sure you're right, honey," Dad says, but he continues to look back at the direction of our house, even though it's far out of sight.

I sigh. "I'm sorry about this, Mom. I guess it's my fault."

She smiles rather weakly. "Do you suppose there's any coffee in here? Could we ask Hakim?"

"Touch the button, Mom," Simon tells her, showing her what she needs to push in order to communicate with our pilot.

Hakim smiles back at us, then says, "Help yourself, but I'm sorry, but there's no coffee, only colas and fruit drinks."

We make do and drink up.

"You can see the news, if you would like, with the green button," Hakim's voice says over the intercom.

Dad punches it on right away. We get to see ourselves coming out of our house, looking like scared bunnies. The ladder bit is really cool, though. It makes us look very brave. According to the news, the crowd is still gathered around our house, and more police have been called in.

"That's enough of that," Dad says as he turns it off.

I wish he hadn't. I want to see what the other channels are saying, but I keep quiet. Unfortunately, Simon doesn't. He whines about watching Captain Jetstream until Dad turns the TV back on.

Thus, when we arrive at Ms. Anderson's estate, we're all sitting like a bunch of kids watching a space cartoon. Hakim, unrolling the screen between us, smiles.

"We are here," he says. "I like that program, too. Is that your favorite, Simon?"

I guess the two of them would have continued their banter about the captain's activities if Dad hadn't put a stop to it.

"Hakim, can you please open the door now?" he asks, and the pilot, looking a bit embarrassed, unlocks the door. Then he scurries out and offers Mom assistance in climbing down. A car is waiting to drive us to the mansion. We slip in and head to what is now becoming a rather familiar place to visit.

Chapter Twenty-Seven

Ms. Anderson supplies us each with a room. Mine is very elegant, done in shades of pale blue and gold, with a full bathroom, including a bathtub half the size of my old bedroom. There's a sitting room, too, in an alcove, which is pleasantly warm from the sunshine streaming in the window. On the wall are pictures of constellations. I greet each one like old friends. I have a small refrigerator with bottled waters and sodas. On top is a cabinet with crackers, cookies, and some dried fruits.

The room is fully wired, too. I check out the computer and find access to everything I could possible want. The drawers are loaded with paper, pencils, pens, and envelopes. I sit down at the mahogany desk and feel perfectly at home. I pull out one of the pads and jot down a few things I want to check on.

I empty my duffle into the extensive closet, finding dresses and clothes all in my size. Shoes of all colors and types are assembled at the bottom in rows of boxes. I check. They're all my size.

Someone knocks at the door. It's Mom checking that I'm okay. She oohs and aahs over the room, too, but then tells me that theirs is much the same. I show her the closet. Even the drawers, where I've put my jeans and tees hastily stuffed into the duffle bag, have brand new items, some still in the packages, as if waiting for me to open them. Like the closet, I'm sure everything was chosen for me.

I wonder how Simon has fared. Mom and I go in search. The halls are long and filled with spare rooms. I open one, although Mom says I shouldn't. They're all empty but decked out with the same elegance as our rooms. I'm positive that Ms. Anderson could hide an entire army in her mansion. I wonder why she owns a place so big when she lives all alone.

Simon's room is between my parent's room and mine. Dad is already with him, being shown all the toys Simon has discovered inside it. Ms. Anderson, for some reason, has acquired every Captain Jetstream toy. I look at Mom, and her eyebrows raise, a sign that something has set off an alarm. Eying Simon's room, with its Captain Jetstream and framed pictures, I agree. The room was specially prepared for Simon.

I walk to the window and look out over the green expanse of lawn. On the right, where it's fenced in, there are several horses grazing. I wonder if Ms. Anderson rides or only keeps horses for show. One of the animals is smaller than the others. At first I think it's a foal, but then when something frightens the horses, and they gallop closer, I realize the small one is a pony. Why would Ms. Anderson keep a pony?

We convince Simon that it's time to go downstairs and meet our hostess. He sighs, puts down the toys, and leaves behind his fantasy world rather hesitantly. "Ms. Anderson's so cool," he tells everyone. We don't disagree, but the three of us are a little uneasy.

We find our benefactor waiting for us downstairs, drinking coffee from an elegantly embossed pink coffee mug. "Are your rooms comfortable?" she asks, her eyes searching each of us.

"Something missing?" she queries my mom, obviously reading the worry in her face.

"No, everything is lovely. It's just, how did you know about the threat on our house? Who told you?"

Ms. Anderson smiles. "Sit down, please. Sergio is waiting to see what you would like. Simon, what's your soda of choice, another suicide?"

He nods his head, but the three of us just want a cup of coffee. It's still early in the morning.

"Money has many privileges," Ms. Anderson says, taking another sip. "I can afford the best of everything, and security is one of those items that's top on my list. When Mattie first came to my notice, I webbed her in for safety. Too many times, our system allows the gifted to be run over by the sub average. Someone is jealous of her fame, her success, or perhaps her desire to create change. They began moving in ways that caused me alarm. The moment my security force informed me of this new danger, I called you. I could not allow her or anyone in your precious family to be harmed."

"We thank you," my dad says. "But isn't this a police matter? Can't they do something about the threat?"

Ms. Anderson eyes my dad peculiarly. "The police?" she scuffs. They only try to find the people responsible *after* a crime has been committed. They don't prevent one from happening. Is that what you want, to look back on what should have been done to protect your loved ones?

"Let me ask you, Mr. Masters Smith, how helpful were the police in removing the horde assembled in your front yard this morning? Why, any one of those people had perfect access to your house. A couple of grenades, a bomb . . ."

My parents sigh and glance at Simon, who's looking at them huge-eyed. He's obviously absorbing everything. They gesture to Ms. Anderson. "Maybe we shouldn't continue this conversation right now," Dad says, backing down from his earlier suspicion that maybe this was all a false alarm.

Ms. Anderson sits back, takes another dainty sip of her coffee, and then nods. "Ah, here's Sergio with your drinks."

So we don't talk about it for a while, and for the rest of the day, we just relax delightfully. For lunch, it's not salmon this time, but barbecued hamburgers that Sergio has seasoned and cooked perfectly. There's also potato salad, a green salad, and chocolate cake for dessert.

Dad meets up with Ms. Anderson's gardener and spends the rest of the day working with him. Mom settles in with Simon, piecing together one of those thousand-piece puzzles. This one has a castle in Germany with lavender blooms in the foreground.

They're all content, but I'm the happiest. I go riding with Ms. Anderson, and she lets me try out her silver-white Arab mare that prances about like a show horse.

For several years I've attended camps where horseback riding is the chief sport. I'm fully comfortable riding English or Western. I adore horses.

We ride on Western saddles that day and head out over hundreds of acres of her property, riding for about an hour. We even gallop across a meadow, and Sasha, the mare I'm on, is amazingly smooth. She's like sitting atop a merry-go-round, except far more exciting.

When we return the horses to the stables, Simon and Mom are waiting for us. I can see Mom's been worried about my ride. I assure her that Sasha was as gentle as the old plugs I always rode at camp. Just that moment, Sasha perks up her ears and her tail and neighs to the other stabled horses. She looks anything but calm. Mom gives me one of her looks but says nothing.

Ms. Anderson informs Simon that she has a pony he might feel comfortable riding. He gets really animated about that, but Mom makes a big deal about how he's never been on a horse. I almost tell her there's a first time for everything, but I figure it's smarter to keep my mouth shut.

After a quick shower, I go help Mom and Simon with the puzzle. It's a hard one. The castle is almost all white and gray shaded. Simon's gotten frustrated and turns the TV on. That's when we see the news for the first time since we've arrived. The picture that flashes is our house, and it says that the police are investigating our disappearance.

"Oh, no!" my mom cries out. "We have to call them and let them know we're safe."

Ms. Anderson is passing by when my mom says that. She glances at the TV and then at our anxious faces. Then she laughs. "The police know where you are. They know to whom the *Butterfly* belongs. This is just a ploy by the media to draw more attention to Mattie."

"I suppose, but. I'd feel better if I called and talked to the police," my mother says, bravely standing up to Ms. Anderson.

"Let's call them now," I say, backing up my mom.

Ms. Anderson waves to the phone. "Of course. Go ahead. They can come here and see you if they wish, but their credentials will have to be well-displayed to get in."

That's why, the following day, Captain Brogger stops by.

Chapter Twenty-Eight

Captain Brogger, a detective with the local police department, comes over no more than an hour after my mother calls.

"We were worried about you," he says. "Is this your daughter, Mattie?" he wants to know right off.

I hold out my hand like my parents have done and pretend that meeting a real detective is something I do all the time. He takes my hand and stares into my eyes.

"Are you all right?" he asks, even though my parents have already assured him I'm fine.

I nod. "Ms. Anderson has been kind to take us in. Is it safe to leave yet?"

His forehead crinkles with puzzlement. "Safe? Why wouldn't it be? You mean from the media? I can't guarantee that. I think there's more of their vans surrounding your house now than there used to be. Give it another day, though, and something else will draw their attention away from you."

"What about the bomb threat?" Dad interjects.

Captain Brogger's eyes flit about. "What?" He swallows and stares at Ms. Anderson. "Your sources?"

She nods, not saying anything. Apparently, that's good enough for the captain. He scratches his whisker residue and thinks about the question for a moment. "Sorry, I hadn't heard anything about that. We don't sometimes. I guess Ms. Anderson's told you that our network doesn't have the money hers does. Trust her. She has a reputation for always being in the know."

Ms. Anderson relaxes then. I wasn't aware how rigid she'd been. I don't know her really well yet, but I think I can feel the difference more than see it. I realize that Captain Brogger has just passed her test. He's been welcomed into her smile. That becomes blatant to everyone when she invites him to sit and orders Sergio to bring in some tea.

Simon's not present at the moment. He's out in the back constructing a fort with one of the servants. Captain Brogger hasn't even asked about him. Doesn't the detective know I have a small brother?

Over fresh coffee, which all of us prefer except Ms. Anderson, we discuss the situation at home. Captain Brogger agrees with Ms. Anderson that we would all be safer behind her secured gates, but Dad argues some. He and Mom need to get back to work. Dad tells the detective and Ms. Anderson that Simon and I need to go back to school.

The conclusion, after several cups of brew and some delicious butterscotch cookies made via a recipe Ms. Anderson inherited from her great grandmother, is that that Simon and I will be flown back and forth each day.

We're just deciding the details when my brother comes in. "Hey, I'm starving," he says, oblivious to the fact that we're all deeply involved in the elaborate planning of what will become our new schedule.

Simon is introduced to the detective who jots down my little brother's name and some other details, which he doesn't enlighten us about. While my brother's scooping up a handful of cookies and pouring himself some orange juice (with my mother's help so he doesn't spill all over Ms. Anderson's elegant tea table,) Hakim is sent for. He is to be our pilot/chauffeur in the days ahead.

Hakim takes down the information, calculates his trajectory, and says, "We will leave at six in the morning. Mrs. Masters Smith will be dropped off first, followed by Mr. Masters Smith, little Simon, and then lastly, Mattie."

Dad grimaces about that and starts to say something, but Mom silences him with one of her looks. In the end, they both just nod their acceptance, as if life has become too complex for argument over trivialities.

"As for the departure," Hakim continues, "I assume you will wish me to make two trips? I will first pick up Simon at 2:00, then Mattie at 2:30. I will carry them to the ranch and then return for the Mr. and Mrs. at 4:00 and 4:30. Is this acceptable?"

Again, everyone nods. Simon between mouthfuls of cookies — he's on his second handful, which Mom has already admonished him for taking — shouts out, "Cool. Can I tell all my friends about it? Can they ride in the *Butterfly*?"

My parents immediately start explaining about the necessity of secrecy and how Simon is not allowed to tell his friends a word about the *Butterfly* or where we're staying. I sigh. They might as well save their breath. "Secrecy" is not a word in a six-year-old's vocabulary.

When they finish their lecture, Simon, who unsurprisingly has not been listening but is instead staring at the detective's sketches of everyone, says, "What are you doing?" Simon crams his last cookie into his mouth and strides over to look down at the detective's notebook.

"Just drawing you. It helps me to remember things," the man tells Simon, turning his notebook so my brother can see it better.

"Cool. You're good. But Mom's got blue eyes. You need to color it. Want to borrow my crayons? Ms. Anderson bought me new ones."

Captain Brogger chuckles. Laugh lines etch themselves into the side of his eyes and mouth.

"I look good," Simon adds, studying the sketches.

"Simon, did you hear us?" Dad asks.

Simon glances over at him. Then he gives a big smile to the detective. "Mattie's prettier than that. You didn't do a good job on her."

I laugh. "Simon!"

"Simon, did you hear me?" Dad repeats.

Simon sighs. "Yeah. I can't tell anyone, but can they ride in the *Butterfly*?"

Dad yells, "Simon Masters Smith!"

Mom takes hold of Dad's arm to calm him down, then says quietly but firmly. "You will *not* talk about the *Butterfly*, Simon. You will *not* tell anyone where we are. You will *not* invite your friends over. You will *not* offer free rides. Is that clear?"

Dad's still mumbling. He does that a lot with Simon. I think, sometimes, that Simon acts up even more because he wants to see if he can get a rise out of Dad, but then I remember how Uncle Theodore used to say that Simon just hears a different song than the rest of us. Maybe Simon doesn't know he's being difficult. Maybe he doesn't feel the way Dad's exasperation keg is ready to blow.

Simon does seem oblivious to the heightened worry in the room. He sighs because Mom has made it clear that his friends won't get to ride in the *Butterfly*. He walks over toward me and puts his hand on my leg.

"You really are pretty, Mattie. Jimmy says so lots."

That silences everyone. The thought of not having told Jimmy about our disappearance suddenly slaps me in the face. Will he think we've been kidnapped? Is he worrying about us?

Dad is looking at Mom, who's looking at me. Simon takes advantage and steals another handful of cookies. Then he runs out of the room, calling out, "Gotta go fix the fort."

The detective says his goodbyes soon after that, and I find myself worrying more about what Jimmy's thinking than fretting about finishing my homework. "May I go call my friend?" I ask Ms. Anderson.

She smiles. "Sure, go call him — only, Mattie — make sure that you keep him at a distance. Okay? I've seen too many females buy into the music of romance. They never get to follow their dreams when they do. Don't be like them."

If it had been my parents who said that, I would have rolled my eyes, but with Ms. Anderson, I just nod and walk away. She's certainly telling me nothing new. Uncle Theodore told me the same thing every day of his visit.

Chapter Twenty-Nine

Jimmy sounds super glad to hear from me. In fact, he actually cries when he hears my voice. "God, you're okay. I was so worried. Why didn't you call me? Darn, you, Mattie. Don't you ever do that to me again. I was frantic."

"I'm so sorry. Honest. I know I should have called sooner, but I didn't know what the media was saying. I never thought . . ."

"I need to see you," Jimmy says, sounding deadly urgent.

I breathe in. Then I attempt to explain about the bomb threat and how we had to go into hiding. "It was scary," I tell him, reliving it as I talk. "We didn't know if they were going to destroy our house or not. We kept looking back as we flew away.

"Hordes of people were crowding the streets, and police flitters were landing on our lawn. It all happened so quickly. We hardly had time to even pack anything. And then, when we got here. We didn't watch the news, not until this morning. We called the police because we found out that they didn't know where we were."

"I'm just glad you're safe, Mattie. I couldn't bear it if someone hurt you. I wish I were with you. I'd protect you if you'd let me. I'd watch your back, anyway."

"I know. You're a good friend, Jimmy. Thank you."

I was sitting at a genuine cherry wood desk, not an antique piece, but certainly a piece of furniture with an exquisite finish that displayed authentic natural wood. The shapes in the desk's top reminded me of a close-up of the storms on Jupiter. I studied them, looking for patterns. Due to the decline of forests, most of us used pseudo plastic replicas. It was not at all the same thing.

"More than a friend, Mattie. I love you, remember?"

"Jimmy …" I said. I sighed and wondered what I could do to stop his *barrage of emotional baggage*, as my uncle would have called it.

My eyes moved from Jupiter's storms to the walls of Ms. Anderson's office. Sketches of spaceships hung in dignified frames of walnut, cherry, and pecan wood. Tasteful and expensive settings surrounded by sky blue mattings displayed them artistically.

Some of the black and white etchings were labeled with statistics concerning dimensions, and others described the materials used. A comprehensive cutaway drawing labeled the parts of a current spacecraft I'd read about. Several blueprints of designs looked like they might be top secret.

"But why would anyone threaten you? That doesn't make sense."

"I know, Jimmy. I agree, but I guess there's a lot of crazies out there."

The landline was the only phone we felt safe to use. I felt honored that Ms. Anderson had allowed me to enter what was obviously her private office. Had she realized that I'd find this room to be the highlight of her house?

The leather office chair I'm sitting in has a health system. It was flashing a warning light informing me that I'm in "High tension zone."

It wanted to know if I'd like a massage or some relaxation music. I pushed the "no" button.

"Let me come to you. I don't care where you are. You need me."

"Jimmy, no. You can't. I told you. It's not possible."

"Don't you trust me, Mattie? Where are you?"

The phone, the newest kind that doesn't need to be held, maintains its steady green blink, letting me know my party is there, but the blink is driving me nuts. I look around for something to cover it with and then toss a magazine over it. That doesn't help. The green continues its irritating annoyance, its light creeping out under the pages.

"I have to see you," Jimmy repeats. "Don't you understand? Why can't I come there? Can you tell me that?"

I close my eyes. I know Jimmy wouldn't be welcomed at Ms. Anderson's house. I don't want to tell him that, though. I don't want to have to explain about what Ms. Anderson said.

"I want to see you, too," I tell Jimmy, trying to soften the blow of my refusal. Then I remind him that I'm far away, hiding out in a secretive place. "But I can't go to you, and you can't come here, Jimmy. You just have to understand that. It's like it'll be at the Academy. I'll be away, but we can still call each other or write . . ."

"I don't have any choice about that, do I?' he snaps, sounding cold and sour. Then he gives out a huge snort. I can't tell if it's a cry of disgust or if he's just clearing his throat. Either way, it doesn't make me feel good. I should have called him before. I should have told him sooner.

The grandfather clock over in the corner is clicking off the seconds. Its hands sweep back and forth, back and forth. My heart is synchronizing with the beat, speeding up as if I'm about to jump up and run for my life. I try to calm down, breathing more slowly, attempting to relax.

But the truth is that I'm nervous. Jimmy's my best friend. Why would I be nervous about talking with him? Yet I don't know how to answer his constant questions. I can shut out my feelings and put them on hold. Why can't he?

This current mode of Jimmy's, always pushing me where I don't want to go makes me edgy, drives me into panic. He knows how it is between us, how it has to be. Why does he keep pushing me? What does he want from me? Does he expect me to give up the Academy after all my efforts to get in?

I don't answer. I can't. My throat closes off. Tears, garnered by the flavor of Jimmy's bitterness, are flooding my eyes.

"I see," he says after a moment with a note in his voice that sends even more guilt through me. I sigh. Then I break down and cry. "I can't do this, Jimmy. You know I can't."

He sighs, too. "I know. I'm sorry, Mattie. I'm driving you away, aren't I? Is that why you ran away? Did you run from me and not from a bomb?"

I sit up, pushing myself out of the soft luxury of the body-molding chair. "No, Jimmy, I told you what happened. The whole family's here, remember?"

I hunt for a box of tissues. I find a fancy box of them on Ms. Anderson's desk.

"Don't cry, Mattie. I know I'm a heel for pressuring you. Please, Mattie. I'm sorry. I know you wouldn't really run away from me."

I don't speak. He can hear me crying. I don't know how to mute Ms. Anderson's phone. I stand up and begin to pace. I've taken my shoes off and the softness of the mutated lawn carpeting feels wonderful. I run my toes through the blades of wool and think of summer and freedom.

"Remember the sparrows, Mattie?"

I nod, but of course he can't see me. Yet as if he can, he continues. "Remember how we watched them build their nest in the tree overlooking my bedroom?"

How could Jimmy ask that? How could I ever forget? We used to watch the sparrows making trip after trip with their beaks filled with twigs. We sat under that tree, the one that Jimmy had once carved with our initials. When he got out of the hospital, his parents placed an outdoor bench beneath it.

That's when Jimmy, still hurting from his operation took out a pocketknife and carved the funny, little heart right next to our names. The heart was wobbly and looked more like a balloon, but we both knew what it was supposed to be. Underneath it, Jimmy chiseled the word "forever."

He's trying to tell me something about the birds, but I can hardly focus on it. I'm remembering the way the sun painted glitter in his hair. Copper glitter. Jimmy turned to look at me afterwards, his chin dark with tiny reddish-brown hairs since he'd missed his monthly anti-shaving treatment. My heart was his at that moment. I'd longed to tell him so, but I couldn't.

"Just a minute," I tell him, and I stab at the tissue box, grabbing up a whole handful this time because my nose is flowing like an open faucet.

When I can listen again, Jimmy tells me how there are eggs in the nest now. "Will you be able to come see them soon?" he wants to know.

"Maybe in another week, Jimmy. Do you think they'll still be there then? How long before they hatch?"

Long ago bird eggs all hatched in the spring, or so we've read. These would have been considered freakishly late, but bird patterns have changed. Now they hatch all year long, even in the same species.

I could almost see Jimmy's shrug.

"I looked it up, Mattie. It's too uncertain nowadays. Today, tomorrow. Who knows?"

"I want to see them, Jimmy. I want to see you, too. I'll be at school tomorrow. I'm being dropped off. Will you meet me at Quad one?"

I can feel his smile then. It comes clear through the phone. "What time, Mattie?"

So we make our plans, and I disconnect. Then I sigh, cleanup my wadded-up tissues, and head for the door. As I open it, Ms. Anderson is standing there, her arm raised, her fist in the air to knock.

"Finished?" she asks.

"Yes, I'm sorry. Did you need me — or the room?"

She laughs. "Neither one. Are you all right?" she asks, staring at my reddened eyes.

I nod and start to walk away.

"Mattie."

I turn back to look at her. "Did you ever wonder why I never got married?"

Of course I had, often, but I lie and pretend I haven't.

She chuckles. "You're a terrible liar, Mattie. I would suggest that you not attempt it often. Come back inside, and I'll tell you all about it — if you have a moment."

I know that I have several hours of homework to do, but an offer like that cannot be refused. I follow Ms. Anderson inside, and once more sit down, attempting to tune out the sound of the ticking of the grandfather clock.

Chapter Thirty

"Long ago I was beautiful and young like you."

"You still are very attractive," I blurt out, and then blush because it sounds like I'm fawning over her.

If she notices my reddened face, she makes no remark over it. "I met the man of my dreams in France. I was studying at the university, a session I'd stubbornly fought my mother over. I used to tell her that life wasn't all about science. I was wrong, Mattie. It is."

She stops, and I see I'm expected to say something, but I don't know what. I swallow and try to phrase something appropriate. Luckily, Ms. Anderson continues.

"Claude de Bonette was darkly handsome. His hands fascinated me. He waved them like a poet or a dancer. Ah, the sound of his voice, his French, his sophistication, all those things wrapped me into the web of love. Within weeks I was enamored. I hungered for the mere sight of him, for the spare moments when I could rush to his side, clutching at his hand like it was my salvation.

"We roamed the countryside. He was rich, as I was. We rode Andalusians, the horses of Spain, which are one part music and one part magic. And everywhere, the air crackled with love.

"I wrote my mother about Claude at the end of the first month. He'd asked me to move in with him, you see. I was willing.

"My mother didn't answer my letter. Instead, she sent thieves in the night. They stole my innocence. They told me that Claude already had a wife and several mistresses.

"This is not the story of your Jimmy. Your friend is as pure as angel wings, but he is far more dangerous. Do you know why?"

Ms. Anderson's story of Claude was very sad, but it was also fairly predictable. I feel sorry for her because it had obviously warped her forever, leaving her a distrustful soul, but I don't want another lecture, so I respond, I hope, suitably. "I know what you're going to say, Ms. Anderson, but that's not going to happen to me. I'm going to the Academy, and nothing Jimmy can say or do will keep me from my dream."

"Good. Remember that, whatever happens. Don't allow him to be the back-up in case you fail."

Of course, I start to argue, but Ms. Anderson raises her hand to halt my words. The look in her eyes closes my mouth. I watch as she walks over to the right wall where a bar unit hides a small utility refrigerator. "What would you like to drink?" she asks. "I have everything, I think."

"Water?"

She tosses it to me and takes one herself. Then she turns back to look at me. "Claude wasn't married, Mattie — not then, anyway. He had no mistresses, either."

"What? Your mother lied to you? How could she? That's horrid!"

Ms. Anderson doesn't say anything for a moment. She returns to her seat and then sighs. "You're so young, my dear, and so very naïve and unprepared for the real world. Jimmy is probably good for you, after all. He's teaching you how to say 'no.' Perhaps, this puppy love of yours for each other will even protect you from what is to come."

"It's not puppy love," I flare up and then realize what I've just admitted to.

Ms. Anderson only smiles. "The world does not like any change to the status quo. You are a threat to his stability. Every trick will be used against you. I have my suspicions about your friend's little appendix problem."

"He was sick. I saw him."

"Yes, someone slipped him something, I would guess. It mimicked the pain of appendicitis. There was nothing wrong with his appendix. I had it checked."

I am speechless. I sit listening to the nonstop beat of the grandfather clock. It suddenly hiccoughs on the hour. I jump, although it hasn't chimed.

"I disabled the clock," Ms. Anderson says, seeing the direction of my eyes. It groans at the hour, but it doesn't make any other noise. I can live with a groan. I choose to live with it because the clock belonged to my grandparents.

I look down at my hands, curled together as if for comfort. "I don't understand where you're going with all this — this story about Claude, the questions about Jimmy and his operation …"

"I want you to be suspicious of everything, young lady. My mother was right to whisk me away from my French boyfriend. I'm sure Claude would have ended up with several mistresses. They do in France, you know, but that's beside the point. The point I'm making, my dear, is that you can't be trusting anymore. Ask yourself 'why?' frequently.

"But if Jimmy didn't need the operation, what was the point of it?" I gasp, puzzling over her words.

She lifts up her bottle and drinks a good portion. Then she sets it down and looks at me. "Ask yourself. What changes did it create between you and Jimmy?"

"That's not fair. No one could predict that."

Ms. Anderson shakes her head. "Oh, it was very predictable, Mattie. When someone you care about becomes ill, the mothering instinct comes into play. So does the emotion of loss. I'm sure it started you thinking about Jimmy's death, and then you realized how much you care about him. Correct?"

I don't like to admit that I'm that easy to calculate, but she's right. "Yes," I say. "You're right."

"So, you see, it has already started. What will they do next, Mattie? What could they do to change your mind about the Academy? Be ready for it. And at the same time, remember that Jimmy is very dangerous. One slip, and the game's over.

"I have work to do now," she tells me suddenly, and she opens a book and begins reading, just like that. I stand and thank her for the water and the advice. Then I leave, shutting the door quietly. As I do, Ms. Anderson looks up and smiles.

"Think about everything I've said, Mattie. You're a smart girl. Start planning for the traps."

On the way up the stairs, I see my mother. She's down at the bottom, holding onto Simon's arm, lecturing him about cleanliness. He's smeared with mud from his ears to his toes, and Mom's face is not showing a lot of tolerance for it. I dash up the rest of the way and head for my temporary room, not eager to feel the remnants of her anger.

Inside my space, I happily pull my schoolbooks out of the drawer where I've stashed them and set to work. The math pages come first, then the essay on Poe. I'm just printing out the latter when Mom peeks in. I pretend I don't hear her to avoid listening to her complaints about my mischievous brother. She retreats without speaking, probably heading for Dad to share what Simon has gotten into this time.

Chapter Thirty-One

That evening the news broadcasts that the situation with the Masters Smith family has been cleared up. They inform the listeners that my parents and I have simply gone to stay somewhere else for a while, since we were being mobbed by well-wishers. I think the news is stretching the last a bit, but it's true that the IAUW (International Association of University Women) has given me an award and several sororities have made me an honorary member. Yet I truly doubt that most other people even care that I've broken down a fence.

Monday morning dawns early. As I yawn and sip my orange juice in the backseat of the *Butterfly*, Dad reminds/lectures Simon about not telling anyone anything. Then he starts in on me. I pour coffee and drink it while I concentrate on not rolling my eyes, something my dad is always accusing me of now.

Otherwise, the drop-offs go well. The *Butterfly* has been camouflaged to look like a *beetleflyer*, so no one gives it a second look. I never knew that such cloaking devices were possible, but when I comment on it, Hakim gives me one of his beautiful smiles and says simply, "With Ms. Anderson, there is no such thing as impossible."

After Mom, Dad, and Simon are dropped off, I slide into the front seat. There I can study the controls and watch Hakim's skillful flying.

"Your father would not like this arrangement," Hakim warns me, but I can see that his eyes are sparkling as if it amuses him.

"Since he is not here to lecture me, it doesn't matter, does it?"

Hakim has a delicious laugh. I tell him so, and he smiles again and then says, "Your school, Miss Masters Smith. Do you need help getting out?"

He knows I don't. I can see it in the teasing shine of his eyes, those dark-brown orbs like sweet, newly made fudge. I sigh as the ship lifts up. Maybe Dad is right. Hakim is more than I can handle right now. Then I laugh at myself and turn to join the other students heading inside.

Jimmy is waiting. When he sees me, he runs toward me and seizes me in his arms. Then he lifts me up as if I weigh no more than a child.

"Put me down," I giggle, embarrassed.

But he doesn't respond. He carries me off to a corner, with all the other students hooting and cheering him on. "Go, Jimmy." "Show her who's boss." "Hey, man, that's the way."

My face paints a rainbow, and I turn angry. "Jimmy if you don't . . ." but his lips cut me off.

When he frees me, I forget what I wanted to say. The hunger in his eyes takes me by surprise.

"We're at school, Jimmy," I remind him.

He sets me down on a picnic bench then hovers over me. "Like that would make a difference?" he says with the same bitterness in his voice.

The double hit leaves me confused. I shake my head. "I can't deal with this right now," I tell him. "One moment I'm fleeing from my life, and the next you're making demands that I can't . . ."

"Knock it off," Jimmy spits out, turning away. "You think I don't know that? I'm the biggest fool in this whole high school. Everyone knows about you, everyone except me."

"Knows? Knows what?" I try to turn Jimmy around to face me, but he stubbornly keeps his back to me.

"You're cold, Mattie. You're either frigid or a girl lover. Which is it?"

I almost don't answer him. The attack is so ridiculous, so unfair. Didn't he feel the way I responded to his kiss? Couldn't he tell that I melt each time he looks at me?

"It's time for class," I say, in an attempt to avoid lashing out with the full brunt of my anger.

"No. You have five minutes yet. Answer me, Mattie. Is it true?" Jimmy's back is no longer facing me. He's turned around and latched onto my arms, holding me with the force of his need. His fingers are pressing bruises into my skin, but I don't whine about it. I look up into his eyes. They're not dark and full of teasing as Hakim's were. Jimmy's eyes look haunted, miserably so. My anger fades, and I meld into him.

"Jimmy, I'm not cold at all. I do feel your love, and I want to respond to it, just as much as you do, but I can't. I won't. If you can't understand that then our friendship is over. I won't be torn to pieces over your needs and wants. I can't. I have to . . ."

"My needs and wants? That's what I'm talking about. What are *your* needs and wants — emotionally, I mean?"

The bell rings. Jimmy's timing is all off. I break away and run from him. It's what I've been doing for months.

I slide into my seat just as the second bell rings. I feel a classroom full of eyes all descending on me. Am I a mess? Has Jimmy's emotional embrace turned my hair into a free-for-all? I reach up and smooth it down, but the eyes are still focused on me.

"Good going!" says one of the girls next to me.

"Yeah, we were rooting for you from the first."

I think they're talking about Jimmy and me, so I'm confused. Heat floods my body. My face must be like a fire alarm, blaring with my embarrassment.

"Hey, cool. Congratulations on your acceptance," says one of the guys at the back. I turn to see who spoke and see almost the entire high school soccer team giving me a thumb's up. Then it hits me. They're not talking about what just happened with Jimmy, but about my going to the Academy.

I just have time to send a short whispered, "Thanks," when the teacher is rapping at the podium. "Students, I'd like the class to congratulate the history-making debut of Mattie Masters Smith, first female Space Academy student."

Of course, everyone claps as I slide lower in my seat

"Mattie, would you please come up and say a few words? Tell us what you did to achieve such an amazing victory."

High school is not the place for recognition. Anonymity is a far better idea. Since I took a front seat in academics, needing high grades to accomplish my goal, my hard work earned me the name "Brain Wave" as a freshman. Now that I'm a senior, the name has more or less faded into obscurity. I'm not eager, in my last few weeks of school, to formulate a new one. Yet, I have no choice but to heed the teacher's request.

I rise up and walk to the front of the room, which reminds me of the many times I was forced to deliver discourses in Public Speaking — definitely not my favorite class.

I make it to the front without tripping over the purse strap lying in the aisle, and the long legs of Johnny Cresto, sprawled as if he owns all the space that lies between the rows of seats. I even manage to step over the pile of science experiments that Carla Gentro always carries from classroom to classroom so she can keep an eye on the various molds and bacteria that she keeps in small, glass petri dishes.

Then I trip on the overhead extension cord. Naturally. Stormy Dalane, the coquette of the senior class and the prom queen, apparently can't stand my minute of fame. She quips, "Oh, isn't she sweet, the first stumblebum on the moon!"

I know exactly what a stumblebum is, even though it probably isn't in the dictionary. I lift my head and respond. "My agility on our lunar satellite will be directly proportional to my adaptation concerning the lack of wind resistance and the absence of external atmosphere. Understand, Stormy?"

It is a mean trick to play on the social queen. Stormy isn't known for her high brain ability, and so she sits frozen to her chair, blinking as if the traffic light inside her has just broken down. I'm sure she's trying to unravel the sentence to see if I've just insulted her. I'm not foolish.

I have always intentionally suppressed my vocabulary among my peers. Maybe it's time for a little enlightenment, I rationalize. Besides, Stormy, as I recall, is the one who first dubbed me "Brain Wave."

I reach the podium and look around the room, reading expressions. I've lost most of the students' good will with the sharpness of my retort. I sigh.

"Sorry. I've been cramming for the Academy exam. I guess I forgot to speak human there for a moment."

That makes the class laugh and wins some of the kids back to my side. Carla Gentro gives me a thumbs up and says, "I understood you."

"Figures," says a voice in the back.

"I may not be able to walk without tripping over cords, but I do understand the mathematics of space. That's why I fought the Academy's blanket decision to exclude females from their program. I am capable, and I need the chance to prove it.

"Mr. Shaker asks that I tell you what I did — well, countless letters, interviews with people from INASA, radio and TV talks, and then, of course, all the Internet BLOGS. Every chance I had I disseminated my viewpoints, and the persistence paid off. They've finally given me my chance. That's all, Mr. Shaker," I say, looking back at him.

Once more he leads the class in applause, while I make my way back to my seat, managing not to trip.

No one says anything then because Mr. Shaker's already giving the day's lesson, followed by a quick write about the merits of tenacity and persistence. That will have everyone throwing mind darts at me, I know, but I sigh and start writing.

When the bell rings, I hand in my paper and head for the door.

"Not bad, Mattie," says the soccer team captain. "I like the package *tenacity* comes in, too. How about Saturday we voyage into space and see the new sci/fi flick about Kurt Chow?"

"She's already seeing that with me," says Jimmy, sliding into a possessive hold as if he has the right.

"I don't . . ." I start to protest.

"Whoops!" chuckles Stan, as he backs away. "Sorry, Jimmy. I didn't know it was like that with you two."

Of course, I've always known that Jimmy is popular. He's the senior class president for one thing. Yet, I still can't believe that Stan gives him that kind of respect. Nor can I swallow the fact that neither guy stopped to listen to what I had to say.

I don't have time to argue about it, though. The warning bell rings, and I rush off to the math department.

Chapter Thirty-Two

The rest of the day is thankfully uneventful. I guess mathematical instructors don't normally lift up their eyes to see the news, even when it's in their own court. Likewise, my English teacher is intent on giving us a pop quiz, when one student whispers, probably the result of not having done her lesson plans that day. We are given a blank lined-paper and told to look up the word "clause" in our textbook. Then we have to write a story or essay that uses an example of each and every item listed. (The list was long, too — adjectival, adverbial, independent, nonrestrictive, etc.)

During physical education, Charlene, Corrie, Zander, and I whip our opposing team in a game of Cribball. It's nice to win.

I run into Jimmy almost immediately after the last bell. I think he's been waiting again. "Well, how about it? Can you go to the movie with me?" he wants to know.

"I'll call you," I reply. "You know how difficult it is right now." I do want to see the movie, but not if Jimmy keeps giving me lectures. I've had enough squabbling for the day. I'm exhausted, so I run out to the front, ignoring his calls to wait.

Of course, wouldn't you know it, Hakim is waiting for me. Simon's in the back, yelling out that I need to hurry because he wants to play in the fort before it gets dark. It won't be dark for another four hours, but I smile at Simon, glad he's there because Jimmy's new mood is no fun.

I hop into the *Butterfly*. Jimmy stands on the curb, waving goodbye. I wave back and wish Hakim would do one of his zero to sound speed take-offs. But he doesn't. He's pretending that he's flying a *beetleflyer* and is slower than even Mom at lift-off.

I take the soda Simon hands me. "You and Jimmy fighting?" he asks me.

"I don't want to talk about it," I snap at him.

"I'd say that was 'yes,'" my brother responds. "I like Jimmy fine, but Hakim flies a *Butterfly*. Maybe you should dump Jimmy."

Hakim is grinning back at me. I can see his face in the mirror. I growl at Simon and tell him to mind his own business. My brother makes one of his clown faces, sticking out his tongue and crossing his eyes.

To avoid his weird looks and Hakim's grins, I open up my textbook and start working on the math. I have it half finished by the time we land at the ranch. I bundle up and start to climb out.

Then I stop. "Hakim, if I needed to go somewhere over the weekend — I mean, Saturday night, could you take me there and pick me up?"

He gives me a measured look. "Did you ask your parents?"

"I'm seventeen, almost eighteen. I don't need . . ."

I stop. Hakim's grinning, obviously aware that as strict as my parents are, he knows I'm not going out without permission. "All right. I'll ask them. But if they say 'yes,' would you fly me?"

"Where would you be going on this date?"

I have two choices — answer his question and the next ones that follow or turn and walk away, but if Hakim's not on my side, would I be permitted to go?

"Just to a show with Jimmy. He's the guy you saw at school. My parents approve of him by the way. He's been my best friend since we were little kids."

Hakim nods, looking at me speculatively. "To see the sci-fi adventure?" he asks. "Sure, I'd be available if I get to see it, too. "

I start to argue about that. I don't need a chaperone.

Hakim holds up his hand to stop me. "I'd sit in the back and ignore whatever you and the best friend were doing during the show. Deal?"

I sigh, then nod.

I know that Jimmy won't like Hakim's presence, but it's better than not going. Besides, an inhibitor might be a good idea. I smile, say 'thanks,' and climb down. "See you tomorrow," I call out as I slide into the waiting car.

"Sure took you long enough. What did you need to talk about?" Simon demands.

I just shrug. I don't feel like talking so I slide back, close my eyes, and wait for our arrival at the house.

Ms. Anderson is not home. I suppose she's working at her company. I wonder how she got there since we've more or less taken over her wings.

At first, I settle down in my room, determined to get my homework done, but the birds are calling. The sunshine is streaming though my window. When I hear a horse neigh, I give up.

I change into my jeans and a tee and run down the stairs. Outside is freedom. I check out Simon's fort. He's hammering under the studied supervision of a servant named Pegwa. I wave to both of them and walk on.

A few horses are running about in the meadow. Those are the ones I probably heard neighing. I watch for a moment, wishing Ms. Anderson were home so I could ask to borrow a horse when Hakim walks up behind me and says, "Care to ride?"

"I wish!"

"Your wish is my command," he says with an elegant bow.

"We have permission to take out the horses?"

"Come, we shall order them saddled and gallop into the wind. It will bring blossoms into your cheeks."

I stop and look at him. "Where did that come from? You sound like a poet."

"All men are poets beside great beauty."

"Right," I sneer. Then I laugh. I know I'm only average. I'm certainly no Stormy Dalane. She's the one who has the perfect figure and the hair to die for.

"Why do you laugh when I speak only the truth?"

"Hakim, I'd love to go riding, but I don't want to hear . . ."

"Your Jimmy does not tell you these things?"

"I don't want to talk about him, either. Are you sure it's okay to take out the horses?"

Meanwhile, one of the grooms is saddling up three horses. I wonder whom the third one is for, but I don't ask. I'm almost ready to cancel the ride and run back to the house. I don't understand Hakim's words. Is it flirting with me? He's so much older than me and movie star handsome. Surely he wouldn't be interested in *me*.

We mount up, and I see, with relief, that the groom is coming with us. Hakim notices my expression and edges his horse over and explains that Ms. Anderson has ordered the groom to ride with me at all times.

Actually, I'm rather relieved. Sandor is an older man. I know he won't suddenly start reciting poetry and give me star-blinding smiles.

We head out, and as Hakim has promised, gallop into the wind. The horses are eager for the exercise, and their gait is smooth. I laugh, bend low over the horse's neck, and listen to the sound of air rushing through my hair and over my body. I will miss this up in space.

Chapter Thirty-Three

I Slide forward a number of days. Nothing happens during them except the usual homework assignments, school discussions, and daily transit.

Then the weekend comes, and Hakim chauffeurs me to the movies on Saturday. I find out then that he's not only meant to be the pilot, but also my bodyguard. He tells us, upon Jimmy's intensive questioning, that he's been trained in judo, jujitsu, karate, and something I've never heard of called pseudo-cha, which he explains as being similar to Chinese acupuncture except using pressure points to deliver a chop.

At first Jimmy's really bugged that Hakim has to chaperone us, but when he hears about the high level of his training, Jimmy asks question after question. I might as well not be on a date. The two of them spend most of the time, including during dinner when we're munching on pizza, discussing it.

I sigh a great deal after we drop off Jimmy. Finally Hakim turns on his smile and says, "Didn't go how you wanted it to?"

"Thanks to you, no."

"But Simon told me Jimmy was pressing you too hard, wanting more than you're prepared to give him. I didn't notice that being a problem this evening."

I don't know why I crawl up into the front. I should stay in the back, sulking, but it seems unnatural. I don't like being *chauffeured.*

"Tell you what," I respond. "You don't talk about Jimmy, and I'll stop sighing. Okay?"

Again Hakim's grin flashes. "Shall I put on the speed?"

I know that he can have us home in fifteen minutes if he wants. I'm really not in to that kind of hurry. "Why don't you let *me* fly the *Butterfly*?" I ask, more to change the subject than because I believe he'll let me.

"Sure. Push the button there for the dual control panel."

I follow directions, and then Hakim instructs me on how to make the *Butterfly* listen. She flies like a dream. I guess we spend an extra hour up in the sky, flitting about, trying out the super charge. Then he says, "Time to get back before your parents and Ms. Anderson worry."

"Could I land her?" I ask, but Hakim shakes his head.

"You'll need a few more lessons before that happens. Of course, you know what you just did was illegal, don't you."

I nod. I hadn't really thought about that at the time, but I remember I'm not yet eighteen, and no minor is allowed to fly, even with supervision.

"You won't tell, right?" I fret with the sudden realization that he could get me into a lot of trouble.

He laughs. "Who do you think would find themselves in a bigger mess, Mattie?"

So we share a secret as we come into the ranch's landing strip. I'm smiling broadly once again, and Hakim takes note. "It is not the wind of the breeze that paints roses on your cheeks, it is merely challenge," he laughs. "Be well, Mattie Masters Smith. I shall see you on Monday."

I don't know how the car that picks us up always knows when to come. It's something I plan to ask Hakim next time, but that evening, I'm glad I don't have to wait. Hakim's right. The thrill of flight has renewed my goal. I can't wait to get up into space.

Chapter Thirty-Four

The mail isn't brought to us until Sunday. That's why I get the notice from the Academy only the day before my appointment. I have to be seen by their physician. I have to be certified as a-okay for space. *The other necessary appointment can be scheduled at that time,* the notice says at the bottom. I know what that means. I'm being warned that my eggs must be removed before August, or I won't be going to the Academy.

I show the letter to my parents and to Ms. Anderson. Unfortunately, that means no school on Monday because my appointment is for ten o'clock in the morning.

Plans are made. Dad needs to be at work the next day, so Mom will take the day off. Ms. Anderson apologizes, saying she wishes she could go with me, but, actually, I never expected her to. I assure her I'll be fine.

Yet, I'm not sure of that. I think about the things Ms. Anderson has warned me about. What if the doctors find something wrong with me? What if they decide I can't go after all? Yet, my own doctor ran tests on me for the university applications. Everything was fine then. Still I worry and get little sleep that night.

I'm up early in the morning. I say goodbye to Simon and Dad and watch them leave. We're served pancakes, but neither Mom nor I eat much.

"You know, you can still back out, Mattie. It's never too late."

I know she means well. I look up and smile. "I'm okay, Mom. I just want to get it over."

Hakim flies us to Washington D.C. He doesn't bother to camouflage the *Butterfly* this time. Before Mom and I can even finish the water bottle we've taken, we've arrived.

I have a pass to get me onto the base. Hakim offers it to the guard and then skims over to the place they've requested him to wait. The *Butterfly* handles beautifully, touching down as precisely as an eagle to her nest. But then, of course, Hakim has great deal to do with that. *The pilot perfects the flight.*

Inside the medical quad, we see guards everywhere. They salute each other, but merely wave us through. When we enter the room where the physical is to be held, several others are waiting their turns. Of course, they're all males. I smile at them, but they turn away, snubbing me.

We're last to go in, or at least, last of those who are present. My mother tries to accompany me, but the doctor orders her out. "Return to the waiting room," he orders gruffly.

Then a nurse weighs me, takes my blood pressure and pulse. She draws out sample after sample of blood — far more than my family doctor ever had. Chills run through me. "What tests will they be running?" I ask her.

She shakes her head. "I only do what they tell me, ma'am."

Another doctor comes into the room then. He checks my eyes, ears, and mouth. Then I go through some balance tests. I need to walk on a line forward, backward, and sideways. They tape one eye and send me around in circles. Then I must repeat it with the other eye, following their directions. As far as I can tell, I pass everything, but when I ask, the doctor only mumbles. "Don't be impatient."

Then comes the part I've been dreading. I'm handed a hospital gown and told to undress. I hate physicals. This one is not much different than my normal one. I get through it and breathe a long sigh.

"I don't quite know how to answer some of these questions on the form," the doctor says with a twinkle in his eye. "I hate to leave them blank, but INASA's just going to have to make a new form for you."

"But is everything okay, otherwise?" I ask.

"Well, according to this, you're missing some parts, but the ones you've got seem healthy enough. Of course, the blood tests and your pap smear will take a couple of days to check."

This doctor takes a moment to check my eyes, ears, and throat. I tell him that's already been done, but he nods his head. "Did anyone check your reflexes yet?" he asks, and without waiting for an answer he knocks my knee with a small hammer. I almost kick him in the teeth. I guess my reflexes are fine.

I get dressed then and rejoin my mother. We're told to go get some lunch, and then I have to come back for further tests.

The canteen is cafeteria style. We walk through the line, choosing whatever we want. Mom and I both select salads and iced tea. We split a piece of corn bread. When we get to the cashier, though, she won't accept our money. "It's all covered, ma'am," she says, looking at the badges my mom and I are wearing.

"Sit over there," the woman tells us, and we look over and see the same guys who were in the waiting room.

"Is that mandatory?" I ask, and the woman nods.

I don't question further, but I'm sure wishing we could sit by ourselves. My thoughts are justified, too. The moment we arrive, setting our trays down on the table, one of the guys says, "I wonder if the little girl's planning on bringing her mommy to the Academy."

I look down at my plate, attempting to ignore him. Both Uncle Theodore and Ms. Anderson have warned me about harassment. I'm prepared for it, but it somehow, it makes it worse to have my mother sitting beside me. I don't want her to have to see what I may be heading for

"Nah, the little girl can't bring her mommy, just her dolls. I wonder how many of them will fit in her trunk limit."

I take a bite of my salad and chew. The salad is like sawdust. I can barely swallow.

"You afraid to talk to us?" one of them asks.

"Are you addressing me?" I ask, pretending I haven't heard any of their attacks. "My name is Mattie Masters Smith. This is my mother, Mrs. Masters Smith. I'm going up to the Academy in August. Is that when you're all going?"

"Yeah, all of us *men* are going in August. I hope we don't have to babysit you. No offense to you, ma'am," he says, bobbing his head at my mother.

"Why would you think I need a babysitter? I've passed all my written and oral exams, just the same as you have."

"Yeah, but I bet you won't pass the physical. You lack the balls to pass that, little girl. Or didn't you notice?"

"I am just about to elaborate on the true definition of courage when an officer steps up to the table.

We all bolt upward — everyone except Mom who's still blushing at the latest insult.

The officer looks us over. "The four of you *men* may not make it up to the Academy after all. Discrimination in any form is illegal, remember? As to whether you have the qualifications needed for Academy training, I seriously doubt that. You are to report to room 746 right now on the double. They're expecting you. Oh, and by the way, they have a full transcript of every word you just said."

Confused, I start to follow, but the officer stops me. "Not you, Ms. Masters Smith. You handled yourself perfectly. Sit down, please, and enjoy your lunch. You and your mother are not expected back for another twenty-six minutes."

I sit down again, but I feel sick. The conversation was being recorded? What did I say? My hands are shaking so badly I drop them into my lap. Then I fight the tears springing into my eyes.

"I didn't know it would get that bad. I never imagined it would be like that," my mother whispers.

I shake my head. "It doesn't matter, Mom. Uncle Theodore prepared me well. I can make it through the hazing. I can make it through anything. I'm going to the Academy. That's all that matters."

So saying, I lift up my fork and dive into my salad. It suddenly tastes delicious.

After lunch there are assorted tests, but I can't talk about any of them. They're secret for some reason. They aren't the important ones, though. None of them challenges me in the least. After all, I've just passed the most difficult of all the tests — Intro to Hazing. The psychiatrist later tells me that I proved myself to be "extremely self-confident, mature beyond my years, and emotionally well-balanced — a highly suitable candidate for the Academy."

Chapter Thirty-Five

A week later, I receive a notice that something has shown up on one of my tests. The notice says that INASA needs me to report back at the medical unit for a cross check. When I show that to Ms. Anderson, she gets very upset and runs into her office to make some phone calls. An hour later, she returns, finding us all, even Simon, sitting around looking like we're in mourning. Ms. Anderson grins.

"False alarm," she says, laughing. "You don't need to go back. It seems that someone wrote "negative" on the line that indicated there was a problem with your sperm count."

"I'm leaving," says Simon, bolting from the room.

Mother and Dad frown, but I'm beaming like the Cheshire cat. "I passed?"

Ms. Anderson picks up the expression of my parents and then starts to laugh. "Sorry, about that. Embarrassed the kid, didn't I. Anyway, your Mattie passed everything they threw at her!"

She stops to hold her arms out to me. "I'm proud of you, Mattie," she tells me, and I step toward her and allow myself to be pulled into her embrace.

"You did really, really well. It seems you very much impressed a senior officer in the cafeteria. That man, Captain Briarfield, has asked for you to be placed in his own platoon. That's quite an honor, because believe me, he's normally a real grump. But you 'glowed with' — what did he say — ah, I remember — good sense."

I remember Captain Briarfield quite well. He was the one who ended the ridicule. I close my eyes and send a thank you upstairs. Are you looking out for me, Uncle Theodore?

Ms. Anderson swings me around and says, "We must celebrate. Sergio!"

When he arrives, Ms. Anderson orders, "Bring us some of those chocolate éclairs."

"As dessert, Madam?"

"Why not!" Ms. Anderson laughs. "You'd like one wouldn't you?"

Dad is very enthusiastic, but Mom only grimaces. She's dieting again. I probably should be, too, but not when I'm being served chocolate éclairs! I nod that it sounds good to me.

That's how the night turns into a party. Ms. Anderson even has Sergio bring in some sparkling grape juice, and we toast to the future.

I think mini celebrations like that make the hard times easier to deal with. For the very next day at school, everything goes wrong.

The media discovers my presence. They can't come onto the campus, but they talk to lots of students who tell them who knows what stories about me. Suddenly the papers are full of it: I am called *fast and easy*. Someone claims that I steal boyfriends just for fun. (Boy is that fantasy!) Someone informs the newspapers that I'm a nerd and wear my hair uncombed and uncared for. She also says that I'm a klutz who trips over extension cords and falls over my own feet. (Gee, I wonder who said that — a certain prom queen?) Someone else labels me a rebel. (I gather that's because I bucked the system.) I suppose I'm lucky the reporters didn't find someone who painted me in black with a witch's hat and a broomstick in my hand.

The worst of it is that Ms. Anderson claims that it's not safe for me to return to school. She says Simon shouldn't go back either. Ms. Anderson believes that we need someone to home school us. There's only three weeks left of school, but strangely, I find I really wanted to attend to the end. I won't ever be going back, not as a high school student, anyway.

As Mom and Dad watch the scene on the television, they agree. Instead of brooding over it, I go out and ride. Hakim goes with me, of course, but he's good about being silent when he thinks I need it. That evening he doesn't talk at all. I don't either, except to thank him for getting me out of the mess that day. It was he who elbowed me through the sixty or so microphones being shoved in my face.

An evening breeze starts up as the sun sets. I don't mind it. I button up my jean jacket and gallop Tristan, Ms. Anderson's chocolate bay Arab. Tristan obviously feels my mood as clearly as Hakim. The gelding's legs eat up the miles as we gallop down to the lake. Then I walk him around and around until his breathing slows, and yet still he wants his head.

"Again?" I ask.

But Hakim shakes his head. "It's going to be dark soon. We have to head back now."

The colors have all slid into the horizon. No more blushing orangish reds. Even the violets and purples have sunk into the far-off mountains. Now grays darken even the wisps of clouds. I nod. I know Hakim's right, but I still feel restless.

Tristan is throwing his head up and down. He paws the ground. "He reflects your emotions, Mattie. You are unhappy that you cannot go back to your school again?"

"You know then," I say, feeling the tears well up in my eyes. "It's silly. High school's not really all that great. It's just that I only had three more weeks to go. It shouldn't be stopping so abruptly. I'm not ready."

"Many times we are not ready when fate delivers our future. But we must accept our Kismet."

I'd always thought each of us made our own fate. I'd believed that individuals had more power than, I guess, we do. Especially when someone throws a monkey wrench into the time stream.

A tear starts its way down my cheek. Angry with myself, I wipe it away.

"The sky grays for a reason, Mattie. It allows the owls and the other night animals their chance to waken. If we rant against its darkness, we do not see that it propels the change."

We are walking back to the stables as we talk, but the horses neigh, and we hear another cantering up.

"You left without me," Sandor glares at Hakim. "I was supposed to accompany the child everywhere."

"She is fine, as you can see," Hakim says, waving his hand in my direction. "We did not see you when we took the horses out. She was safe with me. I would not allow any harm to come to her."

"I'm not a child," I tell Sandor, but he ignores me, too angry, I suppose to listen to my protests.

"Ms. Anderson will be angry with you when I tell her," Sandor says.

Hakim only shrugs. "This is true, but then she will probably fire you for allowing Mattie to go without a chaperone."

"I don't need a chaperone," I tell them both, but they're not listening to me. They're caught up in some kind of game of strategy, each one trying to best the other.

I loosen the reins just a bit, and Tristan takes off. I lean down over his shoulder and let him gallop home. I hear the two men thundering after me, but I don't care. Freedom is such deliciousness. Sometimes it's worth a bit of penalty.

But unfortunately it is Sandor who pays the price for my recklessness. For although I've planned to walk Tristan out until he was cool again, Sergio comes storming out to the stable, insisting that I go inside and eat dinner with my parents. He orders Sandor to put the horses on the hot walker and turns me around, marching me back to the house. Hakim, guarding me as if there were bandits inside the ranch, follows, bringing up the rear.

Chapter Thirty-Six

A retired schoolteacher comes to the house the next day. She is finicky about everything, tearing apart my essays, and criticizing the lack of neatness of my math papers. She is unable to help me with my extension class in nuclear physics, but she more than makes up for it with the way she makes history interesting.

With Simon, she is even worse about neatness. I can hear him in the other room arguing that he's done his best. That brings only more lectures. Poor Simon. He doesn't know his addition facts either, a situation that she calls abominable, so she drills him every hour.

Simon rails against her when she departs each day. Mom and Dad won't listen. Ms. Anderson does, but then she laughs and tells Simon that Mrs. Inger will be good for his backbone. I don't think Simon cares about his backbone. He's very disappointed no one will intercede.

He complains even more about the amount of homework Mrs. Inger leaves behind for him, only half a page, but to listen to Simon, it's more like hours of work. Still, once he stops fussing about it, it only takes him about five minutes. Then he's outside, working on his fort or riding the fat pony named Peanut.

I really do have hours of homework, despite the fact that school is wrapping up. Yet, I don't complain about it. I just sigh and redo my essay courageously, knowing that Mrs. Inger will tear it apart the next day. Then I start a new one, one I'm supposed to present to her orally with visuals like a full-staged production.

By the time I finish my math and the speech, and I polish the latter so it will be ready for Mrs. Inger's attack the next day, it's time for dinner.

Mom's home, so I walk downstairs, find her working on something for the office, and beg to be allowed to ride instead of eat with everyone, explaining that I've been working all this time. She looks at me, calls me closer, and then hugs me to her.

"We have so few more dinners together, Mattie. I won't say 'no' to you, but I will miss you." Then she sighs, and I walk away.

I hate guilt trips. That evening, although the sky is an artist's canvas, and the air is scented with jasmine, not even a good, strong gallop takes away my guilt. I cut the ride short and go running back inside. I arrive in time for dessert.

I sit down beside Simon. Hé holds his nose and says, "Pew!" Ms. Anderson gives me one of her looks that lets me know she doesn't approve of either my lateness or my smell.

"Mom gave me permission," I explain. "I've been inside all day, stuck with my books. I was about to scream, and . . ."

"Really?" Simon asks. "Are you still going to?"

He's hopeful. I can see that, but I shake my head. "I feel better now," I tell him.

Dad's been working in a section of Ms. Anderson's gardens that he's replanted with his genetically altered daffodils. He tells our benefactor that he needs some more bone mix, and the conversation moves away from me. I'm grateful. Ms. Anderson has a piercing eye when something displeases her.

I nibble on a piece of celery that still sits on the appetizer tray. There are carrot sticks, too. I scoop up a handful. I'm just finishing them when Sergio brings in my warmed plate of dinner. I give him a huge smile and begin eating. I manage one bite of the cheese enchilada before the house computer informs Ms. Anderson that Captain Brogger is at the outer gate asking if he can come in to see us.

I take in a fork of refried beans, one of salad, and another mouthful of the delicious enchilada before he makes his arrival. Then, just as I'm about to grab another portion of salad, he says without any preamble, "Someone just bombed the INASA headquarters. We have reason to believe that this is connected with the prior threat you were given."

We all let out startled expressions of dismay except for Simon who merely says, "Wow. That's just like on Captain Jetstream. They're always bombing things on Captain Jetstream."

"But who would bomb INASA?" my father breaks in. "That's like blowing ourselves up. It's the backbone of our country." Dad shakes his head and coughs several times. "And for what purpose? People like that should be gardening or reading a book. It would be better for their souls. Why do they have to be violent?"

Captain Brogger looks Dad over, probably taking in his gardening clothes and his open-necked informality. The detective doesn't quite roll his eyes, but the thought is obvious. He discards my father's words and shifts his attention to me. I see his eyes scanning my jeans and tee shirt. I think his nose even wrinkles a bit, so much so that he suddenly sneezes.

Pulling a brand-new kerchief from his right pocket, he sniffs into it, thumping himself like a woman powdering her nose. At that, Mom and I exchange a quick look and smile, careful not to break up into laughter, at least until Ms. Anderson catches our thought and guffaws exactly like a man.

That's too much to bear. Mom and I crack up, and then, of course Simon follows our lead. For him, laughter is always just a hiccough away.

Captain Brogger apparently has no sense of humor. He glares at us, puts his kerchief away, and says, "It is incomprehensible to me that you would find humor in this situation, especially since it was obviously in retaliation to INASA's acceptance of you in their program."

That stuns us into silence.

"How do you know it's related to Mattie?" Dad charges in, attempting to protect us from the brunt of Captain Brogger's attack.

"Didn't I mention that?" the detective asks, taking out his kerchief once more so he can carefully refold it. He deliberately pauses to rework the thing into a rhombus and then slides it back into his coat pocket. Then he looks up. "The bomber, you see, left a note that said among other things, "Even Captain Jetstream knows that women don't belong in space."

"Captain Jetstream never said that," Simon yells as he bolts up, knocking over his chair.

"Fix the chair, Simon and apologize to Ms. Anderson for knocking it over," Mom says quietly. Then she grabs up a glass of water and takes a delicate sip.

Meanwhile, Ms. Anderson has had enough of the detective's method of doing things. "Exactly what else did the note say? Tell us everything," she orders.

The detective tells us instead that the bomb killed three of INASA's scientists. "One of them," he tells us calmly, "was strangely enough, Dr. Stephenson. Isn't that the woman who tried to talk you out of applying for the Space Academy?"

The few bites of the enchilada I've eaten, which once had tasted so delicious, suddenly invoke their revenge. With a hand over my mouth, I lurch from the table, barely making it to the bathroom before a huge eruption takes place.

"Dr. Stephenson, I'm so sorry," I repeat over and over, sobbing into the toilet.

Chapter Thirty-Seven

Staring down into a toilet is not a pleasant manner of spending time. Neither are bad memories. You see, Dr. Stephenson wrote to me. She wrote several letters expressing her concern for my campaign. She poured out her heart, but I never answered her. I didn't want to. I thought of her as the enemy. Now I see that she was just another woman with ideas that differed from me. But she was a person, one I knew, one I'll never see again.

The thought brings on another spasm, but my stomach is emptied. I have nothing else to give. Only my guilt. I should have written her back. I should have thanked her for her concern.

My mother comes in a few minutes later. I ask her to leave, embarrassed by the way the bathroom must smell, the way I'm sitting on the floor holding the toilet like a teddy bear.

"I'm sick," I tell her. "Please, go away."

"No, Mattie. I've seen you sick before. I've held you in my arms many times when you weren't at your best. That's what mothers do, sweetheart."

She holds a clean washcloth under the faucet and runs the water. Then she stoops down to place it on my forehead. "There, doesn't that feel better?"

Amazingly, it helps. "I lift my head, glancing up at her. "I never answered Dr. Stephenson's letters, Mom. I should have."

Mom sits down on the bathtub rim, and as if this were a normal place to have a conversation, she asks, "Did she die because you didn't answer her letter, Mattie?"

"Of course not, but I should have."

"Maybe, Mattie, but that wouldn't have changed anything. You'd already said what you needed to tell her. You owed nothing more to her."

"But she died because of me, Mom. Don't you see that?"

"I was afraid you'd feel that way, honey, but this wasn't your fault. You weren't the one who planted that bomb. You weren't the one whose hatred caused Dr. Stephenson to die."

"How can you say that? If I hadn't gotten INASA to change their policy, Dr Stephenson would still be alive."

"This wasn't your fault, Mattie. You bear no guilt."

I sigh and sit up. My stomach has calmed down a bit. Shakily I stand and walk over to the sink where I sip a drink of water from the faucet. My mouth tastes wretched. I rinse and wish I could brush my teeth, but this isn't my bathroom. My toothbrush is upstairs.

"Feel better?" Mom asks. "Think you can make it up to your room?"

I nod, and my mother opens the door. I've started shivering for some reason. Mom throws an arm around my shoulder and squeezes me against her body. "Come on," she says. "We'll get you into bed. Then I'll bring you something warm to drink."

I don't argue. I feel weak. I feel like a child. I'm so glad my mom's beside me, holding me, giving me her warmth and support.

Upstairs, Mom even helps me into my nightgown. I insist on brushing my teeth before getting under the covers. She nods and sits on the bed, waiting for me.

Then, I crawl under the covers, and Mom tucks me in, just like she used to when I was just a little child. Then she leans over and kisses me. "No more guilt, okay?" she repeats. We talk about school for a while. Then Dad comes in to see me. He kisses me and sits down on the edge of the bed. I feel like I'm about five years old with both of my parents sitting beside me, but it's a good feeling, a secure feeling.

Dad asks if I'd like to go hang-gliding next weekend. Of course, I agree to that. Mom smiles when we discuss it, but she doesn't say she'll join us. We talk for a few minutes more, and then my eyes start to drag.

"Getting sleepy?" Dad asks.

That's the last thing I remember.

However, that night I have an awful dream. I see Uncle Theodore's ship, the *Jolly Roger,* on fire. The dream starts with a bomb exploding in the cargo room. It sets off a chain reaction that funnels fire through the air vents. I see Uncle Theodore fighting the fire. I watch as the flames engulf him, sending him to his death. Then I see the whole ship implode. There's no sound, yet I smell the scent of burning flesh. When I wake up, I'm drenched in sweat and shaking badly.

There is no school for me that day. My mother insists that I am sick and need to stay in bed. When she comes in to talk to me about it, though, I blurt out my dream.

Mom looks into my eyes and shakes her head. "It was just a dream," she says. "All this pressure and the news yesterday. It was just a dream, Mattie. Put it out of your head."

Not having Mrs. Inger attacking my writing is just fine with me. I eat some hot cereal that the cook sends up to my room on an old-fashioned breakfast tray. I read for a while, but then the prison of my room gets to me. I dress in jeans and head out for the stables.

Sandor is off that day, and because Hakim has taken Ms. Anderson somewhere, there's no one to escort me on a horseback ride. Neither of my parents knows how to ride, nor want to learn. Therefore, all I can do is groom the animals, which I do eagerly. I even help saddle soap some tack, joining a new servant named Sinbad and an elderly man named Philip. I feel quite comfortable as they tell me stories about their childhood. (Sinbad, strangely enough, has never been to sea. He says his mother just loved to watch old movies.)

Around eleven, Hakim enters the stable in search of me. "Why are you not in bed?" he demands, almost angrily.

"I'm not sick anymore," I tell him, laughing a bit. "I've been having fun cleaning tack and grooming horses. Sinbad and Philip have many tales to tell."

Hakim looks me over and apparently makes his own assessment. "You wish to ride?" he asks. When I nod, he inspects my clothes and then says, "You may ride Jazam today. I will saddle him up."

"No, I will do it," Sinbad says, bolting up as if he's been insulted. "Let the young woman drink something cold before she goes out for a ride. She still looks pale."

Apparently, Hakim agrees because he gets me a drink from the stable fridge and holds it out to me.

I drink the fruit juice and wait for my horse. It is close to noon, so the day is at its hottest. Sinbad accompanies us, and Hakim leads us toward the coolness of the woods. We ride through tall trees and leafy bowers. Jazam is full of energy and wants to gallop, but there is no place to do so. Hakim catches my bridle several times to ask if I'm okay with her.

I don't know what he thinks we could do about it. It is too far for me to walk back, and Jazam, although she's jumpy and full of devilment, is exciting to ride. All goes well until an owl swoops down. Owls do not swoop in the daytime, but no one has told this one that. Perhaps that is Jazam's reasoning for rearing and carrying on like the sky is falling. I only know that for a good minute, I have my hands full.

When the explosion is all over, Sinbad and Hakim are watching me with huge smiles. "Well done," Hakim says. "You ride like a Spanish conquistador."

I figure that is overly generous praise, but I glow as we ride back. Hot and sticky from the heat of the day, still as I return to the house, I feel surprisingly recovered from my sickness and from the horror of the nightmare.

After that morning's explosive battle, Jazam becomes my favorite of Ms. Anderson's horses. From then on, I ride her every day.

Chapter Thirty-Eight

On the news that afternoon, we see pictures of what happened at INASA. An INASA spokesman talks about the dreadfulness of it, and how anyone who would do such a thing must be sick in the head. That's an understatement. The three people who died are just scattered body parts, all barely identifiable. The only way they know for sure who was killed was because of the checkout system. Dr. Stephenson, Dr. Perris, and Dr. Fredock were the ones still in the building. The newsman mentions a finger and a nose. He says those things have been taken to the morgue for cell identification and precise conformation.

"Can't we change the channel?" Mom asks, looking worriedly at me. (Simon's no longer in the room, having gone upstairs to play with his Captain Jetstream figurines.)

I sigh, but I'm not feeling queasy any more. I reassure Mom.

"It is nice to see that Mattie has bounced back. I hear she been riding most of the day," Ms. Anderson remarks giving me a smile as she looks up from the papers she's been reading.

I am just about to mention how much I enjoyed riding Jazam when the T.V. newsman mentions me by name. They flash my picture, explain how I've been given admittance into INASA Space Academy, and then go on to say that it's suspected that this terrible crime was committed by someone who has a personal grievance against me.

"Are they blaming me?" I ask.

"Sh!" my dad says, but Mom takes my hand and holds it. She gives me a quick kiss and a smile, shaking her head.

"Maybe it's the pestilence," my father jokes.

"The pestilence?" Ms. Anderson says, and we all start to tell her about the strange woman who left messages on our machine. We're talking all at once when the house computer informs us that Captain Brogger wants to enter.

"All right," Ms. Anderson says, "but his presence here is growing tedious."

Of course, my parents immediately feel guilty because they start thinking about our presence being tedious too. Almost immediately, my dad says that we should move back home and how he doesn't want us to be a burden on Ms. Anderson's kindness. It's the same thing he says every other day. Ms. Anderson, as usual, shoots it down.

"I will not have Mattie and Simon going back home and being bombed. Don't you see that someone is turning violent now? That criminal is no longer just talking about violence. He is doing it. Do you want your children to be the next target?"

My parents sputter for another minute.

I sigh. I know how they feel. They both want to go home, but I don't think Ms. Anderson wants us too — not really. She likes having us here. I can sense that. I think we entertain her.

I tune out their continued debate about whether a week more will be enough and think about the arrival of the detective. What does he have to say this time? Has he found out anything?

I don't like the man. I don't think he likes us either, although sometimes I get the feeling he'd like to become friendlier with Ms. Anderson. Fat chance!

While I'm pondering the reason no one likes the detective, I think about the woman who used to call the house every day. For the first time in weeks, I remember the tape in my bedroom drawer. Should I tell the detective about that?

Captain Brogger swaggers in as if he owns the place. His eyes travel over us. He almost sneers. But apparently we all pass his inspection because he doesn't deride us with his eyes. Instead, he hands Ms. Anderson a VID tape and orders her to show it.

"I beg your pardon," she says frigidly, obviously not caring for either the man or his attitude.

"We need the family to look at it. It's from the INASA. Where's the boy?"

We're all bristling from the man's contemptuousness, but it's Ms. Anderson who responds first. "Do you mean Simon?" she asks coldly.

"I don't know. Whatever. Just get the kid in here. I need the whole family to look at this VID and see if you recognize anyone."

Dad, Mom, and I are sitting on the couch. Ms. Anderson is still in her easy chair with her work spread out on the portable desk she uses. That leaves the stiff, uncomfortable chair for the detective. I doubt he even notices as he drops down into it.

Simon comes running into the room. "The computer told me to come down," he says. "Do you need me?"

"Sit down, kid. INASA wants you to watch a VID," Captain Brogger tells him.

Dad gestures for Simon to sit beside us on the couch. Mom slips Simon in between Dad and her. I'm on the end, but I reach over and tousle Simon's head, and he gives a quick, ready smile.

"This about you?" he asks.

I nod, but he probably doesn't see. We're all watching the beginning flickerings of the VID tape.

There's a lot of boring stuff at the beginning. People coming and going. I see Dr. Stephenson and gasp. Dad squeezes my hand gently. "It's okay, honey. You don't have to watch if you don't want to."

Captain Brogger stops the tape at that point. "What do you mean she doesn't have to watch? Of course, she does. She has no choice . . ."

"Listen, if I think it's bad for either of my kids, they'll be out of here so fast you won't even have time to say, "INASA. You got that?" Dad snaps.

"Tough guy, huh? Maybe you'd like to sit downtown a while. We have a nice stone cell."

"That will be enough, Captain Brogger," Ms. Anderson says with such coldness it makes me shiver. "Your manner lacks sophistication and finesse, and I am finding it increasingly difficult to endure. Would you like me to put in a call and have you removed from this case? It would be very easy to do, you know."

Captain Brogger opens his mouth to argue but then, apparently, thinks better of it. "My apology, Mr. Masters Smith. However, we do need your daughter to watch this. In fact, we're counting on that keen mind of hers to spot someone familiar, someone who might be the criminal. We're hopeful one of you might notice something. Please. Please watch this."

"I see," my dad says, sighing because he really is a non-confrontational person. Will you be okay, Mattie?" he asks, reading my eyes as much as listening for my words.

The sight of Dr. Stephenson has rather unbalanced me, but I understand what Captain Brogger is saying. We have to catch the bomber, no matter what. The three scientists deserve it. I look down and then nod to my father.

I decide to be open with the man. Maybe we should let him know about the crazy lady that always called us. "There's something, Mr. Brogger, that maybe we should tell you," I say. "You see, before we came here, there was a woman who kept calling us. She never made any threats, but she called us day after day, and she kept saying, 'Women belong at home.'"

"What?" Captain Brogger explodes. "Who was she? Did you ever tell anyone?"

Mom takes over then. I guess she's sensing that Dad is pretty close to exploding. He was the one who kept calling the police about it and getting no satisfaction.

"We did call the police, Captain Brogger. They told us there was nothing they could do about it. It seems the woman needed to kill someone before they'd be interested."

The detective sputters about that a moment. Then his eyes light up. "Do you have any of the recordings of her voice?"

I start to speak, but Dad takes over. "No, I erased them immediately. That woman was a pestilence, but she never gave any signs of being violent."

"Damn it!" the detective says, forgetting that Simon and I are in the room.

"Watch your tongue," Ms. Anderson admonishes him.

The man turns a putrid shade of orange, apologizes, and then looks so exasperated that I dive in with my story.

"She called one time that my parents don't know about. She said more or less the same thing as before, except on that call, she talked about being at my uncle's funeral. She said she saw us there. She even mentioned where we were standing. I don't know if she was just bluffing, but it sounded like she'd really been there."

"You never told us about that," Mom admonishes me.

"I was going to," I admit, "but then Dad got so mad every time she called. I was afraid that he'd really lose it if he heard her talking about witnessing us at the funeral."

"So you erased it from the phone computer?" the detective questions sadly.

I look over at him. The lines under his eyes have sagged halfway down to his cheeks. He really looks miserable.

"Yes, I did, but I first made a backup, just in case. I was going to share it with Mom, but I forgot. I guess the tape is still back at the house in my bedroom drawer."

The captain flips open his cell and, once connected, abruptly starts issuing orders. "Get it," he says. "Do we have permission to enter your house?" he asks my parents. "Speak into the cell, if you would," he tells my mom.

She grants permission and returns the phone. Then, everything calms down again, and the detective asks if he can start the VID tape again.

"No," Ms. Anderson interrupts. "I think it's time for some tea. Sergio!"

The servant comes running in, accepts our orders, and leaves.

"Are we ready now?" the detective asks sarcastically.

We nod, but his phone goes off, and he stops to speak with someone. He listens a minute, then disconnects.

"Well, we know now what was used at INASA. We know how it got there, too. I want you to watch the VID very closely. I think we've found a clue."

He doesn't elaborate, and we're all wondering what he means, but at that moment, Sergio returns with the drinks. Everyone takes a glass, and eyes move to view the table in front of the couch where a selection of fresh fruit slices, crackers and cheese, and a plate full of raw vegetables is set out. Despite the detective's pleas, it's several moments before the VID is turned back on.

Simon is busy pigging out, but he's actually the first to see the woman. He cries out, his finger pointing at her. "That's the daffodil lady. That's her, Dad!"

We all agree that the woman in the VID really is the daffodil lady. Then, we have to explain that story to the detective and to Ms. Anderson.

Mainly, Dad takes it on, relating the incident at the airport, the one with Adam Chosky's sister. "What was her name?" we ask each other, searching each other's eyes, but none of us can remember. We've always just referred to her as the Daffodil Lady.

Captain Brogger is suitably impressed with the oddness of the tale, especially since her entrance into the INASA headquarters is full of questionable intent. He flips his cell back on, jots down the frame of the VID where she was identified, and orders whoever is on the other end of the phone to locate the young woman. That done, and the whole crime investigation now heading in a positive direction, Captain Brogger sits back, finishes his drink, and pumps us about Adam and his sister.

There isn't much we can add. There was only her strangeness, the theft, and the hatred in her eyes. We tell the detective that Adam handled her gently as if he'd known she was lying, but he hadn't confronted her about it, wanting perhaps to avoid a scene at the airport. Simon remembers how Uncle Theodore told us that the sister had "problems." That probably meant the mental kind, which is why, I guess, we stopped thinking about her, as if craziness were the only explanation for someone who'd steal daffodils.

The detective probes our recall for another twenty minutes, asking us to tell the story again — each of using our own words. He stops us to ascertain details — the way she looked at that point, the expression of her eyes. But finally, when the story is devoid of further input, Captain Brogger appears satisfied. He stands, removes the VID, thanks us brusquely for our services, and then makes his way to the front door.

"Well," said Ms. Anderson, "I would say we have certainly solved the police department's investigation. What do you say we go in and have some dinner now? Is everyone hungry?

Smiles all around. It's late. We're amazingly tired, but dinner, as usual, is delicious.

A week passes before they catch Nicole Chosky. It's a week of wondering, of worrying, and of watching the news. Then, one night, we see her as they're leading her to the police car. She looks like a frazzled hulk of the woman she once was. Her clothes hang on her.

It's obvious she's lost weight. Her hair is tousled and dirty, and the expression on her face is the classic mad woman's. She's laughing right at the camera as she cries out her familiar line, "Women belong in the house. Do you hear me, Mattie Masters Smith? Women don't belong in space."

Everyone glances at me when Nicole Chosky says that. I look down at my lap. I'm embarrassed, not because of what I've done to achieve Academy admittance, but the fact that a mad woman is speaking my name. I fervently wish she'd never met me and that she didn't hate me.

It's strange to see her again, handcuffed and under guard. I thought the sight would give me a burst of relief that we're no longer in danger, but all I feel is pity. What caused the trim lady in the airport to turn into this sad specter? Why did she latch onto me? What brought her to this?

Ms. Anderson brings in a psychologist to speak to each of us. The psychologist is gentle and non-threatening, but in my sessions with her, she keeps me on the target, probing the subject of how I feel about Nicole Chosky. She keeps bringing up my uncle, too. I don't understand that, but I figure she knows what she's doing. I go along with it, not fighting her.

At first, admittedly, I am numb. Then, I feel the most incredible relief, as if we've been her prisoners and now are free. Still, the woman's eyes haunt me. I keep picturing the wildness of them and the unhappiness inside her. I still feel pity. At least, I do until we find out the whole truth. I think the police told Ms. Anderson the whole truth from the first. I'm sure that's why Ms. Anderson brought in Dr. Connors.

You see, Nicole Chosky, in one of her sessions with the police, broke down and admitted that she bombed the *Jolly Roger*, my uncle's ship. She killed her brother, Adam, and she killed my uncle and the almost three hundred men and women of the crew. It is hard to feel pity for someone who does something that horrible. It's impossible.

I close my eyes and picture my uncle the way he was the last time I saw him. His smile, his bright eyes, the manner in which he joked with us, and the way he made every day alive and better than the one before. Nicole took all that away from us. My uncle and I will never get to have those talks he and I had planned. He was going to visit me at the Academy. And once, he said he'd apprentice me on his ship when I completed training. Nicole Chosky unraveled a whole future.

Dr. Connors talks about how we must let go of our anger, how we must move forward and accept that sometimes bad things happen. I know that. We all do, but something rippled the pattern we'd set inside our memories. Something changed inwardly. Nicole tattered all the pieces.

I sigh lots now. Dr. Connors says we're all grieving again. Newly. Why does grief strike more than once? Why does it seem that Uncle Theodore has just died all over again?

I ask the doctor that, but she doesn't answer me. She just asks me more questions and waits for me to come up with the answers.

Tonight the News is broadcasting a special on Nicole Chosky; it's their attempt to analyze what happened. Dr. Connor wants us all to watch it. Even Simon. Dr. Connor sits in the living room and observes our faces as the special begins. That is difficult at first, but we soon become so caught up in the special, we forget she's even there.

We see the police tapes where they first told Nicole about her brother's death. She doesn't even blink. Nor does she cry. There's no look of surprise on her face. The police at first wrote it off as shock. But now all America knows that for Nicole, it wasn't just a delayed reaction. She wasn't surprised by her brother's death because she caused it.

Later on, another tape shows Nicole laughing over it — a victorious laugh, a laugh so evil our skin crawls with goosebumps of unease.

The special leaps forward, showing Nicole with her attorney. He's an attractive young man in a three-piece suit who looks very frustrated. Poor attorney. His sessions with Ms. Chosky often end in violence, and he has repeatedly asked to be taken off the case, but the judge denies it each time. That attorney finally gets Nicole to plead insanity. I think at that point, no one attempts to dispute it.

The T.V. special doesn't end with Nicole's suicide in the waiting room. They discuss that only briefly, speculating that it was some kind of pill she took, although nothing showed up in her autopsy. An investigator points his finger at the attorney, but there were no grounds for that. The young man was cleared. They've found no cause for Nicole's death. She simply died, presumably by her own hand.

As I said, the special doesn't stop at that point, but leaves several questions for the audience (and hopefully crime investigators to think about.) How did Nicole Chosky come up with a long-set bomb — a bomb that didn't erupt for months? Who gave or sold it to her? How did she manage to plant the thing on the Jolly Roger when she never set foot onboard the ship? Why did she want her own brother killed?

Maybe the biggest question the special addresses is this: Why did Nicole Chosky possess so much hatred?

We've asked Dr. Connors the same things, but she avoids answering. Apparently, psychologists prefer to ask questions rather than answer them. Yet, my family and I have no explanations either. Sadly, I guess, some questions will always remain unanswered.

Chapter Thirty-Nine

After the special, we move back into our own house. That should be a wonderful occasion, full of happiness, but it isn't. Somehow, we've magically become a part of a new family. We miss Ms. Anderson, Sergio and Hakim. I miss Jazam and the other horses. I miss the fresh salmon and …

Sigh. But it's time to return to our own house, our old lives. Except that sometimes, that's not really possible. Mom and Dad still work in the same place. Their commute is now easier, and Simon gets to return to school, but I don't. There's only another week of my school, and what's the point? I've finished all the academic requirements, and my friends are going in different directions. I've even decided not to go to my high school graduation ceremony because both the school and the police have advised me not to.

Because of that, I feel out of the link, like I'm already gone. Maybe I left part of me behind at Ms. Anderson's ranch. When she calls me on Tuesday evening, asking me to come visit, I jump at the chance.

Mom frowns. Dad raises his eyebrows, but they give in when I plead.

"It's only for the day," I tell them.

So I return via the *Butterfly* and flutter back to what now feels like home. Jazam is frisky as a colt. I laugh as he rears and tosses his head. I'm ready for him. I fly with the wind. Everyone should have such an opportunity. Riding is freedom —freedom from time and distance and even gravity.

At lunch, I tell Ms. Anderson that. She laughs, too, and tells me how happy she is to have me back with her. The feeling is mutual. When it's time to return home, I don't want to. I climb into the *Butterfly* and feel trapped by necessity. Yet, I love my parents and my brother. Why should I feel like this? I wish we could have gone on as before, living in Ms. Anderson's house, but I know that wouldn't be fair to Mom, Dad, and Simon.

I do interviews for two different magazines. *Daily Science* and *Changes* both come to my house. For the first one, I have to do all the work, telling them my "route to success" as they call it, but with the second one, the whole family is invited, so we sit around and just talk. That interview is a lot more fun. My brother, Simon, steals the show.

At the end of the month, I need to have my eggs removed. Mom goes with me. It's frightening only because I've never been a patient in a hospital before, but everyone's nice to me, and the doctor who comes in to explain how it will be done doesn't tell me anything I haven't already heard.

Even so, it makes me feel better to hear him tell me what to expect. I'm not going to write much about this is my diary. Mostly, I don't remember since they put me under, and when I woke up, it was all over. I don't really want to know anything more — I mean about the eggs. Someday, maybe I'll be curious, but not now.

The doctor lets me go home a day later. My scar is tiny. Soon, they tell me, it will hardly be noticeable. Other than a bit of itchiness, I don't feel anything. I don't even feel different. How silly to make so much over such a little thing.

Mom cries, though, when it's done. That's the worst. I wish she weren't upset over it. Maybe it's because it makes it all real to her. Maybe she finally sees that I'm going away soon.

About the time that I recuperate from that, ApplePie Studios gets the brilliant idea to open Captain Jetstream to females. To advertise this concept, they decide to do a whole new concept, a show with real people.

They invited me to play the part of the new female astropilot. Simon gets very excited about that. So do I, actually. To think that I might influence future young girls into believing that they can be part of space exploration — that's pretty heady stuff.

What it means, though, is having to get up at five in the morning and flying to Los Angeles again. We're being housed at the Fairmont this time since production is supposed to go on for several days.

No one's as excited by all this media stuff as we were the first time. When the limo comes and picks us up, it's no longer that big a deal. We sit back and help ourselves to the refrigerated beverages, as if we do this sort of thing all the time. Simon crams some cookies into his mouth, but he's not oohing and aahing over the selections like he used to.

At the ApplePie Studio, it's interesting what they want me to do. It's next to nothing, actually — at least, that's what I think at first. I've memorized the script and figure I just have to speak my lines. But after they cut and have me do my lines time after time, I discover that there's a whole lot more to acting than just repeating memorized lines.

Simon gets impatient with me and, stands up and yells. "You have to act like Captain Jetstream is Mr. Important. He's like the president or something, Mattie."

I laugh, but the crew gives Simon a thumbs up, and we try again. I guess I do it better the next time. Nobody yells, "Cut!" for a while.

During the break, Simon gets to meet the man who gives Captain Jetstream his voice. Simon tells his hero that if he ever needs a younger brother or a kid on the show, he'd love to get the part. Peter Jamps more or less rolls his eyes, but I guess one of the big shots is listening because they put in a bit part for Simon. He's supposed to be the nephew who's being transported to school on another planet.

Simon is great in the part. I mean, the kid's really gifted. I think everyone sees that, too, but no one says anything. Simon sits back down, and I finish my part, and that's that. Except when the program airs the following week, I get one line complimenting me in the news, but Simon gets fan mail big time.

The studio, realizing what they've got, offers to give Simon's part a weekly walk-on. My brother gets excited, but my parents don't. They don't want Simon in show biz. The three of them start arguing about it. I stay out of it. In a week, I'll be gone. At least, that's my thinking until my little brother comes and pleads with me to interfere.

What can I say? I write a long letter, explaining to my parents about making dreams come true. I hand that to Simon and say, "Don't give it to them until I'm already up there. Okay?"

The imp nods his head and darts a kiss at my nose — just before he runs away, zooming off into fantasy space.

Jimmy comes over again that night. He's been coming fairly regularly. I think he's finally accepted that I won't be going to Stanford with him. It was rocky for a while when I refused to go for the interview our parents had arranged, but I knew then after I'd received acceptance at the Academy, that I'd just be wasting Stanford's time.

Jimmy and I had a big, old argument where we didn't talk for a couple of weeks, but eventually, the anger faded. Now we're friends again — no demands, no long, guilt-making sighs.

That night, Jimmy brings a movie over, and we sit together on the couch watching it. Simon comes in and joins us. Once, Jimmy would have asked for privacy, but he doesn't do that anymore. We don't need that kind of privacy now. We're back to being just friends.

I like it better this way — at least, I think I do. Yet, sometimes, I wish I could throw my arms around Jimmy. I wish I could kiss him, too, and tell him that I love him, but I won't.

Only time will tell if it's really love we're feeling for each other. And in the meantime, I have too much to do before then. Because you see, tomorrow I'm headed to the Space Academy, one more step on the path to following my dreams.

<div align="center">~~~~~~~~~~~~~~~~~~~~~~</div>